BLACK
DIAMOND
FALL

ALSO BY JOSEPH OLSHAN

BLACK
DIAMOND
FALL

A NOVEL

JOSEPH OLSHAN

POLIS BOOKS

BLACK DIAMOND FALL

For information, address POLIS BOOKS, LLC,
1201 HUDSON STREET #211S
Hoboken, New Jersey 07030
Library of Congress Cataloging-in-Publication
Data is available on request.
ISBN 978-1947993341-0
18 19 20 21 22 RRD 10 9 8 7 6 5 4 3 2 1

First Edition

Quote on p. 116 from "After Apple-Picking" by Robert Frost, first published in *North of Boston* © 1914

Quote on p. 171 from "Ghost House" by Robert Frost, first published in
A Boy's Will © 1915

For Ted and Caroline Robbins

PART 1

In our hearts there is a ruthless dictator ready to contemplate the misery of a thousand strangers if it will ensure the happiness of the few we love.

—Graham Greene, *The Heart of the Matter*

FEBRUARY 11, 2013; CARLETON, VERMONT; 10 DEGREES, LIGHT SNOW

Luc Flanders steps off the cleared skating area and enters drifts of snow that cover the rest of the unblemished, frozen pond. The ice groans beneath his two hundred pounds, cackles and taunts him as he moves across it, and he wonders if perhaps the torrents of summer rain have empowered the undercurrents. Or if his overactive, kinetic brain is once again playing tricks on him. The fickle surface keeps bellowing its complaint. Using the skill he learned as a hockey-playing kid, he lies down and starts moving crab-like toward what he hopes is the ring he lost there earlier. He's batting the snow away from his face, evenly distributing his weight so that he doesn't break through the ice into the dark, deathly cold water.

Then the music starts, the choral music of Rachmaninoff. He pictures the Orthodox processionals, the choking miasma of incense, and cloaked ecclesiastics flooding the nave. He cannot fathom their a cappella plainsong, what it means, or why it chooses him. The music resounds in the evergreen forest. It serenades the winter pond.

He stands again and looks up. A cottony cloud cover has drifted in to shroud the moon. It has become so profoundly dim that even the powerful miniature flashlight does little to bring the shoreline into relief. The area beyond the beam is dark, writhing, hypothermic wilderness, and there's shadowy movement on the shore, a lurking presence. Could somebody have followed him? Could somebody be out here recreationally at this time of night, in this plummeting temperature? Then, struck from behind, he falls forward, his forehead smashing against the ice. He tries to get up but slips and stumbles again, bellowing in pain. It's as if he's being pulled out to sea, his legs reflexively thrashing through gunmetal waves.

He wakes up lying on his back on the ice, staring at the obsidian sky. And then the sense of a string or a rope unraveling. Did somebody actually order him to get up and start walking? Hard to know, really. He reaches for the flashlight but that has vanished and the rest . . . he could be—he must be—dreaming. It's like the accident in the hockey rink when he left his own body and ended up looking down on himself and the officials crowding around him—and doing so in a state of blissful peace.

He sleeps for a while and awakens again to a dreamier world. When his eyes open, at first he cannot see, not even the ice touching his lips, nor the shapes of conifers at the shore, nor his hand right in front of his face. But then light comes back to him. And he thinks of Sam.

He still has some energy, enough to turn himself over and begin crawling. His legs and feet are numb. He waits until he can feel them a little bit and then some miracle allows him to begin moving, a long haul toward shore. Which is like holding his breath and trying to swim into the depths of water. And then the sad, piteous wonder arrives in the middle of his slow procession: *Why did I ever leave him?*

FEBRUARY 13; BLACK DIAMOND FALL, UTAH; 25 DEGREES, SUNNY

If you could be given your youth back, it might have true meaning for a few days, or maybe even a week. A month might allow you to forget that you were ever old, but the whole point would be never to forget—to understand that your visit back in time would expire almost as soon as it began. Sam is thinking this as he and Mike soldier the last ascent up a trail in the Wasatch Mountains, skis on their shoulders, notching their ski boots into steep snowpack, eyeing the flat table above where they'll soon stop and put on the rest of their gear. They've been hiking for an hour in whirring, wintry silence, punctuated by groans of shifting snow and ice and by the soft wailing of the wind. The sun is high, and it's a bluebird day. Looming constantly to their left is Black Diamond Fall, whose headwalls are built up from ice melt that has gathered layers of snow; the slope looks almost vertical in places, dark dashes of rock to be avoided at all costs. It's an extreme descent that only solid, expert skiers can drop into and be confident of surviving. The adrenaline blast of a run to the bottom of the canyon would, to those below them, be almost meaningless.

The night before, pointing to the image of the Fall on the computer screen, Mike said, "You can get into it one of two ways. You can sideslip in, ski straight down the first headwall, then check your speed and pick your way for a bit until it gets wider"—then he grinned maniacally—"or you can just jump off the cornice, which I don't think either of us wants to do."

At forty-five, Mike, Sam's best friend, is four years younger. He lived for three seasons in Tahoe, tuning edges, adjusting bindings, and skiing almost every day, and that regimen has given him a confidence, a fluidity of motion, that never seems to falter, even when his skis combat the eastern ice. He's a tough little guy of French Canadian background; one of his eyes is blue and the other is golden green. Last night, he watched Sam staring slack-jawed at the screen.

"You with me, bud?" he said.

"Yeah, I'm with you."

"Don't overthink this, Sam. You overthink everything. You know the terrain. Now you just have to nail it." Together they had skied all of New England, including Tuckerman's Ravine. In the west they'd conquered Gunsight, Palmyra Peak at Telluride, the Baldy Chute at Alta, Courbet's at Jackson. Black Diamond Fall was not far out of that league and Mike said so.

Sam disagreed. To him, the Fall presented a higher degree of difficulty. Plenty of lesser skiers take on Tuckerman's Ravine's forty-five-degree plunge, which is pretty short and can be dispatched with five turns. Courbet's Couloir in the Tetons is admittedly very steep, requires a ten-foot drop into soft snow, but still a trail marked in bounds—whereas Black Diamond Fall is miles off-piste.

"But whatever you do," Mike spoke up again, "try not to think about him."

Think about him. "About who?"

"About you-know-who."

But how could he not think about Luc? Doing the Fall together was what they'd talked about from the very beginning, was what they'd talked about when Sam had shown Luc the YouTube footage accompanied by a heavy-metal soundtrack of skiers tackling it. "We'll do it, together, we'll do Black Diamond," they had promised one another, hugging tight and cringing, as they'd watched Billy Poole's final moment—miraculously captured on video—when, scouting for a ski film, he died there in '09 at the age of twenty-eight.

Mike and Sam finally reach the top, and without acknowledging their arrival, look around at the sweeping expanse of summit vistas, sheets of snow draping the peaks and folds of mountains nestled close to them, and then begin the mindless drudge of putting on equipment. Sam had been sure to ski several days at Solitude on his rented powder skis so that he was used to them. Mike, who'd brought his Atomics out from Boston, felt he would not need the advantage of extra wide skis. They check their stowed avalanche gear—their probes and miniature shovels— turn on their transponders, secure their backpacks, and approach the lip of the cornice, staring down into what at first appears to be a crevasse but is actually just a break in the fall line. As Mike has pointed out, dropping in off this major cornice is not an option because you'd begin with too much air and might hit a rock face below. You have to jet in from the lip at the side and, once in, ski straight down a headwall through a narrow gate of two squat boulders, then jump-turn down a slim ribbon of skiable terrain and continue until you drop lower into the bowl that will widen before you'll finally be free to turn widely. Nervousness and adrenaline are fine, as long as your brain doesn't go numb.

"Okay, it is a little tricky," Mike concedes as they stand there, studying the slope, "but just set your skis, aim for between the boulders. You'll probably be going fast when you get through, so start turning as soon as you clear those rawks."

His South Boston accent sounds quaint in these western provinces. And for a moment Sam centers himself by taking deep breaths and looking out at the graduation of peaks in the distant part of the Wasatch that unfurl toward western Colorado, and the white parentheses of Solitude's downhill trails, where they hiked in from. Mike, who is pretty laconic, seems slightly on edge, and Sam knows that even Mike is worrying about those first ten or fifteen seconds of the run. They've already debated who should go first; originally, they thought Mike, but then they reasoned perhaps Sam because he, being the weaker skier, should have somebody sweeping behind him. Their ultimate decision: Mike will lead.

"You're going to follow me? Right?" Mike asks softly, still scouring the Fall. "You're not going to psyche out. Which means . . ." He looks at Sam shrewdly with his different-colored eyes.

"I won't think about Luc," Sam fills in the blank. "And he wouldn't stop me, anyway. I will do it," he insists, still not quite sure that he will in the end.

"You have nothing to prove to anybody," Mike now tells Sam. "You've wanted to ski this since college." They'd met at Carleton in a ski club when Mike was a sophomore and Sam, two years graduated, was teaching an expository writing class before going to architecture school. "And we're gonna do it!"

No sooner does the grin on Mike's face fade than he pushes out and grabs several feet of air off the lip before his skis hit and he's already jetting down the narrow path toward the rocks. He adjusts his speed beautifully and begins the quick jump turns down the narrowest part of the face. Sam notices another drop that neither of them had anticipated, but Mike, who has remarkable reflexes, takes it in stride before hitting the slightly flatter, wider part of the fall. And then he's turning great S's through the new snow—Sam can hear whoops of pleasure—making virgin tracks, as though writing words on a blank tablet. And then, ever so faintly, "Awesome!" floating back up to him.

As agreed, Mike finds a good place to stop halfway down and turns his face up to Sam. He yells something, but he's too far below now for Sam to understand it. Sam knows he's got to jump in, that he's going to do it, but hesitates just one last moment to collect his thoughts, to review what needs to be done, maybe even to pray because he's superstitious.

"I'm afraid," he admits aloud to the blustering wind. He

knows it's not just fear of the adventure — it's fear of losing his power, his athleticism, his attractiveness. With Luc gone, he's even more reluctant to let it all go. Ever since he can remember, he's been dreaming of mastering Black Diamond Fall, a notch in his belt before he gets too old to attempt terrain that often intimidates even talented younger skiers. Ripping it all the way to the bottom of the canyon will hopefully slow his decline down another arguably more difficult slope.

The hardest part is to get off the lip and make it down that first schuss, and to continue strategizing while doing so. "Come on," he imagines Luc urging him, and then he's off the lip and in and knows with a flash of exhilaration that it's a good entry. He's following Mike's tracks, gaining speed down the headwall toward the stubby boulders, zipping through them until his shoulder grazes one of them, throwing him off his game for a second. Instinctively, he bends his knees, checks his speed, and then enters phase two: the slightly less steep chute that's maybe two feet wider than his skis. Jump-turning to the right and then the left, Sam is about to enter the bowl's wider field, when one of his edges catches, and with a flash of paralyzing panic, he knows he's going to fall forward.

His skis, high-tech, designed with impeccable precision, release themselves and jet away from him in different directions.

He wakes up to a sky that has cooled, a lower sun, the snowfields taking on rosy color. He's lying at a critical angle, his right leg folded beneath him. He gasps, realizing something is terribly wrong, then glances around and spies his right ski lower down, sticking out of the snow, jackknifed over itself, snapped in half, shocking. He can no longer feel his leg and yet there is pain pulsing everywhere in his body, radiating from a dead zone. But then it fades for a bit; thankfully, it's not constant. Soon it occurs to him that it's more than just the skewed limb, divining a deeper wound. He is losing something, and he's losing it quickly, and he doesn't know quite what it is. And then he hears Mike calling—he'd almost forgotten Mike was there with him. At last, Sam tunes in to the litany, and he's in an echo chamber: "Sam! Sam! Sam! You okay? You okay? You okay?"

Shifting his head to the right, Sam sees Mike a hundred yards down, skis off and crisscrossed at one side, trying to scale the shallower part of the fall, near an outcropping of rocks, having terrific difficulty. "Don't try to get up here! Just call Life Flight," he manages. They've rented avalanche satellite phones that have the number of an emergency helicopter service programmed in.

"So it's that bad?"

"I think so. Stay there, Mike. You can't make it."

Mike had once been a gymnast, but this is one of the steepest slopes on the North American continent.

"Are you cold?"

Sam takes a moment to assess. "Nah, I don't think so."

Muted tones of conversation float up to him and then he hears Mike yell, "Okay, they're on their way!"

Life Flight is coming. When they'd rented the phones, they were told Life Flight was pretty quick, so maybe he'll have to endure only—what?—another half-hour of this? It's in their hands now. They'll know what to do. Sam leans his head back, admonishing himself to rest despite the intermittent screams of his injured body. At first he thinks, *Okay, I can handle it,* but then panics as he did once far out in Grafton Pond, when he was swimming between two islands, growing afraid of drowning, and then turning on his back and trying to relax and hearing the sound of loons, the birds that mate for life, calling out in their haunting lament. And then he discovers wetness, and manages to unzip his jacket and almost passes out when he spies the tremendous pooling of blood. And dimly wonders: *What could possibly be causing this? How much have I lost?*

Somehow, Mike manages to reach Sam; he's there looking down at Sam with composed concern. The pain has preternaturally subsided again, and yet Sam can no longer move, can barely even swivel his head, and realizes, even before he gets alarmed, that his breathing is sharp and fast. And then recognizes he's gone into atrial fibrillation, something that happens only when he's under extreme stress: the episodes sometimes lasting a torturous few hours, his heart racing erratically, his blood pumping inefficiently, the beats scattering like discordant music, making it impossible to climb stairs, to lie down. When it happens, he feels like an athlete who has gone down in the middle of a race. Normally, he'd keep checking his pulse, hoping for sinus rhythm to resume, but now he can't even move his arms.

"How did you get here?" he says, breathless from his fluttering heart.

"I managed—I'm a gymnast, don't worry. I can climb anything. I couldn't be down there just looking up at you struggling. I had to get to you."

"Can't move very much." Sam groans.

Mike's distressed, different-colored eyes are glinting snowy light. "I know, I know. And you've lost blood. But maybe I shouldn't be saying that."

"Already figured that out." Sam forfeits the ability to speak for a moment, and then says, "Why did I?"

"I think you smashed into a rawk. There's an open wound."

"Then don't . . . let . . . me . . . bleed!" Sam wants to add, "to death," but can't bring himself. Not yet. He debates telling Mike about his erratically beating heart but ends up saying nothing about it.

"I don't think it's so bad now." Mike has unzipped Sam's orange shell and lifts his inner fleece to study the oozing wound. Then pivots around and checks the sky. "I don't see them. Where the fuck are they?" The tough little guy shakes his head, and Sam can see tears on his ruddy cheeks.

"Don't worry, Mike," he says.

Mike snorts a laugh and says, "Don't say that. I'm supposed to be telling you that."

"Well, I'm telling you. Okay?"

Mike's voice breaks again. "Okay, Sam."

And then the first of the shadows comes down like a bird of prey with a wide wingspan, or maybe it's a cloud darkening the sun, but it glides over the white parchment on which he lies, over the glistening gorges that have melted in the midday warmth and are, as evening comes on, cooling into quicksilver ice. He feels it in the part of him that can still feel, and thinks of his mother, dead now for a decade, who he could have sworn was breathing on his neck the last time he was seriously injured: mountain biking. That was two years ago when he was lying in a hospital getting pebbles picked out of his arm.

"Road rash," he says aloud, and laughs, light-headed.

"What are you talking about?"

Sam peers at Mike, at a face that is familiar yet somehow strange.

Damn, his heart again, fast-beating like a fiend; he wishes at the very least that it would just revert to normal rhythm; all of this would be much easier and the relief would be almost narcotic. Can't he just deal with one bodily malfunction at a time? He feels stupid now, worrying so much about trivial things, about aging, about being too old for guys he's attracted to, about being too old for Luc. What does it matter now?

Hadn't he read somewhere that men younger than twenty-five were still developing, which meant their assessment of risk was evolving, their sense of responsibility, their dependability? But Luc believed Sam was the risk-taker because Sam rode a motorcycle and actually carried around a note in his wallet that spelled out where he lived, that there was a dog that would need to be let out, and whom to call in an emergency. Luc always worried that the news of Sam's motorcycle wreck would never reach him.

The speck of the helicopter grows larger in the sky and is soon hovering above him. Sam vaguely wonders how they're going to dig him out of the snow and put him on a stretcher. Surely they'll figure it out . . . his breathing is even shallower, his heart still racing crazily, but he's no longer afraid for some odd reason, sleepy rather, and it seems as though he sleeps with open eyes. A spider's web of rope is drifting down; attendants in white jumpsuits seem to be floating toward him. Why are they dressed in white, is it some kind of winter pallor? Their hands seem so soft as they tend to him; miraculously, they are able to create a trench around him and effortlessly pry him out, and he has a halo of snow around him, floating in the air. He's like some weird, crooked angel who fell onto the mountain when he should've been flying overhead on some astral plane. The ropes are finally attached to the stretcher and Sam is lifted gently, rocking in the air. He peers up through the deepening shadows, up at the darkening decline of Black Diamond Fall, and his last lingering thought is: Mike may never be able to get in touch with Luc, the college boy who broke his best friend's heart.

FEBRUARY 11; NORWICH, VERMONT; 15 DEGREES, HIGH CLOUDS

Eleanor Flanders is macerating *Arnica montana*, chopping the flowers finely, adding a tablespoon of almond oil, and grinding them in an alabaster mortar and pestle. She ladles the mixture into masonry jars, which she seals and assembles in the greenhouse just off the kitchen. There, bathed in warm air circulating from a ceramic heater, the lather will cure for at least four weeks. With this unguent she will treat mountain bikers and skiers and hockey players who seek unconventional therapies for their muscular ailments. Luc's friends used to tease him by calling her "The Norwich Witch," but nobody could ever deny her success rate.

The doorbell rings and she answers with the pestle in her hand. The UPS driver has left a small box covered in barcodes, its return address Clearwater, Florida. Eleanor figures this must be *Datura stramonium*, native to the Southern states, a highly effective treatment for asthma when you smoke it; and also atropine, an antispasmodic that relaxes the lungs.

She hears a clattering racket downstairs in her husband's home office. She cocks a practiced ear and listens. Nothing more. She glances at her watch: four thirty in the afternoon; she has yet to see him today. The moment Luc left for Carleton, Eleanor and Giles began occupying separate wings of the house. Any feeble attempt to hide their new arrangement was foiled when their son visited in early October of his freshman year and called the charade foolish; both Luc and his sister, Janine, had already figured out that the marriage had foundered.

Giles is an artist who grew up just outside Montreal. He stopped painting years ago and is now an instructor of studio art at Dartmouth. He hates the university's politics, its rich-kid-jock mentality, and is always insulted whenever students miss his class in favor of intramural sports. A proud French Canadian, he complains that the university's so-called racial diversity is token, that it's a school filled with "tall white boys" and "white professors" who are secretly elitist and homophobic. His most recent rant was aimed at the head of the creative writing program in the English department, who refused to hire a gay black Cuban novelist—whom he and the other hiring-committee members felt was the strongest candidate— because she claimed she "couldn't work with the man." " . . .Which just proves my point once again," he said to Eleanor, "that many Americans are secretly racist and homophobic." He then proceeded to get so drunk that he fell asleep in his office—and inadvertently spilled bourbon on some student drawings.

Several times a year, usually when the seasons are shifting, Giles caves in to depression: withdrawn and unreachable, he drinks recklessly for weeks on end. Any admiration Eleanor once had for his dedication to teaching, his erudition, and his social conscience has been obliterated by his alcoholism. On one glass of wine, he can be charming, two or three glasses, mean as a snake; however, beyond four, he relaxes into a docile, sometimes even philosophical, lush.

Giles has expected far too much of his children. Ironically, he always discouraged any creativity, a stance that had little effect on their daughter, who conquered high school and graduated Phi Beta Kappa from Carleton with a degree in biology, but was crippling to Luc, who inherited his father's artistic talents and whose promise in painting and drawing actually intensified after his frightening head injury during a hockey game.

When Luc's injury first occurred, he suffered weird temporal daydreams. He claimed that his ability to care deeply about his responsibilities and even other people was somehow being short-circuited. The doctors urged Eleanor and Giles to expose him to intense external stimuli, encouraged them, for example, to take their son to hear the Boston Symphony. When they did, Luc complained that the music in the concert hall took on near physical form and he wanted to jump out of his seat and flee. He found city crowds overwhelming, so they visited quiet places like the Fogg Museum at Harvard. There, staring at Rossetti's "Blessed Damozel," Luc claimed that something having to do with the way the light filigreed through the woman's golden hair reconnected him to a deep yearning for his family, even for his father, whom he often seemed to despise.

"I think I'm going to be okay now," he kept assuring them on the drive back to Vermont. "I feel almost normal." But Eleanor's optimism remained guarded until the neurologists did their tests and, while seeming satisfied that Luc's recovery was progressing, warned that these moments of normality might be only short-term. And they were. Soon, disaffection came over Luc again, and he was depressed for months. More susceptible to future head injuries and seizures, he faced off against his doctors who tried to dissuade him from playing any sports, while encouraging him to develop his considerable ability as an artist. But he ignored them. He claimed that drawing and painting now made him feel worse and that playing sports actually distracted him and made him feel better. He took up soccer, considered to be a lot safer than hockey. That he was a smart kid was widely acknowledged, but Luc remained a mediocre student. His stellar soccer skills would barely get him accepted into Carleton, where, as the brother and son and grandson of alums, he'd had an admissions advantage.

Luc is the more beautiful of her two children, and recognizing this, his sister Janine will often say the quality is wasted on him. As the object of affection of so many girls, all too quickly he grew indifferent toward the ones he dated. And the ones who came to love him, loved him, Eleanor suspects, because of his remoteness. Six-foot-two with those piercing light gray eyes and hair thick and wavy and black—he's the finest combination of traits from both his father's family and hers.

A year after the accident in the hockey rink, at the age of fifteen, Luc shocked all of them by going out one night with some of his older high school buddies and never coming home. Frantic with worry, Eleanor began contacting the parents of his friends until she learned that, riding in the backseat of a car, he had gone suspiciously quiet and eventually asked to be let out. When his friends resisted, he began screaming until they dropped him off on the side of the road. He ran several hundred yards, stuck his thumb out, and the very next car gave him a ride. His friends didn't think to follow and get the license plate. They just figured he had somewhere to go.

After forty-eight hours, they and the police began contacting children's shelters in the downtown areas of Boston and Portland and Burlington. But there was no word. They endured a dismal, frantic two weeks and then received a phone call from a woman in Connecticut who explained that Luc had shown up at her family farm and, claiming to be eighteen, asked if they were hiring. He was taken on, given a room, but seemed particularly withdrawn. Suspicious, the woman took it upon herself to search through his things and found a card from the Norwich, Vermont library and was able to track down his parents.

There was a brief window of time that began last summer when Luc actually seemed happier than he'd ever been, when he'd come home from his seasonal job working on a road crew and spend hours in his room lying on his bed, sending and receiving text messages. Eleanor sensed that he'd fallen in love, but when she hinted at this a few times, he claimed there was nobody in his life.

"Probably a man," Giles pronounced to her blithely one scorching evening when Luc was out with his friends, and they were sitting on the screened-in porch drinking gin and tonics, trying to stay cool. In the ebbing light beyond them, a copse of silver birch trees had tarnished to the color of ash.

Eleanor considered this. "Why would you say that? He's had so many girlfriends."

Giles fished the wedge of lime out of his cocktail and looked at her fixedly with his inky dark eyes. "As if the two can't coexist?"

"I suppose they can," she said at last.

"And if so, if it is a man, that would explain . . . his behavior in his relationships with women."

Eleanor found herself doubting her husband's opinion. She'd always felt that Giles was jealous of Luc, competitive with him, and perhaps would be relieved that Luc would at some point stop bringing young girls around, girls who'd make his father feel invisible. She wondered where her son might be at that very moment, tried to imagine him entangled with another man in the same moody light.

"But wouldn't he know we'd accept it?" she said at last. "He knows how tight you are with some of your colleagues."

"But he never tells us anything about himself," Giles reminded her.

"That's because of the injury. He can't help that."

"He was like this before the injury," Giles disagreed, and then pointed out, "so easy for us to blame anything objectionable he does on the injury. But the fact is now he lives in the world of college sports. It's the last frontier to accept sexual diversity."

"Yes, and who encouraged him to live in that world? By discouraging his art?"

Giles looked miffed by her uncharacteristic aggressive tone. He said, "I did in the beginning, I admit. But not after the accident. After the accident, it was up to Luc. He wanted to play soccer." Giles drained the rest of his drink, and then said, "I discouraged him. Of course I did. Because I failed at it. And I didn't—I don't—want him to fail and end up like me." He obviously knew this would effectively table the discussion.

Luc's summer elation turned brackish in the autumn and numb by the winter, and he grew sullen and withdrawn. When he started dating Elizabeth, he seemed to revive. Although she'd met Elizabeth only one time, Eleanor felt drawn to the girl. But then she heard from Janine that the relationship had ended abruptly. She asked Luc why he couldn't have told her himself, and with uncharacteristic candor he said, "Elizabeth wanted way too much, Mom. She was really suffering over it. That's not good for anybody. But I know you liked her."

"I hardly knew her," Eleanor had replied. "But what I knew of her, I did like."

Luc went on to say, "When it isn't equal between two people, the one who cares less never sees the best of the one who cares more . . . Trust me, Mom, my breaking it off was an act of mercy."

An act of mercy? This appraisal startled her; he'd spoken like somebody who'd already traveled the arc of several long-term relationships and was now looking back with the precision of hindsight. She'd realized with a great pang of despair that she didn't know the man her son had become, the man who maybe even knew more about love than she did; she and Giles had married early in their lives.

It's just after six o'clock now. Giles still has not emerged from his side of the house, where they have installed a hot plate that he uses when they don't have dinner together, which is half the time. Eleanor is warming up a lentil casserole that she plans to offer him, when the phone rings. He's calling from his office downstairs. "Can you come to see me, please?" he says, and she can tell immediately that he's been drinking. She turns down the flame under her casserole, takes the stairs down to Giles's office, and raps on the door.

"Come on in."

The room reeks of bourbon as she enters. He's sitting slightly hunched over in his swivel chair, his cloudy black eyes squinting at her, red-rimmed, his body quaking like one of those ceramic sports mascots whose heads rest on springs. He's six-two, the same height as Luc, and his once impressive mass of muscle has softened, not from his age but from empty calories of alcohol; he has become a lanky man with a beer gut. With a glance at his desk, she can spy a sheaf of what she assumes are student drawings that Giles is grading while in his cups. "Dad's a functional alcoholic," Janine has often pronounced. "But as long as he gets his work done, Dartmouth will never get rid of him. He has enough of a name, even though he no longer produces anything of merit."

A harsh verdict against any father.

"What's going on?" Eleanor asks.

When Giles speaks, his words are garbled. "I've had another warning."

"From the dean?" she fills in quickly.

"Right." His expression is pained. "More students . . . complained that I'm harsh. My enrollment has dropped. As you know, if my classes aren't well attended, they can let me go."

She can't help thinking of the shortfall of money this would bring about, and she has her doubts about whether Giles could even get a job at a private high school like Sharon Academy where the salaries are pitifully low, let alone another university. "Maybe you should think about going back to AA meetings."

"I *have* been going. I went today to the noon meeting in Hanover."

Eleanor is puzzled; as far as she knows, he hasn't left his office, much less told her he'd gone to an AA meeting. Maybe when she was working in the greenhouse, he could have slipped out? She points to his cocktail glass. "But you're still drinking."

"They take you in anyway. At the meetings."

Like lost sheep. "Well then, maybe it's high time to stop."

He nods and then announces, "I'm going to get another Antabuse prescription."

In the past, Giles sometimes felt compelled to drink even while on the medication, his body flushing with heat, his face turning blotchy red; vertiginous, he'd lose his balance and fall down, once or twice vomiting all over himself. "I would suggest you cut back on your drinking before you go on Antabuse again," she tells him.

"Good idea. I will," he says with sudden childlike enthusiasm.

Staring at the vessel of her once powerful and domineering and now prematurely aged husband, Eleanor reminds herself how hard it must be for this fifty-five-year-old man to resign himself to the sadness of his failure as a working artist that goes hand in hand with his self-abuse. After all, he's still somewhat in his prime. She remembers their earlier life when he brimmed with ambition and promise and self-confidence, when he was invited to show his work in Boston and Portland, Maine. He's staring into space now, dazzled by drinking, so disconcertingly far away, and her only comfort is that once he got beyond his secondary school hijinks, Luc, at college, seemed to have grown wary of alcohol. Obviously, she can't know for sure, but at least in the summertime Luc never comes home inebriated after being out with his buddies. She thinks back on the past summer and nights he told her he was staying out with friends when he was probably staying with this unknown person — perhaps a man who once, but perhaps no longer, brought him so much happiness.

Waking and sleeping in a hospital bed, his elevated leg wrapped in blue strips of fiberglass, Sam is only vaguely aware of nurses coming and going and asking him what he wants to eat. He is still dreaming of those shadows coming down over Black Diamond Fall and sometimes believes he's still out there waiting for the arrival of the helicopter. He has no idea how many days have passed, but it's early morning now. He sits up in bed and looks out his window, at the white crowns of the Wasatch, a paring of moon slung low in the wakening sky. A bearish, blond-haired male nurse comes into his room to ask, "How you feeling today?"

Trying to assess, Sam says, "I don't know. I guess I'm better, I suppose I'm better."

The nurse looks concerned. "You've been pretty out of it. We think it might be due to the shock you were in when you arrived. Then, of course, there are the pain meds." After a reflective pause, the man asks, "Do you think you feel well enough to talk to somebody?"

"Talk to somebody?"

The nurse looks discomfited. "A police detective is here. He's been waiting to see you."

In the midst of his groggy state, Sam's alarm is muted. "A police detective? Why?"

The nurse shakes his head. "Didn't say why. Just waiting. Now, would you like something to eat this morning?"

Bewildered, drugged, Sam tries to figure out if he's hungry. "I guess. Sure."

———————

In the spring of the previous year, out of boredom and loneliness, he placed an ad on Craigslist, a shirtless picture of himself posted with the stern warning that any response without including a photo would be ignored. Disappointed by the blurry, hardly revealing image Luc sent, he calculated a twenty-six-year age difference between them. But Luc e-mailed persistently until Sam gave in, thinking to himself: *He's close to twenty-three, how bad can he be?* Never anticipating the tall, strapping guy wearing aviators who drove up to the country store in a Mini Cooper. And Sam, on his motorcycle, leaning in the passenger window and asking Luc to take his sunglasses off, awed by the pale-slate eyes against the dark hair, the blond streaks in the young man's beard from having spent the summer working in road repair. And the very quiet moment when two people look deeply into one another and see something at once welcoming and disturbing.

"Your picture almost lies," was the first thing he told Luc, concealing his delight.

"I have to . . . lie, because it's a secret," Luc replied, the first words that Sam, of course, should have heeded.

But Sam had also lied. "I'm actually forty-nine, not forty-four," he admitted.

"It's okay. I'm only into mature guys," Luc told him, then winked and admonished, "But tell the truth next time!"

Sam thought it would be quick and easy. He never dreamed he'd be compelled to tell the young man how beautiful he is or hear Luc say the same thing to him. Or that back at Sam's house, when they were taking a breather listening to an Internet radio station that played tunes from the sixties and seventies, Luc would recognize songs like "Under Pressure" by David Bowie, able to sing the lyrics while they were lying in bed together.

"But this is before your time," Sam remarked.

"Good music is good music," Luc said with a wise grin.

"I can't imagine growing up listening to my parents' music."

"Nobody did that . . . before the revolution," Luc pointed out. "After the revolution everything changed."

"What revolution?" Sam asked with a bit of irritation.

"Free love." Luc laughed, and laid his head on Sam's chest.

Two days later, Luc texted at eleven thirty in the morning and asked if he might visit. It was raining and his roadwork company had called it a day. Sam had already spread some blueprints out on his drafting table: a house in Cornish, New Hampshire that he was designing for a French couple, a minimalist building with walls of translucent glass, a whimsical structure that his clients loved. Due for a meeting with them at seven that evening, he'd promised to have everything finished but figured he might never get such a chance again with somebody like this, somebody so open, so youthfully unguarded in the act of love.

When the young man walked in the door, his Adidas bag slung over his shoulder and a sheepish, slightly frightened look on his face, Sam guessed Luc had probably thought a lot about their first encounter and that sheer carnal compulsion had driven him to the second.

As they were passing Sam's home office, Luc noticed the plans on the drafting table and wandered in. "What are these?" he said, gently caressing the blueprints with a finger.

Sam approached and fit his chin on Luc's shoulder. "House I'm designing. Done a lot for these people. Did their place in France."

"Where at?"

"A town called Lourmarin, it's in—"

"I know where it is. We know a Canadian lady who has a

house there. And that guy who wrote all those books about Provence was really describing Lourmarin. Now our friend says because of those books, that town is overrun—it's ruined." Luc regarded the row of photographs above the drafting table and smiled goofily. "Would these houses be your designs?"

"Yup. All local. Except for the one in France . . ." Sam pointed to a photo of the old stone house whose remodeling he'd overseen. "I've never done anything on a large scale, like an office building."

Luc shrugged it off. "So what? You make a living at it, don't you? Better than bloodsucking on Wall Street or ambulance chasing, right?" He winked. "Plus, you're sexy, mon," he said with a Caribbean accent. "You're Jewish, right?"

"I am."

"Love Jewish guys. You're too sexy, really."

"What does that mean?"

Luc laughed. "I don't know, and don't make me explain it. Just keep being it." And then he kissed Sam.

A lanky man of around forty-five with a trim beard and dark eyes strolls into the hospital room. "Hello, Mr. Solomon. Glad to see you're feeling a little better," he says with a quiet, thoughtful air. Glancing at the cast that ends just below Sam's knee, he remarks, "Tough luck, this injury. Fortunately, you're going to be okay."

Sam says, "You mean that I'll walk again."

"I was told you'll be able to ski again, too, but maybe not Black Diamond Fall."

Black Diamond Fall. How does he know about Black Diamond Fall? "Who are you, anyway?"

The man fixes him with a steady, importunate gaze. He's different, bonier than the Vermont policemen Sam knows—locals, young beer-drinking guys who opt for the academy instead of college. "I'm Detective Nick Jenkins," he says. "I'm from Carleton, Vermont. And I am here on behalf of the college. I'm here because Luc Flanders has been missing for five days. He was last seen on February eleventh."

The news is a slug to Sam's chest, and for a moment he stares at Jenkins blankly. And barely has the presence of mind to say, "Missing as in he took off somewhere?"

Gazing at Sam with a furrowed expression, the detective says, "I'm going to sit down." He grabs a hard chair and perches in it backward next to Sam's hospital bed. A group of chattering nurses passes the door to the room. Waiting until their voices die down, the detective says, "Right now, that seems to be the likeliest possibility."

Sam becomes aware of avian sounds. Twitters, squawks; they must be outside the window. But then his medicated haze burns away with a realization.

"When did you say he was last heard from?"

"February eleventh."

"That's the night I left for Utah."

"Yes, I know. We've spoken to your friend, Mike."

Sam peers at the detective. "It wouldn't be the first time Luc—"

"We understand he disappeared once before."

"The last time I think he forgot who he was—"

"Because of a head injury."

"His parents were frantic."

"They're frantic now," Jenkins says.

This is alarming. "So why are you coming to me? I haven't seen him since December."

There's a pause. "The hope originally was that he might have been with you in Utah. Or maybe you know where he is."

"Might have been with me," Sam repeats slowly. "But nobody even knew about us."

The detective smiles tightly. "They obviously do now."

Sam tries to imagine the parents, whose disapproval Luc always feared, out of their minds with worry and then having to swallow the fact that their son had fallen in love with a much older man. "So where was he last seen?"

Jenkins explains that Luc Flanders had been playing pond hockey with his roommates, left with them and then, alone, went back to the ice later on. "And that was the last anybody saw or heard from him."

"Was there a search?"

The detective nods. "Groups of students and locals. Nothing was found except his and his friends' footprints. We even sent somebody down under the frozen pond."

The idea of a search below the icy skin of a body of water sounds urgent, like a desperate measure, and Sam shivers. "Then . . . surely he's got to be . . . alive somewhere."

Jenkins waits a moment before saying, "I'd like to believe he's alive."

Luc couldn't be dead, just couldn't. Sam looks at his immobile leg in the cast and feels even more trapped.

The detective holds his hands up in calm surrender. "Do you want a break?"

"No."

Jenkins takes out a small pad and jots something down. Then he leans back in his chair and glances toward the window and the blue, flawless curve of the western sky. "So when exactly was the last time you saw Luc Flanders?"

"On December twenty-eighth."

"And you met up where?"

"My place."

"In South Woodstock."

"Yes. He stopped by. Basically to break it off with me."

Jenkins jots this down. "Do you have any thoughts of where he might have gone on February eleventh?"

"I don't."

"Did you get any emails or messages from him before or after February eleventh?"

Sam shakes his head. "Nothing. I texted him a few times after it ended and he never even answered."

"Emails exchanged?"

"Nope. I managed to get him on the phone once in January. That was the only time we were in contact."

Jenkins stares at him steadily, almost appraisingly. "He didn't leave his phone behind, but we got the phone records. We saw the call you made to him. And we saw the texts you sent to him. But since he disappeared on February eleventh, there has been no activity, no texts, no phone calls."

"Maybe he lost his phone. Or somebody stole it."

"Certainly possible," Jenkins says. "So on February eleventh, what time did you leave home to drive down to Boston?"

"Around seven in the evening."

"Do you have any way of proving where you were at six p.m.?"

"Not really. But I was home," Sam says.

Jenkins reaches into his breast pocket and pulls out a folded piece of white paper and hands it to Sam, who recognizes a color photocopy of his own Carleton College ring, which he gave to Luc. "Can you identify this?"

"Yeah, I can. It's mine . . . well, it *was* mine."

"*Was* yours?"

"I gave it to Luc. I let him have it. He couldn't afford one of his own at the time, and he liked the idea of wearing it." Against a blast of anxiety, Sam forces himself to ask, "Where did you find this?"

"He lost it. On the ice. He mentioned the loss to . . . one of his friends. We believe that's why he went back to the pond. To look for it."

The ring: a Carleton College brass signet ring cast by Jostens. Luc recognized it one afternoon in a carved mahogany box on a dresser in Sam's bedroom. Picked it up and saw "1990" on one side and "PANTHERS" on the other, and turned it over in his palm. "Nineteen ninety. Year I was born."

"You gonna get one?" Sam asked.

"Thinking about it, but I'm not what you call sentimental." Luc offered the ring up to the ceiling light like a jewel. "How come you never wear it?"

"My friends were buying them in droves. I just followed them. But I never liked the way it looked. I'm not the college ring sort."

"It's kind of classic. Kind of retro."

"Well, you are kind of retro," Sam observed.

"Anyway, they're at least five hundred dollars. I don't have the dough. And my parents would never pay for it."

"Then just take mine." Sam turned his palms up, grinning goofily.

Luc watched his expression to see if he was in earnest. "Really?"

"Why not? I wore it maybe twice. And took it off and never wore it again. It's been sitting there collecting dust for years. Take it, really, if you think you'd wear it. I know I'll never wear it again."

"Unless they bury you in it," Luc joked, even though he told Sam he often conjured up his death—like from a motorcycle accident—and believed it would be impossible to bear.

"I mean, would you wear it?"

"Of course!"

"But what would your parents say? The ring says '1990' on it."

"They would never notice something like that. And if they did, I'd just tell them somebody found it in equipment storage and sold it to me. I'd tell them I bought it because it was stamped with the year I was born." He laughed.

"I'd hate to see you lie," Sam pointed out sadly.

"In fact," Jenkins now says, "his mother did notice the date of the ring and he did lie to her about how he got it. He also lied about it to his girlfriend, but she figured out that it was yours."

Sam is overwhelmed. "I think I need some water. Can you ask . . . them?"

The detective points at a bedside table holding a large translucent plastic cup of water. "Ah." Sam grabs it and, taking a long drink, glances out the hospital window. The hospital is on the outskirts of the city and is monolithically tall in comparison to the buildings surrounding it. From the bedside, he can actually see the round leavened shape of the Mormon Tabernacle, clusters of people swarming around it like frantic ants.

"I think I need to rest for a bit," he says. "That okay?"

"That's fine. I have to call my colleague back in Vermont, anyway. How about I come back in . . . say, an hour?

"Whenever you want. I'm your captive audience here," Sam tells him.

Once the detective leaves, Sam, woozy and bewildered, switches on the television and starts flipping through the channels. Until he comes upon a men's soccer game.

It brings him back to a lazy afternoon several months after the tsunami struck Japan, he and Luc sprawled over each other watching the Women's World Cup. Luc was rooting for the Japanese team, claiming that the devastated country's morale needed it. Sam was pulling for the Americans. Watching the American team struggle against a disciplined Japanese defense, Luc said, "The Japanese deserve to win. Look at how beautifully they're playing. They're hot!" Sam found himself plummeting into jealous silence.

Then Luc turned to him. "I guess I won't be able to get married," he said wistfully.

"Oh?"

"Can't stomach the idea of cheating on my wife." Luc moved closer to him, his lips now only a few inches away. "With a man. And I would, especially if I had somebody like you," he said sweetly. A roar erupted from the television: Japan had scored a goal. "Yes!" Luc cheered, pumping a fist. He then turned back to Sam with a more confident smile.

"You're right, though." Sam picked up the thread of their discussion. "It wouldn't be fair." And then he watched clouds of confusion and conflict drift over Luc's face. Hoping that this wisdom and self-awareness might come to bear on what was between them. Against his better judgment and against all the advice of his savvy, caring friends, Sam was already dreaming of the impossible: of Luc eventually coming to his senses. And when he did, Sam would be there waiting for him.

The night of the soccer game was the first time Luc stayed over. Sam roasted a chicken, and they sat in candlelight eating and polishing off a six-pack of local beer. Luc explained that he never wanted to join a fraternity, wasn't on Facebook, and spent his sophomore year without a cell phone.

"I like the fact that this is uncomplicated," Luc said at last, candlelight flickering on his face, so that in certain moments he looked older, more mature.

"Is it?" Sam wondered.

"Relatively, don't you think?" Luc looked momentarily bewildered.

"Yes, but only because we get together on your schedule — on your time, not mine," Sam pointed out.

"So are you saying I've inconvenienced you?" Luc carefully lined up the empty bottles of beer, not meeting Sam's eyes.

"Look at me," Sam said, and when Luc did, he declared, "No!"

"Okay." Luc sounded relieved and smiled his sweet, intoxicating smile.

"But this is the sort of thing that can only flourish in . . . a hothouse environment," Sam tried to point out. "We can't be seen together in public. You're not out and . . . the age difference is obvious. I'm nearly the same age as your parents, so they'd certainly never understand."

"I guess what I mean," Luc went on, slightly frustrated, "is that we get together, we have fun, but we don't ask anything of each other. And then we're back in our own lives."

"It's actually a lot trickier. Because even when you don't want or expect things to get complicated, they always seem to. Because even when you remind yourself of all the pitfalls . . ." Sam hesitated, and then said, "In the end, the heart wants what it wants."

The weather had changed yet again in Luc's face; a look of deep affection suffusing it now, he reached forward with a large, chafed hand and took Sam's. "All I know is I really want you," he said.

That night, Luc wanted to be taken more fiercely than ever, coaxing Sam to go harder and harder so that the pleasure felt more like punishment. But Luc's face was slack in the sublime. And then his unqualified "I love you, Sam," in the middle of it all.

Carried away, Luc may not have realized what he said, and although Sam felt compelled to say it back, he didn't for fear of drawing attention to such a precious exclamation and startling this exotic bird into flight. But he carried it with him, the simple affirmation that is chanted over and over again during the life of most love affairs, but which he would hear from Luc only a few times in practically a whisper. And it would have more meaning for him than from all the declarations of people who'd ever loved him, and to all the people he'd ever loved.

And then they spooned, Luc's arm draped over Sam's chest, and Luc fell asleep almost immediately. Sam knew he'd have to extricate himself to get any rest, but held the backward embrace, superstitiously telling himself if he remained this way, they could eventually be a couple. He lay awake all night, until he could spy shadows on the walls of his bedroom, until the sky faded into light. Luc slept deeply, innocently, his mouth slightly open, his breath souring. It was real life now, maybe even real love, named hours before in a sort of fever, a shiny token tossed into a deep well that still glimmered from far below. But Luc was gone by 8 a.m., and listening to his car drive away with a crushing sound of gravel, Sam felt terribly alone.

FEBRUARY 16; SALT LAKE CITY, UTAH; 35 DEGREES, STEADY RAIN

Jenkins manages to find a sparsely populated lounge down the hallway from the hospital room and sits for a moment collecting his thoughts before calling his partner, Helen Kennedy, in Carleton, Vermont. Some sort of hospital orderly in mint green garb appears, pushing a metal cart of what looks like wound dressings—gauze pads, cotton balls, rolls of flesh-toned tape—to a window that views the spokes of streets in the flat city surrounded by a white panorama of mountains. Jenkins can spy a package of Marlboros sticking out of the man's pocket. With a curious glance at him, the fellow extracts a single cigarette and heads toward a bank of elevators.

Watching idly until the man disappears, Jenkins turns his attention once more toward the window and looks out toward the Wasatch Mountains. There's a certain feeling the West gives him—he went to college in California— expansive, magisterial yet starkly prehistoric. The mountains of the West, jagged, monolithic, look as though they recently erupted into existence. Whereas the mountains of the East, softer, rounder, more beaten down, perhaps give a more accurate account of thousands of centuries having passed since the world was formed. Glancing idly down toward the hospital parking lot, Jenkins spies what looks like a sculpture of an American Indian head painted terracotta red and sporting a feather crown. He can't imagine finding something similar in the parking lot of an East Coast hospital.

Jenkins is struck by the fact that Sam Solomon is more or less his own age and, somewhat similarly, still pushing himself to physical extremes. Part of pushing himself was Solomon's risking an involvement with a much younger man who, according to his parents, was conflicted about his sexuality. Like Sam, Jenkins is a skier, although he does more Nordic skiing than downhill, and bicycles in the summer— often with a crowd of younger guys. It occurs to him that they just might be two men trying to hold on to their power, two men afraid of aging. And then his years of investigative experience kick in and he hears the warning voice of some mentor or other in his head saying, *If the suspect happens to be your brother, cut him even less rope.*

"Got there safe and sound?" Kennedy asks when he calls her.

"Yup. Easy flight. No delays. Some bumps on the way in."

"So what's the update?"

"Well, I'm at the hospital."

"And how does he seem to you?"

"Genuinely surprised and upset."

"You believe him?"

"He sounds it."

There is a speculative lull and then Kennedy asks, "So what's his alibi?"

"He claims that, except for that phone call, he and Luc Flanders haven't really communicated since December twenty-eighth."

"But that's not true. They did. Texts. Emails."

"Yup."

"So what do you think?"

Jenkins wrestles with the thought. At last he says, "I think they possibly could have seen each other right before Sam left town. But I'll reframe the question."

"Alibi probably isn't going to change."

Thoughtful for a moment, at last Jenkins says, "I kind of wish it was you out here questioning this man instead of me."

Kennedy asks, "Why?"

"I just think you'd be better at it."

"Better at questioning him?"

"Yeah."

"I don't buy it. There is another reason why you're saying this. Are you going easy on him?"

"Not really. Well, maybe a little."

"Then get over yourself, Nick," Kennedy says.

Jenkins glances at his watch. "All right. I will. Get over myself."

"So when are you going back in to see him?"

"He's doped up right now. I'm going to wait until just before he gets his next painkiller injection. I tried to ask the nurse when it would be."

"And she didn't tell you."

"Of course not. So maybe I'll go and do some sightseeing. Check out the Tabernacle."

"The Tabernacle? You can't get into The Tabernacle unless you're Mormon."

"Then maybe I'll sit outside the Tabernacle and watch the multiple wedding parties."

FEBRUARY 11, 5:15 P.M.; CARLETON, VERMONT; 8 DEGREES, CLEAR SKIES

Skating at night. Flying across the ice under the blaze of a full moon. Wearing baggy snow pants and sweatshirts, Luc Flanders and his roommates, Will McKinnon and Charlie Taft, are playing pond hockey. There's no checking in pond hockey, no fouling, just a makeshift rink carved out of a column of thigh-high snow and goals made out of muck boots spaced four feet apart. Part of the challenge: not to drive the puck deep into the drifts that rise off the pond like frozen waves. They each have come with three pucks, and by the end of the game these pucks will have vanished into sparkling powder.

Luc might have continued playing hockey as a kid if it hadn't been for the head injury that he suffered at the age of fourteen. A point of departure in his young life, when he broke away from solid ground and entered a world of uncertainty, of light breaking into blinding points, of headaches and nausea. Upsurges of intense, almost unbearable emotions unanchored to any event and then numbness to everyone and everything. The doctors surmised that when his head slammed against the ice, his temporal lobes got rattled and that's why he had a seizure in the ambulance. The scar tissue that grew in his brain brought on the plague of vivid, feverish daydreams, and Luc soon began to understand that his body and brain were now tuned to new frequencies. After the accident, whenever he looked at colored plates of paintings in art books, he'd come away with strong after-images of brushwork and mood. He could hear music on his parents' classical music station and then days, even months later, have an exact recall of long melodic passages. Religious chorales in particular unspooled in his head, music in full orchestral flower, ripe with devotion, with light and celestial harmonies. The doctors conferred about these symptoms and then pronounced him mildly epileptic and put him on a daily dose of Lamotrigine.

At first he couldn't bear to think of himself as even slightly brain-scarred and sometimes wondered if he'd ever fully woken up after his knockout on the ice. Too often he felt dissociated from people, from friends, from family.

And, of course, the weird daydreams, the euphony of music that sometimes increases to unbearable volumes in his head. He commits desperate acts to try and wrench himself out of them. He takes freezing showers; he runs wind sprints until exhaustion. When he was younger, he'd do things like joyriding beside a friend driving without a license, underage binge drinking. He once inadvertently set a hayfield on fire.

"Earth to Flanders . . . are you passing?" Taft calls out.

Luc takes a swing and shoots foolishly. The puck goes way wide of the goal. And vanishes into the snow. "Whoa, bro, you out of it again or what?" chortles McKinnon.

"Yup, I'm out to lunch." Luc glances up at the sky, ottoman blue and just beginning to flicker with stars. Even with the moon it's almost too dark to play and they need to wrap it up.

When the game finally ends, they continue skating for the joy of it, circling one another and racing toward either end of the pond and then digging their skates into the ice and stopping before turning sharply with abandon. At some point, Luc hears something tinkling, a sound of skittering. He stops and listens to a faint groan, the perilous cracking sound of ice bridging a dark current fed by the nearby Millstone Creek. Even though people blithely drive their cars and snowmobiles across winter ponds that could in places be twelve feet thick, there will always be those patches of thin ice where even a hundred pounds of weight will cause a dangerous spiderweb fracture.

Luc skates a few feet farther and hears another sound, more brittle now, like a pebble or a loose shard, and flees toward the shore. There he notices Elizabeth, standing in a quilted light blue coat, her head tilted to the side, her long, straight, fair hair feathering back in the cold wind. Taft glides by close to him, and Luc can see the thick eyebrows raised.

Luc and Elizabeth broke off their relationship two weeks ago and have seen very little of each other on campus. They have gone to great lengths to avoid being in the same place at the same time. He glides over to her and stops with a fine spray of ice. "What's going on?" he says, a bit undone.

"Hi . . . don't meant to intrude," she says in a voice of uncertainty, "but I want you to know before you hear it from someone else. Your mom would . . ." she begins and then momentarily breaks off. What about his mother? His mother is actually quite cut up that they are no longer together; could some news about his mother have reached Elizabeth first? He believes his parents have Elizabeth's cell number, but his phone is on him and there is signal, so he resents whatever mysterious bond she might have with his mother—now placing him at some momentary disadvantage.

"Did something happen . . . to her?" he asks and she adamantly shakes her head. "Oh, God nothing like that, Luc, no, no!" And then the ridiculous thought: Could Elizabeth be pregnant? She'd been taking birth control, or so she claimed. Scanning her face again, he somehow can tell it's some other news that has nothing to do with his mother or Elizabeth. She exudes almost righteous patience, whereas she used to show up outside his off-campus apartment in acute distress and text him to say she needed to speak to him.

"I meant to say your mom probably already knows. There's a rumor going around the campus," she says at last. "About the Robert Frost farm. Have you heard it?"

"No. What about it?"

She pauses and takes a deep breath. "It's been vandalized."

"How bad?"

"I don't know. I was told furniture got broken and there's shattered glass everywhere." She hesitates and then continues, "Like a bunch of kids apparently went there to drink or something and then got out of control."

"Really?" Luc croaks.

"A fire was even started, but then I guess it got put out."

Luc slowly kneels on the ice and drops his stick. "That's crazy," he says at last, nervously rubbing his hands through his long, wavy hair, the other three staring at him. Luc's maternal grandmother, now deceased, had been a Carleton college librarian whom Robert Frost befriended. They'd maintained a lively correspondence; she'd been given several signed editions of the author's poetry, all of which his mother proudly displays on the bookshelf in the family room. Both his grandmother and his mother were experts on Frost's life, on his work, and up until recently, his mother had been a docent at the Frost farm. Time after time Luc had been ordered to bring the author's books and correspondence and photographs to show-and-tell at elementary school. It had always been a burden to stand up in front of his classmates and recite all the Frost facts.

Now he thinks that his mother, a Carleton alum, will lose it when she hears, if she hasn't heard already. Luc says to Elizabeth, "Did you call her?"

A pained look crosses her face. "Of course not. I would never call her."

"Get the facts first, Cool Hand, before you upset the apple cart," McKinnon warns, employing the nickname he gave Luc—McKinnon the only one of them to have seen the film, *Cool Hand Luke*. McKinnon has taken off his skullcap, his military-cut bright red hair slick to his skull. The nerdiest of the three and a polymath, McKinnon was accepted to

Harvard but decided—because he is such a rabid skier—to attend this venerable college in the sticks. They all look up to McKinnon.

The path back to campus winds through dense evergreen woods. Taft, with thick hair and the dark features of a Spaniard, the quietest, most introverted—and perhaps most troubled—of the three, and McKinnon stroll ahead, assuming that Luc and Elizabeth might want to talk. It's the courteous thing for them to do, but nothing more to say about the doomed relationship other than the obvious platitudes: that they want different things, and she understandably demands emotional fidelity. This was after she figured out he was suffering over Sam.

As they reach the first exterior lights of the campus, Luc is feeling overheated and unzips his jacket. Elizabeth remarks a bit snidely, "Don't you wear his ring anymore?"

He clutches his throat, feels the nakedness at his neck, then a piece of the filigree chain dangling precariously on his shirt collar like a fine, broken bone. He panics. And remembers the pinging sound, and it occurs to him that the ring must have broken free of the chain, fallen on the frozen surface of the pond and bounced somewhere. Now he has to go back to find it; leaving it there might bring him—well, bad luck, not to mention misery.

"Hey, McKinn," he calls ahead.

His roommate dances a few steps and then whirls around with a grin. "Yo."

"When you get home, can you get that big flashlight? Leave it on my desk."

"Sure, bud, what do you need it for?"

"Lost something—so just do it, okay?" His voice is obviously wound tight, and McKinnon knows him well enough not to press.

When they arrive at the entrance of Elizabeth's dorm, she

turns to him. "I actually have a flashlight in my room. I'll lend it to you."

Flustered, he glances up at the sky. "Nah, it's okay."

"It's small and really powerful," she insists almost angrily. "Wait here just a second. Be right back." He knows she must be glad he lost the ring, so why is she offering to help him find it?

As she rushes into the boxy, gray brick building, eyeing her slim athletic body he thinks: *Shame that she doesn't move on to any number of the kids who were always so envious when we were together.* But then thinks that one of the illogical conceits of love was detecting ambivalence and feeling compelled to stay with a person in order to disprove it. Elizabeth returns with one of those LEDs the size of a small pastille box, hands it to him. "I'll bring it back," he promises.

"No rush, " she says flatly. Leaning forward, Luc hugs her quickly, awkwardly, and hurries off toward the Campus Security Office on South Main Street.

Walking along the cold, empty lanes of the college, he remembers the last time he made love to Elizabeth, the incorporeal sensation of looking down on his own body, on his ass pumping mechanically and joylessly. He went soft inside her, the first time he'd ever gone soft inside a woman, and they'd had to stop and he'd made excuses for it, said he wasn't feeling well.

And afterward they were just lying there in the gloom of his bedroom. A late afternoon at the tail end of January, and trying to transit the awkwardness of their failed coupling, they began talking about how, even though the winter was young, the light was fracturing differently on the snow, wasn't quite as harsh, and days already seemed to be getting longer, or were they both imagining it, even hoping for it? They were talking about taking the shuttle bus up Route 125 and going skiing together the next day and Luc wanting to try a pair of skis one of his buddies who wrote for a skiing website had lent him. But he was so incredibly sad as he lay there, his whole body pulsing in distress. And that's when she turned to him in the midst of their idle chatter.

"Something's obviously wrong. What is it, Luc?"

He frowned and said unconvincingly, "Nothing's wrong. Nothing at all."

"That's what you always say, and every time you say it, I know it's not true. I know there is something." She sat up in bed and then gently turned his head, focused out the window, toward her. And the rueful look in her eyes. "There is someone. You're thinking about somebody else. You love somebody else," she accused at last, the first and only time she'd ever say it.

The confirmation came in the simple fact that he kept his eyes averted when he replied, "No. That's wrong." And yet he knew how transparent his denial probably appeared to her.

And then she reached over to the dresser and grabbed the college ring with the date 1990, which was carefully folded up in the chain from which he wore it and which she'd insisted he take off. "I'm not stupid," she said, banging the ring and the chain against his naked shoulder. "I mean, you're wearing a man's ring around your neck. Why aren't you wearing it on your finger?"

After Luc broke it off with Sam, he couldn't bear to put the ring in a dark drawer. So he'd kept it tight against his body like a hair shirt, a constant reminder that he'd killed something rare and beautiful. "I just don't," was all he said in response.

"That ring is from 1990. Means he's old. Way old. Old enough to be your father!" And then her fury finally unleashed. "Why are you with me if you can't be honest about him?" she hissed.

He was gazing at her now. "I don't want to be with any-body else, Elizabeth. And once you get tired of this, of me—"

"No! You're the one who's tired of it."

He shook his head. "I'm not. And I won't be."

"Luc," she said, "you need to tell me if you want to be with somebody else."

He shook his head and said, "No. . . I don't know."

She pressed, "That's clearly a yes. Which means you've been with him already. And you don't know where he's been when he's not with you."

"He hasn't been with anybody."

"You can't be sure—"

"I am sure." Which, he had to admit, was not completely true.

Moments passed and at last she said, "Just tell me if you love him."

"I did. I did love him."

"You do. You still love him!" she accused, and finally he looked at her full on and slowly nodded his head. "Then why aren't you guys together?" she agonized.

And Luc's eyes had brimmed with tears. "We had a misunderstanding. I left. And now he doesn't want me back."

He is climbing the wooden steps of the white clapboard building. The campus security guard on duty is a portly woman with thinning hair dyed honey-blond and clumsily striated with platinum highlights. He remembers she got involved in an investigation a month or so ago when Portia, Elizabeth's roommate, reported that somebody had broken into their room and stolen a bunch of "intimate garments."

"What can I do for you?" The guard speaks with an accent that is either German or Scandinavian.

"I just heard something about the Robert Frost farm?" The woman remains silent. "That it was broken into?"

She stares at him, suspicious. "And this concerns you how?"

"I . . . I'm . . . My grandmother was a close friend."

Now the woman's flat expression relaxes into questioning awe. "Ah," she says. "You're Flanders, aren't you?"

"Yes."

"The provost called your mother. Maybe thirty minutes ago. Have you spoken to her?"

"Not yet." And then retrieves his phone from his pocket. A text from McKinnon saying the flashlight is primed, but nothing else, no other messages. "I heard stuff was broken? The place was set on fire?"

The woman's hard Teutonic features are set to discourage any further inquiry. "We are instructed not to give out any information right now. I would suggest that you get hold of your mother."

Knowing he's reached an impasse, Luc says, "Okay, thanks," and hurries out into the frigid night. He exhales heavily, his breath curling into the numbing air. The last thing he wants is to listen to his mother ranting on about how she always knew a break-in was going to happen, how she'd been warning the college for years and unsuccessfully lobbying them to install an alarm system. He realizes there is nothing he can do about the Robert Frost house for the moment, but at least he can find the ring.

Outside, the wind has picked up and he stops for a moment to blink grit out of his eyes. The icy pathways and the streets are strewn with abrading sand. It has been a particularly brutal and snowy winter, and the plowed drifts on either side of him rise up into five-foot-high bleachers. Deep winter is something Luc has always loved, even more than the glorious, temperate Vermont summers, but part of his preference is the result of his father forcing him to take on whatever physical labor jobs were offered to high school and college students in the summer: tarring weather-beaten roads with a crew of mostly older and scraggly men, donning iridescent orange vests and directing traffic under a relentless New England sun that tanned his skin so deeply. Winter meant freedom.

He no longer needs to stop at home to borrow McKinnon's flashlight. He pats Elizabeth's LED to make sure it's still safe in his pocket. As he hurries along, the wind is moderate now, the moon lodged above a hill to the west of campus, and he can see a swath of ivory trickling through the trees. The pond lies flat and silver under the moon, and he remembers Thoreau's description of Walden Pond as an unbroken mirror—just like it is now, even in a varnished glaze. Arriving at the cleared hockey sward, he extracts the flashlight and trains it on the perimeters, thinking that, from an angle, he might catch a metallic glint. The shaft of light contours the drifts, and at once he can see a puck lodged there like a small cornered animal. He takes this as a promising sign. Venturing farther out on the ice, he cadges the puck and stuffs it in his coat pocket, feeling a little more hopeful now that he'll find Sam's ring. Then chafes at himself for losing it, for wearing it around his neck, which was always precarious, not to mention chicken-shit. He just should have left it on his finger. Even in the pain of losing him, Sam had said nothing about taking the ring back, allowing Luc to imagine that Sam still wanted him to wear it.

Luc's phone vibrates in his pocket, and he awkwardly yanks it out to see a phone message from Mom. No way will he subject himself to her manic scramble for facts about the Frost farm. Right now he cannot be enlisted in her drama. And he certainly has no desire to explain where he is or why he can't talk, just as he was never able to tell her about Sam. It's one thing to say, "I've fallen in love with a man," quite another to say, "He's actually the same age as you are, Mom, and chances are, in the Upper Valley of Vermont and New Hampshire, you have people—friends—in common." His mother, despite her own misgivings, would have insisted on meeting Sam, and even had Sam agreed, it'd be hard for any parent to accept their child loved someone old enough to be his own father. And such romantic age differences are never dignified unless perhaps an older man is courting a much younger woman whose companionship everybody assumes is paid for, her sex paid for, her love paid for.

But Sam is different. He's probably leaving for Utah just about now, hell-bent on skiing Black Diamond Fall with his buddy, Mike. Didn't Sam once say, "I'm on a timetable, Luc, I'm not getting any younger." Luc imagines Sam taking pictures and videos of the ascent, of the final gratifying run to the bottom of the canyon.

He kneels and the pond is cold on his bones. He lies down and, cheek to the ice, begins sweeping the flashlight beam. Unexpected tears of longing trickle down—he had no idea they were coming—and his wet face momentarily bonds to the cold surface. He rears up and wipes away the frozen salty crud, then lies down again and propels himself around with his legs, his eyes scouring the light's field of vision. He's just about to give up when he notices a glimmer of something and fumbles with the flashlight until he finds it again—an object coruscating on a snowdrift at the far corner near where they'd put up their makeshift goal. The ring! It must have bounced and rolled across the ice. He gets up and starts moving toward it and then feels the warmth of someone's bodily presence behind him.

Sam opens his eyes to find Jenkins sitting in one of the hard chairs, the detective staring dolefully at his notepad, but not writing anything.

"You been here long?"

The detective's large brown eyes come to rest on him. "Maybe ten minutes."

Pointing to his leg, Sam says, "They have me on some good drugs for this. So I sleep a lot." He sighs. "Which is probably a good thing." The man merely nods. "So how long you in Salt Lake for?"

Glancing at his watch, Jenkins says, "Until I fill in some chronology." The detective's curious, colorless eyelashes momentarily distract Sam.

"Oh?"

"If we can go back to February eleventh, can you tell me specifically what you did between five p.m. and the time you boarded your flight for Utah?"

Sam casts his mind back. "I dropped my dog at the dog-sitter a little before five. Went home, sent some emails, finished packing, and left for Boston around seven."

"Did you make any phone calls?"

Sam tries to remember. "Didn't make any, but I did get one."

"From?"

"Heather, the dog-sitter."

"What time would you say she called you?"

"Just after I got home from dropping Panda off."

"Can you give me a time?"

"Around five ten."

"How far do you live from the dog-sitter?"

"Ten-minute drive."

"And the reason why she called you?"

"She didn't think I'd left enough dog food. She asked me for the brand name. It was almost like she sensed that she'd need more."

Jenkins nods. "Any other calls?"

"No. Not that I can remember."

"How long would you say it takes to drive up to Carleton from South Woodstock?"

"An hour and ten," Sam says without hesitation.

"So you've driven it before?"

"Quite a few times."

"Because?"

"To meet Luc for dinner or coffee, or . . ." Sam sighs. "Hang out at a motel."

"How long would you estimate it would take to drive from Carleton to Logan Airport?"

Sam shakes his head, now realizing where the detective is going. "Three at least. Maybe a little more?" Jenkins merely nods. "But from my house in South Woodstock, driving up to Carleton is in the wrong direction from Logan."

Jenkins agrees, peering at Sam unwaveringly. "But for the purpose of discussion: let's say you actually were in Carleton and left Carleton at six forty-five. Do you think that'd be enough time to get to Logan Park and Go by ten-oh-three?"

"I guess. But why do you say ten-oh-three?" Sam asks.

Hesitating a moment, leaning back in his chair and crossing his slim legs, Jenkins says, "We obtained a copy of the parking record. So I know you got there at ten-oh-three."

"Wow, you're thorough."

Jenkins smiles. "As I was saying before, Luc Flanders was last seen around six p.m. Walking back toward the pond where he'd been playing hockey. So let's say you left home at around five fifteen, and got to Carleton at six twenty-five. That theoretically could leave thirty-five minutes . . . for a meeting."

"I guess it could, but like I said, I didn't go up there."

"When was the last time you did go there?"

"Maybe early December."

"So a few weeks before he broke it off with you?"

"Right."

"Was there any warning that he was going to break it off?"

"None at all."

"The last time you spoke to him, was there anything particular he said to you that might have given an impression that he might be thinking about . . . going off somewhere?"

"No."

"Presumably back in December he gave you his reasons for breaking it off?"

"Said he was freaked out about the whole thing. And just needed time away. It's what they all say."

"They?" Jenkins asks.

"What the dumpers say to the dumpees."

Jenkins can't help but laugh. And then Sam watches the detective's eyes flitting back and forth in some calculation. "Could there have been somebody else?"

"He got involved with that girl when he got back to school."

Jenkins shakes his head. "I don't mean her. I mean a man."

Despite the dulling effects of the painkillers, Sam feels a sharp surge of nausea spiraling up through his gut. "Not that I know of. Not that he said."

"Did you ask him if there was another man?"

"Yeah, we talked about it."

"Don't go dark on me," Sam was saying with admirable restraint when he finally reached Luc in January after Christmas break. "I know we're not together anymore. But can't we still talk?"

"Of course we can talk."

"When I didn't hear back from you, I almost drove up there."

"You said you'd never do that."

"I was afraid something might have happened to you."

"Look, it's not the best time," Luc said. "My roommates . . . we're in the middle of Ping-Pong."

"Beer pong?" Sam asked, and Luc actually cracked up.

Then, keeping his voice deliberately low, Luc said, "You know there are times I don't answer the phone or send texts. That I just switch off."

This was, unfortunately, all too true. The longing he felt for Luc was so unbearable, it was difficult for Sam to breathe. And yet somehow he had the presence of mind to ask if there was somebody else.

Luc waited a moment. "There is somebody else," he admitted. "And maybe it has something to do with my being out of touch."

Sam gasped, "Another guy?" feeling a jolt of jealousy.

"No, of course not another guy!" Luc exclaimed almost angrily. Then he softened. "A girl. She's a year behind me."

Lightened considerably by relief that would turn out to be fickle and temporary, Sam said, "So I suppose you're falling in love with her now?"

Quite unexpectedly, Luc got choked up and couldn't answer for a moment, but finally said, "I don't know."

Just then, background noise and Sam heard knocking and "Hey, Lucas, we need your opinion here."

"I really have to go," Luc said. "They're bugging me."

"Don't you think they figured out where you went all those weekends?"

He sighed. "They probably have."

"Can you just keep in touch?"

"Didn't I pick up the phone? Always better to call. You

know how much I hate texting. Anyway, I'm writing an email to you. You'll get it very soon. And then you can reply."

"So he promised to email you," Jenkins resumes.

Sam feels the familiar desolation of rejection. "Yeah. But he never did."

"So you didn't hear from him by email?" Jenkins repeats.

"Nope. Just spoke to him that one time on the phone."

"In January?"

"Right. In January."

And then Sam grows aware that his broken leg has begun throbbing again, the pain taking on a life of its own. He glances at the large red digits of the clock on the sickly green wall and realizes he won't be able to get another oxycodone for another hour. "Shit, this fucker really hurts."

"Do you need a few minutes?"

"No, what I need is painkillers."

At just that moment, an unfamiliar Latina nurse comes into the hospital room holding a clipboard, smiling broadly and warmly. With a glance at Jenkins, Sam says to her, "I think I'm due for something for the pain."

Looking surprised, the nurse peruses the chart and then replies confidently, "Says here not for another fifty-five minutes."

"Well, that's wrong. There was some confusion with the nurse who was here before."

"She went home."

Now Sam knows he can press harder. "She gave me one an hour earlier than she thought. We were talking and she got distracted. I'm due for one now. And I'm in a lot of pain."

The nurse shrugs and says, "Okay, be right back," and leaves the room.

Sam glances sheepishly at Jenkins and says, "It's not going to kill me."

"I know. But I need you to be as clear as possible. Pain-killers blur things."

"Well, I can't be coherent if I'm distracted by pain, can I?" Sam says.

The nurse returns a moment later with a pill and a small cup full of water. Sam takes his medication and thanks her.

Once they're alone again, Jenkins says, "So we gathered that both you and Luc Flanders use America Online accounts?"

"Yeah. It's a dinosaur but it has good instant messaging. Luc prefers that to texting."

"Why did he?"

Sam remembers early on in the relationship and the flurry of inebriated texts he used to get late at night like, *Why is it the way it is with us? Why can't I put my finger on it? Why can't I understand it? Why do I think you can see into me? Why do I hate that? But why do I love it, too? Why do I hear you talking in my head? Why do I love being underneath you? Why do I think about driving down to see you, even if it's only for the night?*

"Texting got us into trouble. We had several misunder-standings this way. With instant messaging, clarification is more . . . instantaneous."

Jenkins says, "Presumably you know that America Online allows one person to see if the other person has read their email."

"I do know that."

Jenkins straightens in his chair. "I'm going to be honest with you. Our IT guys went into Luc's email and found three emails he wrote to you in January. And because it's America Online, they could see that his emails to you had been read. So either you read them or somebody with access to your account read them."

At first Sam gives no response; he's fervently trying to understand what Jenkins could mean. But then begins to piece it all together. "But that can't be. Like I said before, I received no communication from him after Christmas. Electronic or otherwise."

Jenkins insists patiently, "And I'm saying that his account with America Online indicates that you read these three emails."

"I know what you're saying. And I'm saying then somebody must have my password." Sam feels deeply chilled, and the antiseptic smell in the hospital room intensifies.

"Can you think of who might have gotten hold of it?"

Sam tries to think. "No. Luc is the only one I can think of."

"Did you give Luc your password?"

"I don't believe so, but I may have. Sorry, I just don't recall."

Looking weary and leaning back in his chair to stretch, Jenkins asks, "Have you noticed at all that your email has been tampered with?"

"No."

"Did you use that email address with . . . other people besides Luc?"

"That's the thing. I set up the account just to communicate with him. So, no."

"You sure?"

"Positive."

"And did you happen to check this account the day you left?"

"I check it every day. Hoping to get something—any-thing—from him. Especially because the last time we spoke, he said he was writing to me." A rush of anxiety causes Sam to begin shivering. He crosses his arms for warmth and stares at his interlocutor. "I check the emails so much that I would have noticed they'd been read. They still would have been in my inbox."

"Unless somebody—or you—deleted them," Jenkins says.

FEBRUARY 12; ROCHESTER, RIPTON, CARLETON, VERMONT; 17 DEGREES, LIGHT SNOW

Eleanor's mother had once been a close friend of Robert Frost, and until recently Eleanor was a docent up at the Frost farm. The current docent has asked her to come and help evaluate the damage from the vandalism.

Driving along Route 100, Eleanor tries to imagine whirlwind violence committed in a sanctuary whose objects are historical relics of a man who wrought the sublime out of language. She sees a flash of priceless, jacketless books arranged alphabetically on simple pine shelves flung everywhere; the destruction of nineteenth-century pharmaceutical vessels of various hues lined up against the windows; the shredding of painstakingly sewn samplers that the poet hated and that were brought out and framed after his death—to make the place seem more cheerful and homey. She wants to cling to the idea that the invaders had no idea of whose house it was that suffered their vandalism.

This incident is exactly what she has been dreading: Vermont has one of the highest per-capita heroin problems in the United States. Drug use plagues its population, scores of people who got hooked and scrounged desperately to buy more. She imagines how underage kids, to maintain their habit, would rob the Frost farm of anything valuable: first editions or old records or some of the lovely, faded turn-of-the-century watercolors. She pictures the stolen objects pawned at junk shops across the border in northern New York State.

She is now passing Rochester, Vermont, a small town with a tightly knit clan of inhabitants and cluster of a secondhand bookshop, a bakery, a bike shop and a ceramic studio. As the road ribbons out of town, she reflexively glances at the phone lying next to her to see if Luc has responded to her text. Gently touches the forbiddingly blank screen that, for her, symbolizes her uncommunicative child who should at the very least have responded to her last message, a banner brightly announcing "Lucas," her grandfather's name that he always claims to hate. He rarely answers the phone and is often slow responding to her texts, but usually by the next day would have. His silences always make her uneasy.

As she ascends Route 125 through the Carleton Gap, the snow level rises with elevation. And yet curiously, the temperature on her car gauge also rises, meaning that there is some kind of inversion layer: the higher elevations are, for once, warmer than the lower ones. She passes Carleton's ski area, which looks surprisingly crowded. Just ahead, a shuttle van from the college is pulling into the parking lot. She wonders if Luc, who probably spends too much time on the slopes, may be among the students en route to Saturday skiing. She hates the idea of being the cloying, doting parent—the woefully out-of-touch parent. At last, Eleanor drives past the snowy Robert Frost trail with its wooden placards engraved with poems, precious stanzas now lacquered in hibernal ice.

On the secondary road that leads to the Frost farm, a fresh dusting of overnight snow is trampled by a large number of vehicles that by 11 a.m. already have traveled back and forth to the farm. On a normal midwinter's day, her car tracks might be the only ones cutting the soft blanket of white dust on this class three road. She can see the barricade from a half mile away, a single patrol car parked at a diagonal in the middle of the lane. An officer in a starched Statie uniform stands rigidly in front of it, his arms crossed, and once he catches sight of her car rumbling toward him, begins striding swiftly, almost aggressively, toward her, no doubt itching to discourage her officially from going any farther. When she comes within fifteen yards, he jabs his finger toward the side of the road. She rolls down her window.

"Good morning," she says. "You have my name on a pass-through list. I'm Eleanor Flanders."

The rosy-cheeked young officer, who looks not much older than Luc, regards her at first with skepticism. "Just wait right here." He stalks back to the patrol car, reaches in and grabs a clipboard. He scans it for her name and then returns walking more slowly, as though reluctant to say, "Yes, I have it here. Can you get around that vehicle? Or do you want me to move it?"

She studies the space between the patrol car and the five-foot-high pile of plowed snow. "I think I can make it."

Several two-toned state police cars are parked in a neat, choreographed line, and the officers stand in a scrum just outside the front door of the nineteenth-century farmhouse. She spies Beverly, the current docent, in a maroon down jacket off to one side talking to a slim, wizened-looking man with thick, unruly hair. Beverly squints when she notices the civilian car and waves her up.

Mindful of the ice beneath the freshly shoveled path, Eleanor begins heading up the cleared walkway toward the farmhouse. Although the poet spent a good deal of time here, this was actually the residence occupied by his caretakers and, sometimes, supernumeraries. Frost spent most of his time higher up on the property in a stark bare-bones shack, now boarded up and permanently locked away from public access and, presumably, untouched by the despoilers.

She dreads seeing the state of the farmhouse, a place of reverence she'd first visited as a child, old books that smell of maple and dust, watercolors of hardscrabble New Hampshire with tiny smudges of human figures painted in great mountainous shadows, battered antique kitchen utensils, the pine floors, beeswax-polished to a high glaze. All those years ago, she invented a game in which she committed to memory every single object in residence and then tested her own recall. She's certainly the daughter of a librarian.

Beverly gives her a quick perfunctory hug and then introduces the man. "This is Detective Nick Jenkins," she says. "He's from Carleton."

"Hello, Mrs. Flanders." Jenkins's voice is soft and articulate. He's handsome in a sharp-featured, wizened sort of way with strikingly sad, dark eyes. There is something at once familiar and odd about him; he doesn't exactly fit her vision of a detective. He seems to be possessed of some weighty uncertainty, even fragility.

Beverly faces her. "Elle, I told Mr. Jenkins that you would have a . . ." She smiles and says elegantly, "A better read of what might be amiss."

Eleanor turns to the detective. "Is it really a mess?"

"Unfortunately, yes."

"Let's all have a look," Beverly says somewhat brightly, as though suggesting that perhaps the cabin won't be as bad as they're imagining.

"I just wanted to prepare myself," Eleanor tells them, nearly breathless from a sudden rash of anxiety, and Beverly gives her an understanding look, as if to suggest that Eleanor will find the desecration more upsetting than she does.

The farmhouse windows are blackened from smoke and Eleanor gets a hint of the sulfurous smell of charred objects never meant to burn. Arcs of yellow—probably urine—stain the fresh layer of snow. Inside, books are flung from shelves, shards of dishes strewn everywhere, the fabric of the furniture torn and spiked with silverware. There are coverlets and sheets bunched on the floor, also yellow from urination. There is even a brassiere—God knows whose—lying on the ruined sofa, and a bull's-eye welter of red wine in the middle of a cable knit rug.

The detective asks if they notice anything missing.

"The catalog will tell us," Beverly says.

Eleanor drifts to the bookshelf in disarray. "I don't know why, but I think some of the books are gone."

Back in her car, she feels inexplicable numbness toward the wreckage she has just witnessed in a place of reverence that she, herself, has helped care for. It makes no sense at first. She wonders if it's because her phone reveals neither a text nor a phone call from Luc. Then again, there is only one bar of service and she wonders if positioning herself in better range will grant her some shred of communication from him. So, holding her phone in one hand like an offering, she drives down the deserted snowy road, glancing back and forth between navigating the car and the phone, scanning for signs of better coverage. By the time she reaches the state police roadblock, there seems to be no cell service at all, and the young trooper who'd been initially intimidating happens to spy her staring at the phone and now has sufficient grounds to scold, "Please just put that down when you drive."

Frightened, furious, she nearly, uncharacteristically, tells him to "fuck off," but manages to contain her reaction and, holding her phone down by her hip, continues driving until she glances down to see three bars. She promptly pulls over to the side of the road and holds the phone out the window, angling it, shaking it, positioning it properly as if some celestial intervention will bring in a bright message banner from Luc. But the screen remains black, insolently remote. She isn't young enough to believe that messages will always reach their intended recipient, won't be expunged by some atmospheric fluke. She tells herself she has no choice but to continue driving the nine miles to Luc's apartment in Carleton.

Eleanor spent most of her childhood in Carleton. Her father died when she was five, her mother, an alum, landed the college librarian job when Eleanor was eleven, and they moved to Vermont from New York City. The town kids immediately embraced her and she grew up in their ranks, hanging out at the Congregationalist Church, watching boys drive by and, when she got older, riding with them and hanging out at Chapman Hill, the local ski jump, in the winter, and going with busloads of kids down to Lake Dunmore in the summer, where she lifeguarded and taught swimming. Later on, as the child of a staff member, she attended Carleton College tuition free. But then she had to deal with all the snotty coeds, many of them wealthy girls from the city she had left.

As she's driving through the town, she sees a poster, "Save the Town Hall," which she knows is the local pushback against the college's expansion, against its annexation of local land, its exemption from state taxes. She'd actually wanted Luc and Janine to attend Dartmouth, but Giles, ever resentful of his employer, convinced her that their children would get a better, healthier education at Carleton.

Luc's battered, secondhand Mini Cooper is parked in front of his apartment building; it's Saturday, so there won't be class. Once she occupies the space behind his, she calls again. This time Luc's phone cradles immediately to voicemail, which makes her assume that since her last attempt, he's turned it off. She composes herself for a moment, picturing his predictable annoyance at her unannounced appearance. Then the front door swings open, and Will McKinnon comes hurtling through it. Eleanor grabs her keys, leaves the car, and starts walking toward him. Wearing a black down jacket, a dark green woolen cap pulled halfway down his florid face, McKinnon seems shocked to see her and stops. "Oh, Mrs. Flanders," he says, scratching at the bright red scruff on his several-day unshaven face. "How . . . are you? I heard about what happened up at the cabin."

She explains that she's just driven from the Frost farm and, assuming McKinnon knows what has happened, tells him the place is crawling with police. "But now I'm actually looking for Luc. I haven't been able to reach him."

McKinnon hesitates before saying, "He's not here. Actually, I haven't seen him since . . . I don't know, maybe five thirty yesterday afternoon. We played some pickup hockey on Skylight Pond."

"So you mean he never made it home?"

McKinnon shrugs and looks cornered. "No, he actually didn't."

She puts her car keys in the pocket of her coat. She has left her gloves in the car, and the cold metal stings her fingers. "Doesn't that concern you?"

"He was doing that a lot when he was seeing Elizabeth. And he did go off with her last night after we played hockey."

"So they're they back together?" Eleanor's thoughts are firing in many different directions, propelled by an unexplained yet palpable anxiety.

McKinnon shrugs. "Might be. I don't know."

"So then he could be at her place?"

"Or with her somewhere. Maybe skiing." And yet McKinnon looks uncomfortable. "I actually have to go," he says. "But let me get your number." McKinnon whips out his phone. Eleanor is so unused to giving out her cell number that she can't recall it at first. But then she remembers and rattles off the digits, amazed at how fast McKinnon's fingers record the data.

Eleanor already has Elizabeth's contact information. Elizabeth offered it surreptitiously the only weekend that she and Luc visited Norwich, offered it while Luc and his father were outside chainsawing a fallen apple tree. When Eleanor had complained that her son was impossible to reach sometimes, Elizabeth, *sotto voce*, said, "If you need to get him and can't find him, like in case of emergency or something," dutifully writing her number down in beautiful handwriting that Eleanor rarely saw in people younger than forty, penmanship no longer being taught in schools. And while she had appreciated the gesture of trust, Eleanor couldn't help wondering if Elizabeth was doing this to curry favor, remembering Luc's comment that his girlfriend often tried too hard.

Elizabeth answers, Eleanor announces herself, and there is a confused beat of silence. "Oh my gosh, hi. This is a surprise." Eleanor doesn't even need to ask; deflated, she divines that Luc isn't—and hasn't—been there.

Nevertheless she says, "I'm sorry to bother you like this. I've been trying to find Luc. Will said he might be with you."

"No, he isn't," comes the plaintive reply. "I did see him last night, briefly. I mean, I'm sure you know . . ."

"Yes, of course. He told me. And I wouldn't have bothered you if—"

"I'm talking about the vandalism," Elizabeth clarifies.

"Oh, I'm sorry. Of course."

"No, *I'm sorry*. Honestly, I wouldn't have seen him if I hadn't heard about what happened at the farm and thought he should know." And then she explains about showing up while Luc and his roommates were playing pond hockey. "Did you check at his place?"

Eleanor now reveals her location, her conversation with Will McKinnon, swallowing before she mentions—because now she is bound to—that Luc actually never returned to the apartment. She can feel the discomfort on the other end. "Wow. Really?" Elizabeth says softly.

After a few moments of strained silence, Eleanor says, "Would you mind having a cup of coffee with me?"

Elizabeth takes this in for a moment, as though weighing her options, and then replies, "Okay. Sure."

Elizabeth, whose cheeks are stung crimson from the cold, is standing just inside the door of the student union. She is wearing a stylish aqua-colored parka, and her long, fine, sandy hair is tightly pulled back in a ponytail. She looks fearful, blinking, as though stupefied. Eleanor's very first impression had been that this was a solid, sorted-out girl who knew what she wanted. Even though Elizabeth might still be hanging on to the notion of a relationship, Luc surely will be a blip on the screen of her romantic history.

Soon the two are sitting in a quiet corner, each with a latte in a tall white paper cup. "Did they find out who broke in out at the farm?" Elizabeth asks, carefully sipping her coffee.

"They're still gathering information."

"A lot of damage?"

"Quite a bit, yes. It's all so disgusting," Eleanor says. "Probably one kid came up with an idea and then it spread. And then there was drinking. Funny—I was thinking that Luc was never like that. He never willfully destroyed anything."

Elizabeth stifles a yawn and then, pursing her lips, blows a stray tendril of hair out of her face. "Sorry if I seem a bit out of it. I hardly slept at all last night."

Sensing this might be a lead-in, Eleanor says, "Everything okay?"

Elizabeth's hands are shaking and she's fidgeting in her chair. "Not really. After I saw Luc and talked to him and then he went off without me, I felt . . . well, you know—it's only been a few weeks."

The distress is palpable. Eleanor reaches across the table and momentarily covers Elizabeth's hand with her own, wanting to convey understanding, but then withdraws it, reluctant to display too much sympathy. Appreciating the gesture nevertheless, Elizabeth says, "I'm okay. Hoping to catch a nap later on after I study. If I don't fall asleep in the library."

A tall, beautiful black woman with cornrows drifts into their presence and places an elegant, perfectly manicured hand softly on Elizabeth's shoulder. Piling her hand on top, Elizabeth says, "Hi, Portia."

"You all right?" Portia asks.

"Sure." Elizabeth suddenly looks awkward. "This is Luc's mom, by the way."

Portia looks bemused. "Why, hello there, Mrs. Flanders. How is Luc?" she asks in a rancorous tone of voice that Eleanor takes to mean she has little if no interest in the well being of her son.

"That's what she'd like to know," Elizabeth says, smiling forlornly at Eleanor.

"Oh, okay, then I'll leave you to it and I'll see you in a bit," Portia says, and with a graceful turn, walks away.

"My roommate," Elizabeth explains.

"She seems concerned."

"I was . . . crying last night. And to be honest, she's not wild about Luc."

"I get that impression," Eleanor says, and then after a moment, "So do you have any idea where Luc might have gone after you saw him?"

Hesitating, Elizabeth replies, "Well, he was going back to the pond. Because he lost something."

"Lost something," Eleanor repeats.

Elizabeth nods. "The ring he was wearing around his neck."

"What ring around his neck?"

"The Carleton ring."

"Oh, okay. That ring."

Elizabeth continues, "After I found him at the pond, Luc was walking me back to my dorm. His jacket was open and I noticed the ring was gone. I told him and he freaked out." In a no-big-deal tone of voice that Janine often uses when she makes a significant pronouncement, Elizabeth goes on to say, "The ring belongs to the guy he's been involved with."

Eleanor is stunned into silence, her head muddled with clashing reactions to this news. "So you think Luc is involved with a man?"

"I think he was involved with a man before we got together, and I think he's still involved with that man now."

The girl can no longer hide it; her face is flickering with anger and Eleanor knows that even though alternative sexuality is more widely accepted these days, Luc rejecting Elizabeth for another man is probably still an assault to her self-esteem. Eleanor explains that she and Giles have wondered about Luc, bewildered why he never would have said anything. "It's not like we're these . . . I don't know, rednecks who'd disown him."

A deep flush has suffused Elizabeth's face. "Do you remember when Luc brought me to visit that one weekend, when I asked you where his friend Sam went to school?"

Eleanor nods. "I do. And I think I said I didn't know any friend named Sam."

"Well, I asked you that because I once saw a yellow Post-it Note on his desk . . . he didn't realize I saw, and it said . . ." She recites from what has clearly been committed to memory. "'Sam, why do I think you can see into me? Why do I hate that? But why do I love it, too?'"

The words are a jolt. And Eleanor's first flash is: Can they even be Luc's words? Is he this passionate a man? He often strikes her as so buttoned up. But then, it occurs to her that sometimes the most passionate people are—buttoned up.

With reluctance, Elizabeth informs her, "I happen to know there isn't a single student at Carleton named Samantha. I checked. There are plenty of male Sams, obviously."

Wow, and just a little obsessive, Eleanor concludes with some concern.

"Did you know that the ring is dated 1990?"

Eleanor stares back at her and now begins to realize. "Yes, I do."

"Well, that's probably the year his guy graduated from Carleton."

Even though she finished Carleton College in 1985, Eleanor finds herself momentarily unable to even calculate the age of somebody who'd graduated in 1990. But then she does with a shiver: fifty years old, more or less. Thrown off kilter by this revelation, she finds herself saying, "Last summer I had this feeling that Luc was having a relationship. Sometimes he didn't come home at all. I sensed he wasn't at a friend's house. And he was always vague. Lying doesn't come easy to him."

"But that's where you're wrong, Mrs. Flanders!" Elizabeth says a bit too forcefully for Eleanor's liking. "Luc *is* a liar. For example, he lied to me about that ring. He told me he bought it from his friend who transferred to Tufts."

Eleanor feels obliged to admit, "He told me the same story."

In fuming silence, Elizabeth nervously runs her finger along the edge of her white paper cup. Then, with an abrupt gesture, she swills the last dregs of her coffee and sets the cup to one side. "If you saw how Luc was last night when he realized he lost the ring, if you watched his face as I did . . . you'd know exactly how he was feeling. And that's why I couldn't sleep last night. Because I saw this . . . devotion in him, devotion toward someone else that he's never shown to me, and it makes me feel so awful." Tears glaze her eyes. "And I just want to get over it. I just want to get over him."

FEBRUARY 12; ROUTE 23, DONNER'S FIELD, WEYBRIDGE, VERMONT; 20 DEGREES, LIGHT SNOW

Daylight is gathering at the edge of the sky. For so many hours he's been caught in a crippled vagueness, walking slowly along Lemon Fair Road in the early morning, every foot of snow and ice crossed a sort of triumph. The four-mile journey to warmth and safety seems longer than the longest White Mountain hikes he's made up Jefferson and North Kinsman, Moosilauke and Madison, all distant summer memories now. The chill at these mountain summits was tropical in comparison to the agony of this penetrating and punishing cold that seeps into bone ache, making him want to sleep off the pain even though he knows that sleeping will probably kill him.

Trying to remember how he came to this place, Luc stops and looks across the wind-blown, snow-bound meadow that unfolds for thousands of acres in flat white patchwork toward Snake Mountain, which stands between him and the shores of Lake Champlain. He faintly recalls falling and struggling and waking up and feeling compelled to walk through curtains of snow and sleet and the brutish gales rising up around him. He remembers the tamarack trees bent over with their mighty plumes of white. Miraculously, the night is almost over and he is now looking at the cobbled split rail fence of a farm's perimeter.

He's woozy from his fall on the ice, flooded with misimpressions. Has it been a long march, or did he actually get a ride here? He just can't recall precisely but knows somebody has been in his company. Was it more than one person? He's just not remembering. But he wants to believe that Sam somehow came to him, even made love to him, when he lay on the ice back at Skylight Pond. Why couldn't he have told Sam that he now craves the warmth of what he rejected, the warmth that made him feel the peril of his own neediness? Sam's body heat would keep him alive if only he could find him again in the midst of this endless wilderness of wax.

And then he spies the enormous pinwheel hay bale left out in a field, a bale that should have been gathered in months ago. It looks broken apart, and he can see fresh yellow tendrils of straw and then a curious gaping hole inside it. Had an animal dug it out, a bear perhaps? Dig in, climb in, curl up and try to stay warm—this is what the survival guides would suggest for these extreme circumstances.

As Luc musters all his strength to climb over the plowed wing of snow and hobbles toward refuge, he hears the muted music of the Millstone Creek, which runs just beyond him. Closer he sees that the hole in the bale is fairly large, maybe even hospitable enough to shelter him without his hollowing it out much more. But then he wonders: could this be a place where he might wither and die? Could this be a trap?

The thought of a trap recalls a movie Sam insisted they see called *In the Bedroom*, the title referring to the rear of a lobster trap in which a pair of caught lobsters, after a time, turn fierce and try to slaughter each other. While they were watching it, Luc was shocked to hear the Eastern Orthodox choral music that he'd been hallucinating intermittently since the hockey accident actually playing in the movie. He grabbed the remote and stopped the film and confessed to Sam about hearing religious melodies when they were together, that he'd begun hearing them after his helmet came off during the hockey game, after his head hit the goal post. He described his blackout, the strange syncopated lighting and rising up above his own body in a kind of euphoria, looking down on the officials and the medics crowded around him, watching himself being carried to the bench, and then the delicious daydream ending with a slam, and falling back into the uncertain world of concussions and CT scans, scrambled thoughts, the daydream lock. How the doctors diagnosed mild epilepsy brought on by the shock of the injury. How they said there was nothing he could do but wait it out, how they said perhaps his body would slough off the disturbances like an unwanted electrical skin.

"How come you've never really told me about this?" Sam asked, looking perplexed.

"I don't like to talk about it. I don't want anyone to think I'm not normal."

"But it sounds more like a gift, being able to hear that music."

"It's not a gift. Not when it comes on involuntarily."

Sam considered this for a moment and then said, "You might have gone to an Orthodox church when you were small, heard that swell of music and just don't remember."

Luc disagreed. "If music made that kind of impression on me, I think I would definitely remember it."

Sam actually went out and bought the choral music, thinking that if Luc actually listened to it, his auditory hallucinations somehow would become easier to bear. Luc felt nervous the first time they heard the recording and worried that the melodic passages might bring on one of his dissociative states. But the music sounded no different than when he hallucinated it. And it didn't make him hallucinate.

But then, shortly after they begin listening, Sam began suffering from his own fit, of atrial fibrillation, his heart fluttering as the real music swelled through the house. Luc lay next to him and stroked his chest with calm resolution, knowing this affection would help the episode to pass. This strong, vital man momentarily incapacitated, and Luc wanting so much to take care of him, thinking this is what it must be like when carnal love ripens into devotion. And Sam accepted him, and unlike Luc's father, Sam didn't try to change or criticize him. But then, as Luc laid his head on Sam's chest, as he listened to the discordant rhythms of his lover's erratically beating heart, he grew petrified of losing him, afraid that their powerful love possibly might be compromised by the unforeseen.

Now, nestling into his makeshift straw shelter, Luc removes a glove and tamps some of the snow down into an icy curd and with a finger scrawls his lover's three-letter name. And then he notices a deep purple and yellow bruise blooming where his palm ends and blotching its way over his wrist. He pushes back the sleeve of his jacket to see the dark lesion's territory continuing up his arm. It frightens him enough to take his phone out of his pocket, to call someone—his mother, or maybe even Sam—but the battery appears to have died.

Helen Kennedy is a small-framed woman with deep blue eyes and brush-cut silver hair. She arrives at Jenkins's office with two cups of coffee and sets them down on the corner of his desk. With an index finger, she wipes a black-and-white framed photograph of Mount Mansfield that is hanging on his wall. "You need to spruce up this place," she says, glancing around the small, windowless room. Jenkins grunts an unintelligible reply. "That light enough for you?" she asks about his coffee, grabbing and taking a sip of hers, which she drinks black.

Glancing at his steaming cup, Jenkins says, "Um. Caffeine."

"Well, don't expect miracle brew. The coffee machine is still on the fritz."

"What about the new one that's incoming?"

"Incoming probably means two years from now." Sitting down in the chair next to his desk, Kennedy says, "Got some good news. An ID on the DNA we found at the Frost farm. Something was in the database." Jenkins now faces her and he can see the trace of a grin that is trying to cross her freckled Celtic face but that she suppresses. "It points to a pair of twins, two forty-one-year-old guys living down in Bethel. Howard and Mark Newcombe. Who once got booked on a drug bust."

"Bethel, the meth hub of Vermont?"

"But they didn't get busted for meth. It was steroids."

Jenkins is surprised. "Steroids, huh?"

"Never told you this, but my brother used to do and deal them. And he eventually got slammed for it."

"I assume all this is from Barb Kessler?"

"We just got off the phone. Apparently, these guys had/ have a very small, select clientele. Some hard-core cyclists. Some gym rats. By the way, they work out at V-tech in Randolph. Gimme your keyboard." With a few strokes, Kennedy brings up a picture of a pair of tanned, bodybuilder-jacked twins dressed in identical flannel shirts cut off at the shoulder. They have huge biceps and wear their hair in long, blond dreadlocks.

"They hardly look Vermonty," Jenkins says. "With those fake tans, they look like they walked off Venice Beach. Blond Rastafarians."

"You're close," Kennedy says. "They're actually Trustafarians."

"Come again?"

"They live on an inheritance. And not a family one either. Some rich geezer whose farm they lived on left them a shit-load of money."

"So if they have money, why do they sell steroids?"

"Barb says they do it for sport. I guess they like seeing other guys get big."

"Wait, are they gay?"

"No. Not according to Barbara. She knows one of their ex-girlfriends."

"So what the bleep were they doing breaking into Frost's house?"

"Well, Frost was a rock star poet with lots of followers. And probably also lots of detractors."

"They broke in because they hated his poetry?"

"I don't know! Maybe the poet was secretly bonking their mother. I guess we'll find out when we find them. One of the neighbors saw them a week ago throwing duffel bags in the back of their camouflage Jeep Wrangler and presumably heading out of town."

"Camouflage Jeep, huh?"

"I fed them to the DMV and got the plate number. I just put out an APB."

"So I guess we sit tight."

Pausing a moment, Kennedy says, "I was actually thinking that maybe Mrs. Flanders, knowing chapter and verse about Robert Frost, might have something on these jacked-up twins."

"Let's ask her."

FEBRUARY 18; ROUTE 89 NORTH, VERMONT; 13 DEGREES, LIGHT WINDS, SNOW

I-89 north of White River Junction has always been desolately majestic: long stretches of uninhabited conservation land, gentle rising cerulean mountains softly contoured with snow. Giles is driving and Eleanor looks out onto the mantle of snow, imagining what lies beneath it: frozen fields flayed down from late summer haying, the remains of small animals that have perished trying to cross a desert of ice. On the side of the highway she sees the yellow cautionary signs for moose crossing. Medical care may have evolved since her childhood, but if your car strikes a moose at more than 50 miles an hour, your life will be forever altered. If you live, paraplegia, and if you die . . . ?

Once afraid of colliding with such brutally dense animals, she cares little now. For in death there would at least be a disconnection from this inverted daytime nightmare that is only alleviated when she drugs herself to sleep.

She is now one of those mothers waiting for news about a missing child. That Luc had gone missing once before does little to dull the persistent worry that he may never return. The last time was in summer, only a year and a half after his injury, when he was still suffering frequent headaches, spells of feeling withdrawn and alienated.

Since his first disappearance, Luc has consistently promised to be in frequent touch. Aware of the potential risks of driving with anybody who is drinking, he reassures them that he would never put himself in this sort of situation. He always promises that if he ever gets stuck in a place where nobody is sober, he'll call—no matter what time of night—for a ride home. Which is why this disappearance seems so out of the blue, and why she can only conclude that something or someone lured him away from Skylight Pond. Most likely Sam Solomon.

Back on Sunday, when he'd been missing for only forty-eight hours, Giles had said to her, "I mean, think about it. If, like Elizabeth suggests, he's been having a secret affair with an older guy, he probably would be off the grid whenever they were together. So maybe they just recently got back together. And . . . I don't know, right now are celebrating their reunion. So before we report him missing, why don't we try and figure out who and where this . . . Sam guy is?"

With great reluctance, but knowing they had little choice, they invaded Luc's bedroom. Luc had never been the sort who liked putting up posters, and his only wall adornment was a series of drawings he'd done as a high school senior of the Calvin Coolidge birthplace over in Plymouth, various photorealistic studies of vintage stone-and-wood buildings and rambling, magisterial barns. Approaching his son's mounted and framed creations, Giles studied them. "These are really pretty good, you know."

Luc's desk was decoupaged with a brightly colored map of the world. Cautiously, they began to open its drawers, surprisingly neat inside, with stacks of sports gear catalogs, several antique rulers, tiny hubcaps from his miniature car collection, a stack of Flash Gordon comic books, golf balls and tees, old schedules for high school soccer seasons, all the talismans of a young man, certainly nothing to give any hint of sexual preference—no porn magazines or DVDs. But then, beneath a driver's education manual, they found a sketchpad with all the pages torn out.

"Must be one of his old ones," Giles said.

"No, look." Eleanor pointed to the flip side of the cover, and a series of recent dates: 10/3/13; 10/19/13; 11/3/13; 11/27/13;

12/5/13; 12/12/13; 12/21/13. "I thought he'd stopped draw-ing," she said sadly.

"I guess he hasn't."

Below the sketchpad lay a book of colored plates by Cara-vaggio. Eleanor glanced meaningfully at Giles, who nodded his approval, and they acknowledged a certain irony in find-ing this, the great painter able to invest religious images with a kind of male eroticism unequaled in any other artist, including Michelangelo. She flipped through it and found a small, penciled scrawl of notes under several paintings: "Crazy light, wow. If only I could do something like this. He's rogue. Loves men but a real man." And then a whole entry under the painting of *The Death of Saint Lucy* in the duomo of Siracusa. "My favorite. Got to get to Sicily. Naked men digging a grave, never saw that before. Got to be the best painting about death I've ever seen."

Reading the short description, Giles nodded and agreed, "He's probably right. Probably is the best painting about death."

"Did you ever discuss it with him?"

Giles shakes his head. "No. We never did."

"Maybe you should have!"

Giles turned to her, his features pinched and his silvery dark hair cascading into his eyes. "Trying to be an artist. Spending four years at art school and then having to make it in a world that's a lot more competitive now than it was when I graduated. Is that what we want for him?"

"Perhaps he could use the training to do something prac-tical but more meaningful. Like graphic design. I would hate to see him do what his friends are doing: going to work for some money organization or some consulting firm. You've always been so . . . black and white about education." Black and white about where their children went to school.

"He's still in college, Elle. It's not too late."

"Still in college," Eleanor muttered. "His last year of college. And he hasn't taken a single class in art or art history. All econ and poly sci. No wonder his grades aren't good. He probably hates what he's studying."

At last, under a stack of crude India ink drawings that dated back to when Luc was ten, they found a cloth-bound diary filled with his barely legible scrawl. With a quick glance, Eleanor determined that the dates of the entries were recent. "Wonder why he didn't take this with him back to school."

"Just look for Sam."

She flipped through the pages quickly, both afraid to read and horrified of what she might find: not about his romantic life so much as harsh and unforgiving words about herself. When she saw the name, she closed the book and held it against her chest, her heart clattering. "Okay. Sam is in here," she whispered. "Sam Solomon." And then words flipped by: "Beautiful man. I've woken up, finally." They'd located a Sam Solomon, Architect, on Giles's computer. Noah Wood Road, South Woodstock, Vermont.

Giles looked up the telephone number, called and left a message that it was an emergency. "Probably a landline he doesn't answer on weekends. Probably where Luc is right now. He'll probably drive back up to Carleton later on tonight in time for school tomorrow."

"He doesn't have his car."

"Well, then maybe Sam will drive him back."

Cleaving to this new hope, Eleanor wiped her tears. "You think so?"

"You always assume the worst is going to happen to him," Giles reminded her. "You were never that way with Janine, even during her rebellious period when she stayed out all night and we didn't even know where she was."

"But Janine never had a head injury. She never just took off like Luc did."

———

They're now entering the town of Carleton, a town Eleanor has known for forty years. It seems almost a travesty that Luc has disappeared in the place she grew up but left many years ago. As Route 7 doglegs and runs through the middle of the town, Eleanor notices the blazing white spire of the Congregationalist Church; next to the entrance is a sign painted in rainbow LGBT colors with the phrase "God is still listening." She parses the words over and over, trying to understand what they mean. Could it be that the church is reminding its parishioners (and the general public) that God speaks to anyone of any sexual persuasion, and that these souls deserve to listen as well as be heard? And yet she can't be sure that the words "God is still listening" actually mean what she thinks they do, and Eleanor's anxiety ratchets up to an even higher level.

They come to a red light, and after the car comes to a brief halt, Giles says, "I'll be honest. I've been wondering if maybe he just decided to blow off college once and for all and just took off somewhere."

This annoys Eleanor. "Well, if he 'took off,' he was bored. Because he wasn't studying what he really loved."

Giles looks over at her. "Sounds like you're blaming me for this misbehavior."

"Well, you've made him feel bad about himself."

Glancing over at her, Giles said, "Like how? How did I make him feel bad about himself?" The light goes green and he begins driving again.

"All those jokes you used to make about him going out and blundering his way through girls to get experience."

"But fathers joke around like that with their sons."

"Yeah, but I remember you when started talking about it . . . and he wasn't even fifteen. Can you imagine how that must've felt . . . if he was struggling with his sexuality?"

"No, but he already had that girlfriend."

"Oh God, Giles! He's always had girlfriends. Clearly that doesn't mean very much." And then a thought comes to her. "Now I'm thinking that maybe his running off that first time had something to do with the fact that there was something he felt he couldn't discuss with us."

"Yes, I suppose that could be possible."

As they pass the old train depot on Seymour Street, make a left turn under a railroad trestle and then another left to get to the police station, Eleanor, for the first time, sees one of the flyers with Luc's face on it affixed to the side of a beverage and liquor market. HAVE YOU SEEN THIS MAN? At first she feels an almost electric jolt. But then retreats from the impact, and the image she sees becomes a refraction, a backlighted scrim that both clarifies the image of her son and obscures it so that he's staring back at her like a stranger, like somebody she's never known or perhaps vaguely recognizes from a different life. It takes another moment for the acute recognition and then nausea, and then bewilderment and then fear. "Have you seen this man," she actually whispers to herself. "Have you seen my son?"

FEBRUARY 18; CARLETON, VERMONT; 18 DEGREES, SNOW

Jenkins enters a quiet waiting area with a potted bottle palm tree, where Mr. and Mrs. Flanders have been shepherded, deliberately removed from an unusual melee going on in the dispatch center. After shaking Eleanor's hand, he says to Giles, "Good to meet you finally," and Giles, staring down on the detective from his six-foot-three height, shakes his hand reluctantly. *He may be the problem,* Jenkins surmises to himself. "If you'll follow me, I have a nice quiet place that we can talk." He leads them back to a small conference room with an oblong table, where Kennedy has been waiting. She jumps out of her chair and comes forward to introduce herself.

Once everyone is seated, Jenkins says, "The trip okay? No pockets of bad weather?"

"A little bit of snow around Sharon," says Giles.

"Well, last I looked, there is nothing predicted, so it should be smooth sailing getting back to Norwich," Jenkins says. Both parents are staring at him like frightened children. He can tell they want to dispense with small talk. "Anyway, as I was saying to you on the phone, the difficulty for us is that your son took off once before. So after we completed our search around the pond and took his exiting footprints into account, our only option was to put the word out everywhere. Now we have to wait and see if anybody spots him or comes forward with something. "

Mrs. Flanders pulls a sketchpad out of a canvas book bag she has brought with her. "We found this in his room." She shows Jenkins and Kennedy the dates written on the inside cover. "We're thinking these might correspond to a bunch of drawings he did recently. But obviously the drawings were ripped out of here."

"Which is . . . unusual because he supposedly stopped doing drawings," Mr. Flanders explains. "He claims drawing makes him feel weird—after his accident playing hockey."

"Well, there were no drawings or personal art of any kind in his room at Carleton," Kennedy tells them.

"So do you have any leads at all?" Mr. Flanders asks. "Heard anything from anyone?"

"Nothing credible," Kennedy says.

"But wouldn't it be worthwhile to search the entire area around Carleton?" Mrs. Flanders asks. "Rather than just the area around Skylight Pond?"

Kennedy answers, "We searched a thirty-mile radius. We announced the search on the local radio and in the local paper. We have posters up everywhere with his picture and a hotline telephone number."

"I know," Eleanor says despairingly. "I just saw one."

"So if by chance he is holed up somewhere, somebody should recognize him when he decides to go out in public," Jenkins says.

"But like the last time, he might have gone farther away," Mr. Flanders points out.

Mrs. Flanders says, "The people he was staying with that first time he went missing didn't even ask him any questions for over a week."

"Could also be the case here," Jenkins says. "His picture has been sent to a national register."

"What about foul play?" Mr. Flanders asks. "Didn't you tell us it looked like there could have been a struggle?"

Jenkins says, "Yeah. Maybe two people wrangling. Snow all churned up with footprints. But then a single trail that matched his shoes left the pond and went to the road. Nobody else's footprints there but his."

Jenkins notices that Mrs. Flanders has suddenly gone extremely pale. "Do you want to stop for a bit?"

She shakes her head and seems to be fighting back tears. "No," she replies at last. "I'm sorry . . ."

"Don't be sorry," Kennedy says. "You're his mother."

Mr. Flanders turns to Jenkins. "But why would Luc go back to the pond from a different direction than he went the first time . . . with his friends?"

Kennedy replies, "Because when he went back the second time, he went specifically to look for Sam Solomon's ring. That's where and when—we surmise—a struggle occurred."

"How do you know the struggle wasn't with Solomon?" Mrs. Flanders asks sharply.

"We don't know for sure," Kennedy answers.

Jenkins goes on to say that Sam Solomon conceivably could have driven from South Woodstock to Carleton, had a half hour encounter with Luc and then continued to Logan Airport. Therefore, Solomon would be the likeliest instrument of harm. "We're keeping an eye on him. We've asked him not to leave Vermont."

"What was your impression of him?" asks Mr. Flanders.

Jenkins replies, "He and his story seem credible. He is liked and admired down in Woodstock, vouched for as being a model citizen as well as a gentle, honest man who treats everyone with kindness."

"You hear that about a lot of people," Mrs. Flanders says, "who then change stripes when it comes to love."

"Absolutely true," Jenkins agrees.

Kennedy says, "We also spoke to Sam's Canadian ex-partner of five years. An established Toronto lawyer for a multinational with a twenty-four-year-old daughter. Apparently, Sam confided in him about the relationship with your son, and this man consistently warned Sam that the affair could not possibly last. This Canadian man insists that Sam wholeheartedly agreed with his assessment. He says that Sam knew that Luc had a lot of conflict about the relationship as well as the age difference, and Sam figured/assumed the affair would come to an end." She glances down at her notepad.

Jenkins says, "Sam claims he didn't fight it when Luc broke things off."

"Well, I don't have any suspicion about Sam Solomon," Mr. Flanders says.

Surprised, his wife turns to him. "I didn't know you felt this way."

The man stares at Jenkins. "Maybe it's that I just don't want to consider the idea that somebody who supposedly really loved my son could've . . ." The possibilities hang in the air.

"That's why it would be good to rule Sam Solomon out entirely," Jenkins says.

"So you haven't yet?"

"It's hard to because, like I said, logistically Sam could've gotten himself up to Carleton."

"I can't take this anymore!" Mrs. Flanders cries.

"We're almost done," Jenkins says. "But—"

"Just go on!"

He continues quietly, "What I am about to discuss cannot go outside this room. I need your assurance."

"You have it," Mr. Flanders says.

"And mine, too," says Mrs. Flanders.

"Your son is of age, so we had to ask a judge to grant us access to his email accounts. One of them was an America Online account. In that account there were three emails that your son sent to Sam Solomon right after they spoke on January sixth. One was sent on January seventh. Then one on January eighth. And the last one was sent on January ninth. American Online customers are able to see if the mail they send to another American Online customer has been read by the recipient. The three emails I refer to—that were sent to Sam Solomon—were all marked as read; however, Solomon claims he never got them, never read them."

"And you believe him?" Mrs. Flanders asks with understandable skepticism.

Jenkins says, "When he found out about them, Sam seemed genuinely distraught."

"But what do the emails say?" Mrs. Flanders asks.

"All very passionate. Describing Luc's love for Sam. Luc asks for a meeting." Jenkins pauses, and then adds, "Wanting to reconcile."

There is considerable silence following Jenkins's pronouncement.

At last, Mrs. Flanders says, "So maybe they had their meeting and Sam is just not confessing to it."

"No, Elle, I disagree. If they'd had the meeting, they'd probably be back together right now." Mr. Flanders turns to Jenkins. "You did say the breakup was one-sided, correct?"

"According to Sam," Jenkins says.

"And so what about these emails, if Sam claims he knows nothing about them, then who read and deleted them?" Mrs. Flanders asks.

"Somebody could have hacked into Sam's email," Kennedy says. One theory we have is if somebody else did read the emails and deleted them, this person wanted Luc to think that Sam had read them and just hadn't bothered to respond." Looking from one parent to the other, she asks, "Is there anyone you can think of? A close friend or former friend who could have done something like this?"

Mr. and Mrs. Flanders glance at one another. He shrugs and she shakes her head. "No. Not really," they both say.

"Can we read these emails?" Mrs. Flanders finally asks.

"Do you really want to read your son's love letters, Elle?" Mr. Flanders asks his wife.

Mrs. Flanders peers at Jenkins fixedly, as though he might be able to answer the question. "I don't know," she says finally.

After a short silence, Kennedy says to her, "I wanted to ask about something else, something having to do with the Frost farm."

"Oh?"

Kennedy grabs her laptop and pulls up the photograph she showed Jenkins. "We have a lead on these guys. They're a pair of twins around forty-one years old. Their names are Howard and Mark Newcombe. They live in Bethel. They were once competitive bodybuilders. Do those names or descriptions ring a bell?"

"Are you suggesting they have a personal connection to Robert Frost?" Mr. Flanders asks.

"Perhaps, but not necessarily," Jenkins says.

Mrs. Flanders stares at the photo, blinking rapidly. "Well, I don't recognize them," she says, "however, as I think back, I believe there was a guy, a gardener who worked for Frost back in the very early sixties, maybe a year or two before Frost died. I think I heard from somebody in Carleton that this guy had twin sons late in the sixties, maybe 1970."

"They were born in '71," Kennedy says.

Mrs. Flanders politely nudges the laptop away. "I remember my mother saying that Frost had a major altercation with this . . . gardener, who I guess would have been their father."

Jenkins interjects, "Do a lot of people know about your family's—and Luc's—connection to the poet?"

"People in Carleton do."

Mr. Flanders says, "So let's just say these guys are the ones involved in the break-in. Are you now suggesting they also might be the ones who could have . . . waylaid Luc?"

"That's something we obviously need to look into," Jenkins says. "When we locate them."

FEBRUARY 14; DONNER'S FIELD, WEYBRIDGE, VERMONT; 22 DEGREES, HIGH CLOUDS AND WINDY

It's probably been at least two days, maybe more than two days. Everything has slowed, something is not right. Luc has been able to slake his thirst by sucking on the snowy halo all around him, so he has plenty of water if nothing to eat. But he's not hungry and feels the way he feels in the morning when he wakes up and his stomach is dead, before intense hunger sets in. Or when he's waiting to hear from Sam, the phone call that is supposed to come in at 10 p.m. but is, for some reason, delayed for an interminable fifteen minutes. He retreats into his room to wait—often to the dismay of Tate and McKinnon. Anxiety builds brick by brick until its weight is unbearable and smothering. Sometimes he'll even call Sam instead just to short-circuit his worry that something has happened, something gone irrevocably wrong, like Sam hooking up with somebody else, and sometimes Sam doesn't answer and the dread grows even worse, truly frightening, so all-consuming in the real estate of Luc's brain, that he begins to desperately think of ways of breaking things off with Sam—which, of course will be painful and self-destructive and yet will prove to him that he can at last take control of his passion. Sometimes he'll look at Taft and McKinnon, whose dalliances with women seem so enviably blithe and carefree. They never pine over anyone.

Here he is, huddled in this cavern of frozen straw, doing nothing but daydreaming. Although he feels no chill or shiver, he wonders if he might be febrile, like Ivan Karamazov. He feels the all-too-familiar ringing in his head, the relentless sonority of an injury that never seems to completely heal, as if too many complicated parts have been deranged and scattered like shrapnel. The day seems to go on endlessly.

He remembers the day back in early September, right before he returned to school, when he was studying Middle Eastern politics in Sam's office, after having made love to him upstairs. Sam was somewhere outside, chainsawing a fallen tree, the sounds of metal chewing into green wood ferocious and guttural. And episodic. And in the crashing silence between cuts, Luc ventured out into the hallway and peered around the downstairs, the old pine floors, the dusty bookcases with ceramic vases on top of them, the paintings of North Sea landscapes that were made by Sam's best friend who lives just outside of Newcastle, just south of the border of Scotland. The house and its furnishings struck Luc that Sam had a whole life from the past that he, Luc, was not part of, that there was a great swath of Sam's life, still separate, and it made him sad. Scared. Once again, he glanced out the window at the long late-afternoon light in the pasture behind the house, and the light lacerating his eyes and making him feel once again strange, as though one of his fits might come on.

Then Sam came back into the house and into the office and kissed him on the head. He reached beneath a scattered folio of blueprints, pulled out the thick paperback of *The Brothers Karamazov* and gave it to Luc, saying it was a new, definitive translation by a husband and wife. Disoriented, daunted at first, Luc took the book, turned it over to read the synopsis and said, "I've never read Dostoyevsky."

"There happens to be a great Russian lit professor at Carleton."

Luc looked up at him. "How do you know?"

"I studied with him."

"Really?" Luc grinned. "And he's still there?"

Sam cuffed him on the shoulder. "Smart ass. I'm sure there are other professors I studied with who are still there. Anyway, I was thinking if you like this, maybe you'll take his course in the spring."

"It's my last year," Luc reminded him. "I still have classes for my major. And I don't know if this one is even offered."

"Oh, it's offered. I checked."

"Ah." An awkward moment, and then Luc said, "Funny how my parents never suggested I take even a single course."

"Well, you're into econ and government. They probably figured you don't have the time for something like this."

Luc laughs. "I almost took—I wanted to take—art history. But I didn't . . . because, well, I'm not going in that direction anymore, so what's the point."

"You can always take that, too, in the spring." Sam looked hopeful and Luc couldn't help wishing his own father had shown this sort of concern.

"If I take art history and Russian lit, I'll have to come back in the summer. To finish."

"Wouldn't be the end of the world. It's your only college education, after all."

Luc said, "But you understand why I'm studying what I'm studying, don't you?"

"I think so."

"Not always but too often whenever I try to go back to drawing, I start to feel the electricity thing. It's like that part of my brain doesn't want to be disturbed anymore, and bites me if I touch it. Does that make any sense?"

"Sure . . . it does." But Sam's tone was skeptical.

And so, wanting to please him, back at school, Luc sat down with Dostoyevsky one Sunday. He was resting a pulled thigh muscle as the result of a scrimmage. The warmth of late summer wafting through his window, he was lying on his bed and feeling unusually calm, even happy, knowing that he loved somebody completely and deeply, a man who lived only an hour away and whom he could visit whenever he wanted.

The book was different from anything he'd ever read. It moved slowly but had an urgency that he recognized and that seemed familiar. Then it came to him: of course, this is the work of an epileptic mind, a mind like his, a mind that breaks down into blinding flashes and sounds, constantly flirting with a fit that might or might not give warning of its appearance. And what struck Luc was that every major character in the book seemed to come close to the edge of insanity, even crossed the border into it, but finally at the last minute stepped back to reason. What compelled him to keep reading was that he felt understood for once—ironically, by someone who'd lived in another century.

When Luc told Sam he was well into it, Sam suggested paying attention to Smerdyakov, the epileptic servant. But it was really Ivan whom Luc warmed to, well before knowing that Ivan would be afflicted with a brain fever and told by a Moscow doctor that hallucinations would quite likely be in his condition. Ivan has already dreamed up *The Grand Inquisitor*, when Christ returns during the inquisition and, recognized, is sentenced to death. Then, later on in delirium, Ivan meets with the Devil, who, dressed like a dandy, actually tells him that he wants to enter a church and offer a candle in simple-hearted faith. Reading about this hectic encounter makes Luc felt a bit more at home with the kinetic episodes of his off-kilter brain.

But there's no electricity circulating now. He's in the doldrums one moment and in terror the next. He hears the wind sluicing above his head, the groans of winter, snow heaving and softly bellowing in the rising and falling temperatures. At a certain time of day, he can spy a glint of frozen field,

the dapples of sun and the shadows of fence rails that elon-
gate, then vanish as light ebbs away. And the murmur of the
Millstone Creek grows louder at night. He knows the sound
will increase in the melt, with the shore coming nearer and
nearer. But it will be months before the river arrives and
surely he'll be somewhere else by then.

PART 2

Men outlive their love, but they don't outlive
the consequences of their recklessness.

—George Elliot, *Middemarch*

FEBRUARY 18; BOSTON; 22 DEGREES, 20 MILES VISIBILITY, LIGHT WINDS

Sam doesn't know if it's the increased dose of painkillers that the hospital has given him for traveling, or just his restive mind, but he finds himself narcotically daydreaming. He's at an art opening in Lebanon, New Hampshire, noticing a plump woman with salt-and-pepper hair held in place with a girlish beret, a woman with a grave, florid face carrying a pitcher of red hibiscus tea with the nametag "Eleanor Flanders." He can't help staring at her, desperate to see Luc's likeness in his mother's face. Can she really be out in this harsh world so early in her grief? How can she get out of bed every day knowing she'll never see her son again? Sam has stared at her for too long, and she catches his gaze and migrates over to him.

With a slight air of annoyance she asks, "Do I know you?"

And he thinks: *Grief has cracked open her soul, she'll talk to anybody now because she's so distraught, her life is ruined, it will never, ever be the same for her.* As his own tears come, he tries to stanch them and manages to say, "I heard about your son. I'm so sorry for your loss. I was just thinking about . . . well, I lost . . . one, too."

"Your son?" she asks, incredulous at such a coincidence.

He nods his head and says, "Yes," and immediately feels the shame of his lie.

Her response is a fluted sigh, like a soul that keens every time it breathes. "Ah. I'm so sorry. I just hope people have been as kind to you as they've been to me," she says, and then adds, "I wish you'd known him, I wish you'd known Luc."

"I wish I did, too," he says.

But then a day later she calls him at home, railing at him. Somebody has told her Sam never had a son and why would he tell her such a blatant, awful lie? He can say nothing to explain himself.

"And you did know Lucas," she accuses, her voice stinging Sam with the sound of Luc's proper name. "He was in your life in a way . . . I guess I have to try to understand that now, too, don't I?"

"I guess you do," Sam confesses.

"Because I think . . ." She falters and then proclaims, "Because I think he loved you."

"No," Sam says, "because I loved him."

Sam wakes up with a shudder just as the plane begins descending. Looking out the window, he could swear that, just ahead of its wings, he spies a strand of lights illuminating a coastline, and then an ultramarine membrane stretching out before him in the early evening shadows. But then the ocean reshapes itself as land, as lights and matchbox houses, like the mirage of an inland sea. Maybe the painkillers are wearing off.

Mike is dozing peacefully in the seat next to him. After cashing in some mileage points to upgrade Sam to first class, Mike flew out to meet him in Salt Lake City. With ample room for his leg and the cast, Sam has been able to get up during the five-hour flight and move around to prevent the possibility of a blood clot, which is always a danger when one travels with a broken leg. Gina, Mike's girlfriend, a tough-minded nurse practitioner from predominantly Irish Southie, will be meeting them at Logan's curbside with a rented van, and the three of them will drive up to Vermont. They will get Sam reestablished and figure out what outside help he will need until he is able to get around on his own without crutches.

Snow falling steadily over Boston softens the edges of the grittier neighborhoods, bringing yet another frozen stratum to a city brutally besieged by winter. During the final approach over icy Winthrop Bay, Sam remembers that a plane went down there in 1960 after its engines inhaled a flock of starlings; he imagines colliding with the bracing waves, almost like a transitory death wish. During landing he can see the dirty floes left by plows that have run out of places to push what looks like an urban glacier. During the eastward flight, Mike described people in tantrums feuding over parking spaces, slashing tires, threatening bodily harm. Sam wishes for the luxury of worrying about where to park his car, anything to stem the relentless anxiety plaguing him over the disappearance of Luc Flanders.

In their last conversation in the hospital before Jenkins returned to Carleton, Sam was warned that, despite the evidence that supports Luc's walking away from Skylight Pond, he would likely be damned in the court of public opinion. Jenkins explained that local people, unhinged by an unsolved disappearance of a university student, might feel the need to indict somebody. Even in a place supposedly as liberal as Vermont.

Arriving back in South Woodstock close to midnight, with Gina and Mike, Sam sees a familiar Volvo station wagon parked in front of his house, clouds of exhaust blooming in the sub-zero air. "That looks like Pete's car," Mike says.

"I think it is Pete's car," Sam agrees.

Gina says, "What the hell! Why is this guy out here in the middle of the night?"

"He's somebody we went to school with," Sam explains.

"Somebody *you* went to school with." Mike gently reminds him that their age difference is four years.

Sam tells Gina that Pete is a local reporter for the *Valley News*. "I guess he wants to talk to me."

"It's pretty late. Isn't this a little aggressive?"

"I . . . don't think it has to be," Sam says as they pull up to the Volvo, and Mike, on the passenger side, rolls down the window. "What's going on, Pete?" Mike says in a flat tone, deliberately forbidding.

Bundled up in a tan Carhartt coat, Pete Skalski is a short, compact, exceptionally fit man with widely set light gray eyes and buzzed blond hair.

"Hello, Mike. I'm here to talk to Sam."

"Because?" Gina asks from the driver's side.

"Don't worry," Pete says. "I'm here unofficially."

"Pull up a little bit, please," Sam says to Gina. When she does, he manages to open the van's sliding door to meet his friend's uneasy gaze. "Hey there, Pete."

Pete's attention immediately trains on Sam's cast. "Holy cow! How long will that be on?"

"They say I'll be free by the end of April."

"You're lucky it's your left leg and not your right. At least you'll be able to drive."

"That's some consolation," Sam says.

"Can we get you inside?" Gina's protective, nursing instinct has kicked in.

"Just hang on thirty seconds, okay?" Mike asks her quietly.

Sam waits until he and Pete are looking squarely at each other. "What's going on?"

"There were other reporters hanging out here earlier. I told them you weren't coming back until tomorrow."

"How did you know I was coming back tonight?"

"Heather Finlayson," he says. "You forget that she takes care of my dog, too. I figured Panda had to be there."

"Just tell him to come inside," Gina insists. "We need to get you inside, Sam!"

Pete smiles sheepishly and tilts his head. He has quickly figured out that Gina is in charge. "I'll help him," he offers after Gina has pulled into the freshly plowed driveway. Turning to Sam, he says, "You can use my shoulder instead of a crutch from here to there, right?"

"Yeah, no problem." Sam puts his arm around his friend. Once they are close and hobbling their way toward the side door, Sam says quietly, "So what's going on, Pete? Why were you waiting?"

"Hoping to talk to you. My editor wants me to interview you."

Sam draws back a little. "But how can you interview me? You're biased. You're my friend."

"Simple. I'd disclose the fact that we know each other."

Mike is now unlocking the door to Sam's mudroom.

After a moment of consideration, Sam says, "Look, as you can see, I just got home. How about I'll think about it?"

"That's fine," Pete says as he hands him off to Mike, who is standing just inside the door.

Once they are all inside, Sam says, "How's Meagan, by the way?"

"She's well," Pete says. "She sends her love."

"You almost lost it there," Mike tells him the following morning. "Again. I wish you wouldn't try and do everything yourself. Just let us—let people—help you." He's referring to Sam's maneuvering around the kitchen, nearly collapsing with his crutches while trying to pour from a thermos of freshly made coffee.

Gina crosses her ample arms and admonishes, "If you fall and do any more damage to that leg, you may never walk right again, much less be able to ski."

"I know. I know," he says with exasperation. "I just hate not being able to take care of myself."

She shakes her head and informs him, "You are going to have to rely on other people for a while. If you'd only stop resisting, you'll make it easier on everybody else."

"Okay, but it's still going to be difficult finding anybody

willing to come here and help me," Sam says, referring to Jenkins's "court of public opinion."

"We just won't look in the redneck pool," Gina suggests.

"No, it's not about rednecks," Sam insists, going on to quote Jenkins that liberal as the region might seem, many New Englanders still sit in silent condemnation of love between men, and especially love between an older man and a much younger one.

"Even in this day and age?" Gina asks, dubious.

"Yes, believe it or not, " Sam says.

"Besides, you can always get a visiting nurse."

"I can't afford a visiting nurse. My insurance won't pay for it."

"Well, we need to get you somebody's help!" Mike insists as Sam hands him the metal crutches and sits down heavily on the sofa. Pain shoots up his leg so that he can't help whimpering. "The only alternative is coming down to my house in Boston and living there. And I know you don't want to do that."

"I can't do that!" Sam says, his temper flaring up in frustration. "How will I get my work done? I need to be at my desk, I need to see clients and have all my files, my plans, and my special printers. I'm already way behind. Besides, who'd take care of my Panda?" His black dog, an Australian shepherd mix, has drifted into the room. She looks at his cast and then at him with great worry in her intelligent, calculating eyes.

"She's always welcome. You know that," Mike says.

Although she had seemed jubilant earlier that morning when Mike went and fetched her home, Panda had greeted Sam more tentatively than usual. As though aware that he was injured, she even refrained from jumping all over him as she usually did whenever Sam returned from being away. Now she rubs her long fur coat against him, and he hugs her tightly, listening to her groan and whimper in pleasure. God, does he love this wise dog. And yet he thinks how desolate it's going to be when Mike and Gina leave, just him and this big creaking house, a place where he once happily spent days and nights alone, until he met Luc, who filled the rooms with chatter and mirth and then left him to a profound, aching emptiness that made him feel even lonelier than when he had no romantic attachment in his life.

Gina resumes, "We just need to find you somebody around here to come in every day."

As it turns out, the dog-sitter, Heather Finlayson, has a friend whose daughter, just out of high school, is looking for part-time work. Around noon, a sturdily built girl, fair-haired and slightly walleyed, arrives, and Sam can tell that she's a bit of a misfit and, rather taciturn, not prone to making idle conversation. This, he decides, is probably a good thing. Gina speaks to her at length and, when satisfied that the girl can perform the needed tasks, spends the rest of an hour showing her how to help Sam up and giving tips on dealing with somebody relying on a pair of crutches.

It's agreed that this young lady will come four hours a day, two in the morning and two in the afternoon, and that Sam will pay her in cash. Once Gina formalizes the arrangement, she and Mike start organizing their return to Boston. Sam, in the meantime, has managed to propel himself upstairs to his room and sits on his bed with his leg propped up. Mike follows behind, drops down next to him and grabs hold of his shoulder. "You going to be okay without us, buddy?"

"Got to be okay. No other choice."

Mike looks nervous and Sam imagines he's reliving the nightmare of the accident in the Fall when they both thought Sam was going to die. "You were given a second chance. At your life. So don't blow it. Go easy on yourself."

"I'll try. Not so simple when I keep thinking about Luc being gone and maybe being dead."

"I know. I understand. But no matter what, in spite of everything, you still got to get yourself better. You got to focus on that. On doing your rehab exercises and taking one step at a time."

Nodding, Sam goes quiet for a moment. "I'll admit there is part of me that doesn't want to do anything, part of me that just wants to give up. Part of me that just wants to let go."

The words fall heavily between them, and Sam can see Mike stiffen with alarm. "What are you telling me, Sam?" he says at last.

"I'm telling you, Mike, that sometimes I think about not going on."

Mike has fallen into dismayed silence.

"But don't worry," Sam manages to say with lightness in his voice. "You don't have to put me on suicide watch. Not yet. I'm just trying to tell you that whenever I think he might actually be gone, dead, it's . . . And now these letters that he supposedly wrote me and seem to have been read and deleted by somebody. I have to see them."

"Why haven't you?"

"Something about forensic people looking at how they were sent or accessed. Because they were deleted after they were read—supposedly by me—they had to be retrieved. And I had no way of doing that, of retrieving them."

"They told you what was in them, didn't they?"

"Not the words, themselves. Just that the emails were . . . conciliatory. And passionate." A slimy, nauseous feeling comes over him. "I don't remember if I gave my password to Luc or not. How could somebody else have gotten it?"

"Maybe the person didn't have a password but was able to hack into your computer anyway. Accessing, reading and deleting somebody's email is probably not that hard for a computer geek."

"That geek would have to know when Luc wrote the emails

and be able to read them before I got to them. I checked that account fairly frequently. At least a few times a day. Three different emails were read at three different times."

Mike ponders this for several moments. "Ah, so that's why it's harder for you to prove you didn't read them."

They can hear Gina moving around downstairs and then seem to stop moving, almost as though she's listening for them.

"I can tell she's about to call me down to leave . . . Babe?" Mike calls out. "I'll be there in a second. Just finishing going over something with Sam." Then he turns to Sam. "But if Luc took off once before—"

"When he was fifteen—"

"I guess we can't assume anything until . . . they find him, right?"

Sam nods at the grim thought. "But you know what?" he says. "As hard as it is for me, can you imagine what it's like for his parents, waiting like this? What kind of hell is that?" Sam sees Mike looking at him with his downcast, different-colored eyes.

Mike says, "My mom's younger sister died when they were kids. She told me my grandmother never got over it."

"I'm sorry. I know I've gotten us on a downer."

"Yeah, I think you have," Mike says with a laugh.

A bounty of newly fallen snow thunders as it plunges off the roof, and hearing it, Panda begins barking nervously downstairs. "Jenkins mentioned that Luc's mother might want to see me," Sam says softly.

Mike looks bewildered. "Really? Why would she want to see you?"

"Who knows? Any number of reasons, I guess." He pauses. "When we were flying back to Boston today, I had this weird dream about her." Sam goes on to describe the dream that he had of meeting Eleanor Flanders at an art opening and confessing to her that he'd lost his own son and how she'd gotten really furious when she found out he was lying.

FEBRUARY 19; CARLETON, VERMONT; 31 DEGREES, UNSEASONABLY WARM, CHANCE OF FREEZING RAIN

The police department's IT forensic division has finished combing through the hard drive on Luc Flanders's computer and Jenkins has dropped in to see his roommates to clarify a few of their findings. At a kitchen table stacked with thick textbooks and some small bullet-like aluminum cans of Red Bull, Will McKinnon and Charlie Taft sit slumped in their chairs with an air of defeat. Already they have given their version of the last few hours they had spent with Luc Flanders, how they'd left the apartment for Skylight Pond armed with a blue tooth speaker, some beers, and their hockey sticks. According to both Taft and McKinnon, Luc had seemed untroubled, certainly more upbeat than he'd been a few weeks earlier when he and Elizabeth had broken it off. When that had happened, for several days running he'd returned to the apartment, drunk a six-pack of Pabst Blue Ribbon, and fallen into a babbling, incoherent sleep.

Jenkins begins reading through a list of student names furnished by Taft and McKinnon and Elizabeth Squires; all of these students have been contacted, and in some cases, questioned, about their acquaintance with Luc Flanders. They've been asked the last time they saw him, and if he'd said anything that seemed noteworthy or alarming. Bits and pieces here, snippets of casual conversation there, had yielded no clues at all. After Jenkins finishes reading through the list of names, he says, "Now, did anybody come to this apartment other than people on this list?"

A few moments of reflection pass. Finally, "Yeah, a girl

from my hometown," Taft offers. "Named Courtney Markwell. A student at UVM. She's been down here a few times."

"From Newport?" Jenkins clarifies.

"Right."

"How much time has she spent here?"

"Let me think." The young man stammers and looks discomfited. With dark hair, dusky skin and large brown eyes, he looks like a highborn Latino, maybe a Spaniard or even a patrician Argentinian. Jenkins concludes that the Latin blood must derive from the mother, Taft being such a New England-sounding surname. Beefy and muscular with a thick neck, he doesn't have the ideal physique for a soccer player. "She spent the night a couple of times."

"Part-time girlfriend?"

"Not really. We hang out."

"So when she spent the night with you, Luc was in his room?"

"When he wasn't with that dude," Taft says with unmistakable rancor.

"So could he and Courtney Markwell have had a conversation or"—he searches for a better word—"an 'interaction,' without your knowing about it?"

Taft looks taken aback. "You mean like hooking up?" His face is flushed and purposeful, and Jenkins finds this noteworthy.

"Not necessarily. Perhaps more like saying hello or . . . maybe even chatting when you weren't necessarily in the room."

"You know what he's saying," Will McKinnon tells his roommate irritably.

Taft is clearly the beta in this situation and, probably, in the roommate hierarchy. McKinnon, the alpha, on the other hand, seems awfully cocksure of himself in the way twenty-two-year-olds can be before life intervenes and they get broken or, at the very least, taken down a few pegs. McKinnon is finely hewn like any college athlete, but like his roommate, almost unnaturally muscular.

"Well," Jenkins says, "you cast a wide net with the hope that some related facts turn up. Sometimes you even stumble on them." He watches the expressions change on the faces of Luc Flanders's roommates. "So"—he turns to Taft—"Courtney Markwell is at UVM?" *Easy to stop by and have a word with her,* he thinks.

"Not there anymore," Taft informs him. "Dropped out."

"Because?"

Taft looks cornered. "Couldn't hack it."

"What year was she?"

"Freshman."

"You'll get me her contact information?"

"Sure." Taft grabs his nearby phone, scrolls through it effortlessly, then reaches around a fat tub of protein powder with the hologram of a bodybuilder on it and grabs a yellow Post-it in the middle of the kitchen table, as well as a pencil with a sharpened point but whose eraser has been chewed off, and writes the name and phone number carefully. Jenkins notes the meticulous care he gives to his handwriting, not necessarily what he'd expect from an oafish jock. But then again, this was Carleton College, number eight in the *U.S. News and World Report*'s ranking of small colleges. Once finished, Taft places the note on the table, adhesive side up.

Jenkins takes out the legal pad with his notes and peruses them. Then, looking between both men, he says, "So we got access to Luc's email," noticing that the news makes both men flinch and stiffen. After all, this must seem like a dire measure that reinforces, in a far more concrete way, that something has gone terribly wrong in their friend's life. "Somebody signed on to his college email account at seven p.m. the evening Luc didn't come back, and we've traced the computer to where the email was accessed. It was in Morrell Student Center."

Both men are staring at him, zombie-like.

"Is there any reason to believe that Luc didn't come back to your place but showed up at the computer center at seven p.m. on the night he went missing?"

Taft and McKinnon look at one another quizzically. And McKinnon shrugs and says, "No."

"Did he have a habit of going there?" Jenkins asks.

"Not that I know of," McKinnon says. "Far as I know, he always worked in his room." He turns to Taft.

"Ya, I suppose he could've gone there."

"Or somebody just logged in under his name," Jenkins suggests.

"Then they would have had his username and password," Taft says.

"That's stating the obvious," McKinnon says.

Jenkins continues, "He has two email addresses, his Carleton account and an AOL account: Flandersman@AOL. com. So at the same time that Luc or somebody with his sign-on information logged into his Carlton account at the student center, they also logged into his AOL account. And an email that was sent at two p.m. and not yet read was then unsent. Which, you both probably know, can be done with AOL if the intended recipient hasn't read it."

"I have an AOL account," McKinnon offers. "Unsent plenty of drunken emails. Push of a button."

"Exactly," Jenkins says. "And this particular email that was sent and then unsent was to Sam Solomon." Jenkins watches the reaction of discomfort this evinces. Both of these men seemed bewildered to learn that Luc had been carrying on an affair with another man, a man old enough to be his father. "And the email urgently requested a meeting."

"Maybe Luc unsent the letter because he had second thoughts about it?" McKinnon says.

"Certainly possible," Jenkins says, sitting on the fact that three other emails sent by Luc Flanders to Sam Solomon were actually read. "Now, according to both of you, Luc's car never left the street, is that correct?"

"Yes, that's right," Taft says.

"So if Luc met up with Sam Solomon on the night of February eleventh—"

"The guy picked him up," McKinnon interrupts.

"The guy?" Jenkins asks.

"Sam Solomon," McKinnon says snidely.

Jenkins waits a few moments, knowing the next question is crucial to his investigation. "That name make you angry?"

"Of course it does," McKinnon says.

Jenkins keeps his eyes squarely on McKinnon, whose face has colored deeply. "And why is that?"

"Why is that?" Taft interjects. "He probably killed Luc."

Now looking at Taft, Jenkins says, "One thing we do know. Even if Sam Solomon came up to Carleton, he would not have had enough time to . . . kill Luc and dispose of his body and get to where he was going in Boston and arrive when he did. Anybody dumped on the side of the road would have been found by now. The ground is frozen. The lakes are frozen. And a deep layer of snow is not easy to get through, especially after it has settled and congealed. That's why I'm told, not too long ago in rural parts of Vermont, people who died up here during the winter were stored in barns until they could be buried in the spring."

"I'm from the Northeast Kingdom, so I know all about that," Taft says. "My grandfather died in December and they couldn't bury him until April."

"So where did they keep him?" McKinnon asks.

"In an old car."

McKinnon bursts out laughing.

"Could he have killed Luc and then dumped him in Lake Champlain?" Taft asks. "Parts of it never freeze."

"Too far north," Jenkins says reasonably. "Certainly not enough time for him to go even farther north to get rid of a body and then head south to Boston."

"Maybe he drove the body all the way to Boston," McKinnon says. "Then tossed him in the ocean."

"Obviously possible, but from our point of view, again, hard to justify time-wise. He'd still have to stop in some place like Revere or Southie and drag the body to the beach."

"Or carried him," Taft says thoughtfully.

Then McKinnon says, "Okay, this is getting gruesome."

Jenkins, ever mild-mannered, says, "Back to emails. Let's say somebody and not Luc Flanders logged in to his email accounts, then we'd like to find out who this person is."

After a short silence, McKinnon turns to Jenkins and says, "And what about Elizabeth?"

"I plan to speak to her next."

"I spoke to her yesterday," McKinnon says quietly. "She went home for a couple of days. To chill out. All of it was really getting to her."

Jenkins leaves the apartment building and, heading toward his car, stops and pivots around to glance up at the kitchen window. He can see the silhouettes of Taft and McKinnon sitting where he left them, in quiet discussion.

They're notably defensive and curiously agitated. Angry. There seems to be a pronounced bubbling over of anger in university kids these days. Jenkins doesn't believe this anger was so manifest when he went to college back in the 1980s. Many of his former FBI colleagues remarked how hard it has been to wrap their heads around the rash of campus shootings that occurred in recent years, much less the decision of some universities to allow concealed weapons—to give the students a way of protecting themselves against unstable and violence-prone contemporaries who lose their cool over academic pressures or rejection in a world distorted by opportunistic social media.

A freezing drizzle slows Jenkins's travel up Route 7 to his home in Burlington, and the trip takes close to an hour. He listens to the icy hiss of the drops striking the windshield. Looking out into the decreased visibility of the roadway, he thinks about text messaging and photograph posting, instant pastimes that lead to self-absorbed kids, demanding and impatient kids. A hierarchy of cool and uncool. Among the uncool are always the campus shooters, who blame their violence on feeling invisible among the ranks, or the lack of interest shown to them by the opposite sex. As far as he knows, none of the perps in the history of campus shootings were gay.

And as far as he knows, Carleton College itself has never

had a single homicide or violent assault other than fights between drunken kids or horned-up guys trying to aggressively coerce reluctant coeds to have sex. Abduction and possibly murder would certainly seem beyond the ken of this particular place. And yet in 1971, a Carleton freshman had been on her way to take an exam when she stopped and told her friends she needed to run back to her dorm to get a pencil. Then she completely disappeared. Back in her room, the police found her wallet and all of her possessions. There were no computers with email and Internet histories back in 1971.

Jenkins makes a note to himself to ask one of his IT forensic guys to research campus disappearances to see if there might have been any pattern among the disappearances of forty-five college-age male students who, over a period of years, were found drowned and inebriated mainly in the Midwest—but also at a few campuses on the East Coast. A theory advanced by two retired New York City detectives: that these forty-five men had been the victims of serial murders committed by a group of people who identified their crimes with "smiley face" graffiti found scrawled on buildings or roadway signs near the bodies. The FBI, while Jenkins was a member of its corps, had debunked and vilified the theory.

Four people might possibly have found a way to access Luc Flanders's computer: Will McKinnon, Charlie Taft, Elizabeth Squires, and Sam Solomon. However, there could be yet another student—or even professor—on campus, someone with whom Luc may have had a secret relationship and who then found a way to gain access to his personal particulars. Jenkins has spoken to the soccer players who know Luc, and there seems to be nothing about any of them that would suggest a meaningful relationship. The general consensus is that Luc Flanders is a bit of a loner.

Just after eight in the evening, Jenkins arrives at his house on South Willard Street, a brick Victorian that has been in his wife's family for generations. Because Connie is a medical researcher at the University of Vermont, she keeps long hours—deliberately long, Jenkins has always surmised. It was her job that brought them back to Vermont from the Washington, D.C. area, Jenkins already on the verge of retiring from the FBI and therefore welcoming the change. He'd grown up in Bucks County, Pennsylvania, and has always yearned for a quieter, rural life.

While he was in Quantico and Connie at the NIH, they'd postponed having children. Neither at the time could commit to taking a substantial sabbatical from work, and they didn't want their child raised by a nanny. Beyond this, Connie always professed—sometimes proudly and sometimes with regret—that she wasn't the maternal type and therefore did not consider herself a good candidate to be a parent. Around that time, Jenkins got caught up in an investigation of one of the lesser-known religious cult mass suicides in which several children were involved and died innocently, and this only amplified his fear about being a father who conceivably could lose a child and be destroyed and dismantled by grief. With what he now realizes was impulsivity, without mentioning it to his wife, Jenkins made an appointment to get a vasectomy.

Connie, understandably, was furious that he'd never even consulted her. And yet she never asked him to have his vasectomy reversed, which, to him, definitively proved her ambivalence about having children.

She is home when he arrives, lackadaisically stirring a pot of black bean soup with chicken sausage that Jenkins made two days before and that they've been dining off of the entire week, neither being a big meal planner. Knowing he'd gone to question Luc Flanders's roommates, she asks, "How did it go?"

Before he responds, Jenkins grabs a decanter full of bourbon and, in a gleaming crystal tumbler, pours himself a finger full. "Both seem disgruntled."

By contrast to bright-haired McKinnon, Connie is one of those lovely auburn-haired types whose skin freckles—to him appealingly, although she claims to hate it—whenever she spends any time in the sun. She laughs flatly and says, "Welcome to my world. Medical students: frazzled, drama-ridden, and always pissed off. With what they put themselves through, it amazes me that they can even focus."

"So what do you think it is . . . with all of them?"

"Well, many of them are on Adderall, thinking that will give them an advantage. Allow them to work with less sleep, to focus better. But the drug makes them really irritable."

Connie starts ladling the thick, steaming soup into two deep white bowls. She has set the table in the dining room: two round rattan place mats, pale blue plates and mustard-colored cloth napkins. She sets the bowls down carefully and hands Jenkins a soup spoon. They both sit.

As they begin the meal, Connie says, "I told you I'm going to Athens next week."

"Athens?"

"Ohio Athens. For a conference."

"Oh, yeah, I guess you did tell me a while ago," he says just as he notices a delicate gold chain on her neck that he's never seen before. He is fairly certain he never gave it to her.

She takes a spoonful of the thick soup and nods to say that it's good. Eyes on her bowl, she says, "I would say 'come with me' but you sound pretty tied up right now."

"I am, pretty much," he says, sensing that her invitation is halfhearted. "How long will you be gone?"

"Three days," she says breezily.

No, she definitely doesn't want my company, he perceives.

Connie stops eating her soup and looks at him squarely. "So this kid who's missing? You said he took off once before?"

"Yeah, when he was fifteen."

"How long has he been gone this time?"

"Eight days."

He can sense Connie is pondering something and he waits. At last, she says, "There is something interesting that came up at the lab today. Related to a report on a science website. I watched it on my laptop. I'd like you to see it."

"Would it help this investigation?"

"It very well might. I'll let you determine that."

She gets up from the table, disappears for a moment and returns with her silver laptop, which she opens and brings over to Jenkins. She awakens the screen and he is staring at a red play arrow on a YouTube video. Connie clicks on the arrow.

The story that unfolds is about a Swedish man who'd entered a mysterious state of human hibernation after driving off the road and down into a ravine in the dead of winter. "Most people would have frozen to death overnight," the commentator points out. "However, when this man's car plunged off the road, the impact of the collision knocked him unconscious. His breathing slowed and so did his heart, and he entered what scientists at the University of Stockholm describe as a twilight state requiring very small amounts of oxygen. And very little water. The man survived for an entire month like this until he was found. He completely recovered. He had no bodily damage. No frostbite. He wasn't even dehydrated."

Bewildered, Jenkins turns to Connie. "Is this really legit?"

"The YouTube video reported other cases as well. An Austrian woman who was skiing off-piste crashed into a frozen pond and went under the ice for well over a half hour and survived without any brain damage. Then there was a Japanese guy who went hiking in December and slid down a steep slope. He went into the same state of hibernation and lived for six weeks in a snowbound welter and wasn't found until January."

"And your colleagues. What do they say?"

"We're looking into it. It may be relevant to something we're doing. But I thought it might be relevant to you."

FEBRUARY 19; NORWICH, VERMONT; 25 DEGREES, SNOW SQUALLS

Eleanor Flanders is back to reading the poems of Frost, the poems of her childhood; they seem to settle her, to soothe her more than Walcott. Perched by the bay window in her kitchen with the first edition Collected Poems she inherited from her mother, she looks out at their red, dilapidated barn that long ago began to look sculptural, in the beauty of its decay. A frozen spume of snow clings lightly to the wooden flanks.

Essence of winter sleep is on the night.
The scent of apples: I am drowsing off.
I cannot rub the strangeness from my sight.
And then later in the poem, the lines, of course, strike her.
One can see what will trouble
This sleep of mine, whatever sleep it is.

Because, of course, with Luc missing, she is sleeping fit-fully, waking up to the knotted nightmare of where he might be, whether he's alive or dead, and, wanting to stay in bed, feeling forced to begin another endless day that needs to be gotten through. Janine keeps calling, wanting to take off from work and just come up and devote herself to helping her mother get through it all. But Eleanor keeps refusing, dread-ing the disruption of her daughter's life—for her daughter's sake.

Eleanor is on autopilot. She now spreads chamomile buds on the fine mesh of one of her herb-drying racks and sets the rack out in the thermally warm greenhouse. Back in the kitchen, she begins a preparation of hawthorn, a dark, watery extrusion with which she will make an alcohol tincture to

help regulate erratic heartbeats. She adds freeze-dried calendula to a glycerin gel for burns and rashes. And then begins
her most popular item: arnica salve for tired and aching mus-
cles, something that she had always pressed on Luc, who
used it reluctantly. If she has time later, she'll begin another
batch of atropine for her own asthma, which has been acting
up under the stress of waiting for word.

On one hand, she yearns for this terrible period to end with
some definitive news of him; and on the other, she is afraid
to hear the worst and is tempted to prolong her ignorance, to
cling to the shred of hope that somehow he will just walk in
the door, as if returning from some nonsensical adventure,
his pale eyes full of mirth and affection. She has imagined
this sudden euphoric appearance again and again, prayed for
it in her own Unitarian way. She was recently encouraged
by the story of a mother in Alaska who was mistakenly told
her son had died in a car accident, only to have him show
up at her door six weeks later. But Eleanor's hope has always
shrunk to a small aperture of light that only for a moment
plumbs the dreaded darkness of his being found, his death
confirmed, and the wretched hopelessness with which it will
surround her. She feels the chimerical desire to switch with
him, to bring death upon her as long as her death will sustain
his life. And then the guilt over unwittingly discouraging him
from avowing his lifestyle, for somehow giving the impression
that she'd have difficulty accepting a man as her son's lover. It
occurs to her that any sexual or identity struggle would have
been a lot less of a conflict had he gone to a different school,
maybe an "art college" like Rhode Island School of Design,
where a substantial percentage of the student population
identifies as bisexual or gay. But instead, Luc got caught up
in the patriarchy of Carleton athletics; nearly all of his close
friends are nerdy jocks like McKinnon and Taft. So had Luc
needlessly imprisoned himself with his secrecy? Had he felt

shame? Eleanor has done her own digging, contacting the head of a New England chapter for sexual equality on college campuses and was told that Luc's making a secret of his sexuality was still quite common.

Jenkins told Eleanor that when he questioned the roommates, he could see how uncomfortable they were when the subject of Luc's affair came up, that they hardly acknowedged it, much less were willing to talk about it. She could well imagine Luc hiding his comings and goings from them, so that his not showing up on any given night—such as the one on which he disappeared—was not in any way unusual and certainly not questioned. She has the feeling that early last autumn he was away many evenings, trekking back and forth between the college and South Woodstock, maybe driving over the Carleton Gap in one of those freak October snowstorms.

Eleanor wonders if Luc even mentioned his head injury to Sam. She wonders what Sam thinks might have happened to Luc. And then she realizes what she really desires is to know that Sam is genuinely tormented at Luc's vanishing, to get her own piece of mind that Sam Solomon has had nothing to do with her son's disappearance

Imagining the start of any conversation with Sam Solomon, her heart pounds and she can feel the pulse in her neck. Abstractedly, she looks over the kitchen, over the vessels and crocks of her naturopathic and homeopathic preparations, jars full of herbs and oils with neat labels—now throbbing before her eyes like foreign bodies, and the appliances she's operated for years glinting strangely, looking as alien as moon rock. Eleanor wonders if there is anything she could tell Sam about Luc that he doesn't yet know—like how Luc had wound his way to Connecticut the last time he took off. And maybe if she told Sam how it all happened, he might remember something Luc had said that could indicate where he'd gone this time. But then she seesaws back into: Luc didn't go anywhere. Sam is hiding something. Whenever this thought crosses her mind, she grows frantic.

Then again, if Luc ended that eight-month relationship around Christmas, if Luc withdrew to the point that Sam was barred from his day-to-day, that must've been pretty unbearable. And all this business of emails sent and retrieved and —supposedly—deleted, she tends to distrust it. Then again, if, as Jenkins says, they are unalloyed love letters, maybe she doesn't want to see them, just like she wouldn't want to know the intimate details of her children's sex life. Luc not responding to Sam's messages but for that one phone call is certainly plausible. After all, he rarely ever answers her messages.

She now realizes that Luc failed this man, and what her son ultimately withheld from him is similar to what he has withheld from her. And she certainly doesn't want to hear confirmation of this. It strikes her that when children Luc's age fall in love, as much as they might seem caught up in the object of their desire, in the end, when things settle down, they probably don't behave much differently toward their lovers than they do toward their parents.

FEBRUARY 19; PORTSMOUTH, NEW HAMPSHIRE; CARLETON, VERMONT; 10-20 DEGREES, FREEZING RAIN,

A New Hampshire state policeman spots two men matching the description of the bodybuilder twins entering a residential warehouse building on the wharf in Portsmouth. They have bleach-blond dreadlocks flimsily concealed by loosely knit Rastafarian caps. They dress like lumbersexuals and they walk like apes. Jenkins contacts the building landlord, who verifies that Mark and Howard Newcombe leased the building on February 13, three days after the vandalism occurred. He asks the Statie to find their apartment, ID them and detain the brothers until he arrives.

Halfway along the 207 miles between Carleton, Vermont, and the coastal New Hampshire city, Jenkins hears from the Statie who showed up at the loft with backup. He is now calling from the street and tells Jenkins they've just finished searching the apartment. "No hostages," the officer says. "And also no furniture. Just two sleeping bags, two inflatable mattresses, and a black nylon duffle with clothes, a few books and a zip-lock full of large hypodermic needles."

"Large hypos, you say?" Jenkins says.

"Definitely large," the Statie says.

"Any vials of anything?"

"Nope, just the needles."

"What are the books?"

"Three books of poetry."

Jenkins is startled. "Come again?"

"Three books of poetry," the Statie repeats.

"You get the names of the poets by any chance?" Jenkins asks.

"I wrote them down. Let me find them." Jenkins hears some rustling. "We have books by Marianne Moore, Ezra Pound, Amy Lowell."

"Well, blow me down," Jenkins mutters.

Inside the posh, upscale warehouse apartment building, the detective finds the twins sitting on the floor on opposite sides of an empty open plan great room whose old wooden floors look newly bleached and pickled. They look at him inquisitively, their eyes a pale, cruel blue framed by voluminous, medusa-like blond dreadlocks. Deeply bronzed by what looks like uneven spray tans, they are dressed identically in military pants and thick, fitted flannel shirts. Two tightly rolled sleeping bags are lined up next to the black nylon overnight bag.

Scrutinizing them, Jenkins says, "You guys are traveling light for having just rented an apartment."

"That's what we do," says one.

The Statie who made the arrest now enters the room. He's young and pasty and has a sizable gut. "Inflatable mattresses in the closet," he informs Jenkins.

"So I guess you guys were planning on staying for a spell." "We like Portsmouth," says one of the twins, who looks a bit walleyed.

"Really?" Jenkins says. "You think Portsmouth, New Hampshire is a step up from Bethel, Vermont?"

"You ever been to Bethel?" the twin asks.

"I have, indeed. I helped shut down a meth lab there. You got some real sketch hanging out in your town there. Never saw so many missing teeth in my life. Smile for me," Jenkins says, and both of them show perfect rows of white teeth. "Well, I can see meth is not your drug of choice. So what's with the hypodermics?"

"No crime to carry them around," blurts out the other twin, whose gaze is steady and sharp.

"You're Howard, right?" Jenkins asks.

"Yeah," the man says.

"And you're Mark," Jenkins says to his slightly walleyed twin brother.

"That's right."

Jenkins turns to the Statie. "Books still in the bag?"

"No." He lumbers over to a cardboard box turned upside down to make a wobbly surface upon which the three slim paperback volumes are resting. When the Statie hands them to Jenkins, he glances at them and then says, "Marianne Moore, Amy Lowell and Ezra Pound. You guys certainly have highbrow taste in poetry." Silence follows his remark. "Where did these come from?"

Howard says, "We don't have to explain anything to you."

"One way or another you'll have to," Jenkins tells them. "We have a DNA sample from a crime scene that matches both of you."

"Well then, I think we're going to have to call our lawyer."

"You can certainly call your lawyer. Do you want to use my phone?" Jenkins offers his with a gesture of sincerity.

The twins don't respond to this but rather stare at him vapidly.

Turning to the New Hampshire Statie, Jenkins says, "I'd rather not leave these guys together on the ride back. We'll also need to get forensics to go over their car. Ever been to Carleton, Vermont before?"

The Statie shakes his head.

"Quaint town. I think you might like it. Can I get you or another officer to drive one of these guys back?"

"You'll have to talk to my lieutenant about that."

Sitting in an observation suite with a two-way mirror, Kennedy looks at the bodybuilder twins seated at an examining table. They are facing Jenkins, who is questioning them with an unnerving calm. "So you have a website," he is saying to the twins, his voice piping into Kennedy's headset. "When was the last time you updated it?"

The brothers look at each other. And then the one on the right, the walleyed one, says in a slower cadence of speech, "Maybe a year ago." Through a microphone, Kennedy says, "Just want to make sure: this one is Mark?" Jenkins nods slightly and then asks the twins, "And what was the occasion for the update?"

"A new workout program," they both say in unison. And then Howard says, "One of the kids at V-tech saw us doing it at the gym and asked about it."

"So we decided to post it," Mark says.

Kennedy says to Jenkins, "Notice how big their heads look? Especially their foreheads? That's human growth hormone. That's what happens when you take too much of it."

"Are you guys still working out regularly?" Jenkins asks.

Both brothers simultaneously flex through their loose flannel shirts. By the way the fabric drapes on them, Kennedy can see the peaks of their biceps and a hint of cleanly defined pectorals. "Still pretty buff," she murmurs. "Nicky, I'd just cut right to the cheddar and ask if they're still 'on the juice.'" Jenkins blinks in auditory pain and adjusts his earpiece as though lowering the volume, and then rolls his eyes as if to say, *You don't think I'm going to ask this?* Ignoring him, Kennedy says,

"And then tell them we know how loaded they are. Why do they need . . . to illegally supplement their income."

They hear Jenkins say, "Regarding the paraphernalia you guys had in your bags. Are you on the juice?"

Both men stiffen simultaneously and Mark Newcombe says, "No."

Kennedy says to Jenkins, "Press them."

And Jenkins, poker-faced, says, "Just tell me what you're on, all right, and save me the time of having your blood drawn."

"Okay, we're on test," Howard says.

Jenkins looks confuses and Helen clarifies, "Testosterone. Ask them if they're on a stack."

"Anything else. On a stack?" Jenkins adds.

Both twins look startled. "D-ball," Mark says.

Kennedy says, "D-ball is injectable, usually smuggled in from Mexico. D-ball and testosterone are often taken together. A combination of these drugs is known to increase aggressive behavior dramatically."

Because Kennedy knows more about steroids and steroid use, Jenkins had originally suggested that she be in on the questioning. But Kennedy demurred. "I would get nowhere with these guys. They hate women like me. They're guys' guys and women they respect are bodybuilders with small waists and big, fake tits." She'd jammed her hands on her hips and said, "That's hardly me, is it?"

Jenkins now says, "I need you to cooperate. The more you cooperate with me, the less jail time you're going to do."

"Jail time?" Mark Newcombe asks.

"Yes, jail time. Your DNA is linked to a crime scene where a historical monument was trashed. So I don't imagine either of you will deny being at the Frost farm on the night of February tenth."

Both men stare at him, indignant.

Jenkins says, "Where does your father live?"

"He's dead," both say in unison.

"Did he work for Robert Frost?"

The twins glance at each other quickly. "Yes," Mark New-combe says.

"For how long?"

"Two years."

"And when was this?" Jenkins asks.

"Around 1962," says Howard.

"And they had a dispute?" Jenkins asks.

The twins are silent for a moment. "Seven-hundred-dollar dispute," Mark says.

"That Frost owed?"

"A tidy sum way back when," Kennedy remarks to Jenkins.

"Was your father ever able to collect it?"

Howard says, "He tried. Twice. But Frost refused. After that, Dad was too offended to ask again."

"Frost was a shit," says Mark Newcombe.

"Nobody ever said he was a model citizen," Jenkins comments. "Just a great poet. And speaking of poetry, what did you think you'd gain by taking those three books we found in your bag?"

"Because they weren't his?"

"His?"

"Frost's?"

"How do you know?"

"Dad lent them to Frost. Dad complained to us that he never got them back."

"So your father lent books of poetry to the Poet Laureate of the United States."

"That's right."

"Where did they ever meet?"

"At Carleton. Where else?" says Mark.

"Your Dad went to Carleton?"

"Yes."

Seeming to pause for a moment in order to collect his thoughts, Jenkins resumes, "So you leased an apartment in Portsmouth. On February thirteenth. Is that correct?"

"Yes."

"Did you think we wouldn't find you there? A hundred and fifty miles away?"

"We weren't thinking about that. We like Portsmouth," Howard says. "We're thinking about moving there permanently. We like the water."

"If you like the water," Jenkins says, "you can always go shopping up at Lake Champlain."

"We like ocean."

"You like ocean," Jenkins repeats. "So when was the last time you actually were at Carleton College?"

"Been a while," says Mark.

"Were you in the area of Carleton College on the night of February tenth?"

"No."

"The night of February eleventh?"

"No."

"February twelfth?"

Then Mark blurts out, "Look, we don't know anything about that missing kid."

"Missing kid?" Jenkins asks. "Who suggested you did?"

Kennedy is carefully watching Howard Newcombe, who is glowering at his brother. "Look at that face," she remarks.

"Have you ever met this 'missing kid'?" Jenkins asks.

"We read about him," Howard says finally. "It was on the news. That he disappeared on February eleventh. From Carleton."

"You didn't answer my question. Have you ever actually met 'this missing kid'?"

"No," the twins say simultaneously.

"Will you take a polygraph?"

"Not without a lawyer," Howard says.

"You'll get your lawyer, no worries about that," Jenkins tells them.

FEBRUARY 21; DONNER'S FIELD, WEYBRIDGE, VERMONT; 20 DEGREES, CLOUDLESS NIGHT

Luc has sculpted a little cave for himself inside the giant hay bale and he can hear the winds. The wind of sleep. He can no longer feel anything: the temperature, his hunger, his extremities. He has no idea how long he has been here in this hovel, tasting snow, melting it in his mouth to slake his thirst. Just beyond him lie the snowfields, splendid in the shadows of the sun, which slips behind the ragged peak of Snake Mountain. He knows he's approximately seven miles from campus, and yet feels worlds away from the broken terrain of his own life, of his own heart.

One thing constant is Sam, always Sam circling slowly around him. They're making love, and while people like Taft and McKinnon joke harshly about men with men and make it sound like depravity, he knows that there is a naturalness to it, a rightness, and that his wiring, his craving again, is almost spiritual in nature. That's what he could never convey to anyone: that between the right people, irrespective of gender, sex can be a journey, a transcendent journey.

That he was born to receive and not give, although he can give and has given to many women and made them happy. In so doing, he has made himself only partially happy because he knows it's what a man is biologically supposed to do; celebrated among his friends, bantered about in the locker rooms, and ironically, any guy who can resist falling into the trap of a relationship is always worshipped as a hero. Because down the line is marriage with all its constraints and commitments. Until then, you were supposed to have a grand old time.

When Luc would come back from those weekends in

South Woodstock and McKinnon and Taft greeted him, they always imagined he'd been with an older lady somewhere, a neglected married woman, housebound, with a husband who traveled. Sadly, he'd never try and contradict them. And yet whenever either of his roommates described a romp with a woman, the adventure, recounted with delight, sounded less significant somehow than his lovemaking with Sam. Luc wondered why this was. Shouldn't the act of love between two men have less meaning, less power, because it has no real biological imperative? Because it's not powered by the instinct and compulsion that might, for example, induce penguins to travel hundreds of miles over hostile wintry terrain to mate and have children, or drive soldiers through the perils of war so that they can return home to their brides?

Taft and McKinnon know Luc has disappointed some of the women in his life. They know that he hasn't cared enough and actually think he's cool because of it. They think he's just another guy who likes to keep his distance, a guy who likes to get as much as he can from a woman without promising anything. From his perspective, though, even if women like Janine have taken some of their power back, in general, young men like him still get away with being callow and cavalier. If he were only able to love women the way he should, or the way he loves Sam, he certainly would never have jumped from one woman to the other. Certainly, someone like Elizabeth deserved better than what she got from him.

And Sam, of course, deserved better, too. He'd failed Sam. Luc has been asking himself what it was that made him cut loose finally. Could it be that Sam reminded him how fragile the balance is between living and death, between health and illness? And that due to Luc's accident, due to the strange electric, epileptic spells that plague him, as unforeseen as the spells of atrial flutter that affect Sam, could it be that Luc always felt the possibility of ill health looming over both of them? Or maybe because Sam, the rugged, outdoorsy guy, was about to turn fifty, and that distant decade seemed a lot closer to death than birth. Having been seriously injured once, Luc finds himself preoccupied with how something in the body can suddenly go wrong, can leave you defenseless, can leave you sometimes without hope.

During one of Sam's arrhythmic episodes, to stem his own worry, Luc managed to overcome his fear that doing line drawings would bring on some kind of unwanted aura of his misfiring synapses. While Sam lay on his bed, eyes closed, doing yogic breathing to slow down his fitful heart rate, to bring his cardiac rhythms into a sinus pattern, Luc took out an unlined notepad that he'd found in Sam's office and began to sketch. It was late fall and Sam, who felt chilled due to his erratic heartbeat, was wearing a fleece jacket and corduroys. But after sketching Sam's supine form, instead of copying the drapes and folds of his lover's clothes, Luc drew the naked body he knew so intimately, the body that brought him every pleasure he could possibly want. And after such a long time away from drawing, once Luc began to sketch Sam, the technique and perspective all came back. It was like wheeling a bicycle out of a dark hallway after years of neglect, listening to the tires click, click, click as they venture forward, spewing dust that has collected during months or years of disuse. The ability to balance on two wheels is still there, the knack of steering second nature.

And somehow, this one time, Sam's state of alarm over his heart in revolt subsided enough so that he fell asleep and he gratefully woke up with a slow, regular heartbeat. Sam claimed that whenever the fit of arrhythmia ends and his heart is finally beating as it should, the feeling is euphoric, like finding religion after some sort of revelation.

Luc left the finished drawing on the coffee table downstairs, and later on that evening, when Sam first saw it, he didn't even make the connection. "Where did you get this?" Sam held up the drawing.

"What do you mean, where did I get it? I did it."

"Really? This?" Sam's eyes hungrily reverted back to the drawing, studying it carefully, microscopically, as he would one of his own architectural renderings. "This is really well done." Then he regarded Luc skeptically. "I thought you didn't draw anymore."

Luc shrugged. "I don't."

Sam gently waved the drawing at him. "Obviously, you do."

"Special occasion," Luc said. "I wanted to make sure I drew you in case . . ." He paused, realizing what he was about to say might be misconstrued.

"What, in case I croaked?" Sam asked with a hearty laugh.

Luc looked down at his hands. "Don't say that."

"Only thing is this doesn't really look like me."

"What do you mean?"

"I mean, yes, I recognize myself, but you've . . . made me look a lot better than I do."

Luc got defensive. "What are you talking about, that's exactly how you look."

"You airbrushed your perspective, let's put it that way."

"Bullshit I did!"

"You know what I'm saying." Sam sat down opposite him and reached over to touch Luc's arm, but gained nothing because Luc instinctively wrenched away.

"No, I don't," Luc said at last. "I don't know what you're saying."

"I'm sorry, maybe I should have said the drawing is flattering."

Luc remained resolute. "No, the drawing is you, Sam. And the problem here is that this world that you've lived in, this competitive world of guys rejecting each other because of some — or one — ridiculous physical imperfection, has dented your self-image."

Now Sam got angry. "Okay, whoa, that's a lot to insinuate."

"What do you mean? You've already said it yourself. And what bugs me, Sam, is that is the world that's waiting for me."

"Well, you have nothing to worry about because you're lovely and young," Sam said, sounding flippant.

"What a dumb ass thing to say," Luc told Sam with hurt incredulity, and Sam, who, at first, stiffened angrily in his chair, suddenly went slack, realizing his mistake. "You're right," he capitulated, "you're right. I'm sorry."

"It's okay," Luc said. "And you wonder why I still think about being with a woman."

"Well . . ."

"Women aren't as critical as men. At least about the physical body. They're much more forgiving. They don't sit around and take men apart because their ass is just a little too big or because they walk funny.

"I'd agree with that," Sam said. "However, if you don't have the gut desire for the person you're with, man or woman, you won't have the patience to put up with them for the long term, for the rest of your life."

"Sex isn't the be all and end all," Luc said.

"I don't believe you really think that," Sam told him.

And, of course, Sam was right.

FEBRUARY 21; CARLETON, VERMONT; 15 DEGREES, HIGH WINDS

Elizabeth Squires and her roommate, Portia Dominic, meet Jenkins at the campus police office. As far as twenty-two-year-old Carleton coeds go, Elizabeth seems rather typical: flaxen-haired, slight of build and yet with muscular legs that strain against her corporate-looking navy blue pantsuit. Portia, however, is a lovely, exotic woman of mixed race with long limbs and a natural grace of movement.

The two women have arrived punctually, whereas traffic on Route 7 from Burlington delays Jenkins's entrance by ten minutes. Greta Thornhill, the blowsy Scandinavian woman who was the last person to see Luc Flanders before he disappeared, meets him.

"Ms. Squires and Ms. Dominic are here already. And you are late," Thornhill tells him with a tone of admonishment that seems to come easily to her. She leads the way into a small, whitewashed, book-lined room where Elizabeth and Portia are already seated at an oblong, highly polished cherry wood table. In between them is a yellow legal pad with handwritten notes. Both rise slightly to cordially shake his hand and sit down again. They are trying to maintain an officious, businesslike air, but he can detect nervousness and discomfort radiating like waves of heat in this chilly room that is, like many of the old campus clapboard buildings, draughty and poorly insulated—particularly on such a blustery day. He hesitates a moment before beginning, feeling a bit sorry for Elizabeth as well as for all the people in Luc Flanders's life, the people who love him.

He begins, "Elizabeth, Will McKinnon mentioned that you took a break for a few days and went home."

"Yeah, I did." She looks down at her nail-bitten hands. "It was all getting to me."

Portia is meeting his gaze with a confident glint in her eyes. "It gets a bit much, you know, people coming at her all the time. Telling her how bad they feel. Parking their sympathy on her."

Elizabeth shrugs and, sticking out her lower lip, blows some stray tendrils of hair out of her eyes.

"A few things have come up since we last spoke," Jenkins tells them. "First, I want to talk about Luc's email being accessed the evening of his disappearance."

"I wouldn't know what to say about that," Elizabeth says.

"Understood. But have you any idea of who might have gotten into it?"

Elizabeth states the obvious: that most people would keep this kind of information on either their smart phone or their computer.

"But Luc didn't really—consistently, I should say—carry around a phone like other friends of his, did he?"

Elizabeth replies, "I would have to say more often than not, Luc didn't use his phone much. If he did have it on him, whenever I spent the night with him, whenever he took off his pants, he left it in there."

"Do you think he might have been hiding . . ." Jenkins hesitates. "Messages?"

"I do."

"Did you ever see any messages flash?"

She blushes deeply. "You mean, like, from Sam?'"

"Right."

"Once or twice I saw 'Sam.' I even asked Luc about them, but he lied and said they were from a school friend. School friend, Sam," she says bitterly.

"I mean, you've got to know," Portia breaks in. "That Luc Flanders is quite a liar. He lied about the ring. He lied about who gave him the ring. And until Liz browbeat him into it, he completely lied and covered up his relationship with . . . Sam." She pronounces the name with almost musical emphasis. "And Luc should've told her. He had, at the very least, a responsibility to inform her that he was having sex with a man right before he and Liz got together."

Jenkins can't help agreeing with this, although he does nothing except glance questioningly at Elizabeth. "Your friends call you Liz?"

"No," she replies. "Portia's the only one. So please don't get in the habit," she instructs Jenkins. "Anyway, Luc told me eventually about Sam."

"Eventually," Portia repeats with sarcasm.

"Okay, enough, Portia!" Elizabeth retorts. "You might be easy on somebody, too, if you fell in love with them."

"As if I haven't?" Portia replies.

At this, Jenkins hears a phone vibrating. "It's mine," Portia says, grabbing a blue canvas book bag. With a look of annoyance, she says, "Can we hang on just a second?"

"Of course. Take your time."

Portia reaches into her bag, at first looking inside and then glancing up at the ceiling and feeling for the phone, which continues to vibrate. At last, it's in her hands, and she shrugs and says, "Hi," and then to Jenkins, "It's my dad."

"Go ahead and speak to him," Jenkins tells her. "I'll take a little break. I have to speak to the lady in the office anyway."

Portia nods and says to her father, "Hang on, the detective is just going outside."

Greta Thornhill looks startled when Jenkins arrives at the chest-high counter. "That was very quick," she says.

"She had to take a phone call."

"Ah, okay."

"But I also wanted to speak to you."

Her face darkens for just an instant before she turns to him with a calculating look. "How can I help?"

"You were the last person to see Luc Flanders before he went to the pond."

"Okay."

"Was there anything about him that day that struck you as odd or off?"

"Well, I hardly meet him before this." Thornhill clings to using present tense. Strange, because up until this moment, her English seemed perfectly correct.

"I thought you told Randy James you'd met him before." Jenkins refers to a personal friend of his who, until recently, had worked for Carleton Campus Security.

"Oh, so you know Randy?" She's clearly jostled. "I didn't realize." She takes a deep breath. "Anyway, hardly a meeting, but I spoke to him briefly when the girl who . . . lost some of her intimate garments."

"You're talking about Portia Dominic?" Jenkins asks, tilting his head toward the conference room.

Momentarily ruffled, Thornhill says, "Yes . . . I didn't know if you knew who it was. We have campus policies here to discuss these things with outsiders as little as possible."

"Oh really? Even if it's with a local detective investigating a possible crime?" Jenkins asks, incredulous. Thornhill stares at him until he continues, "So back to Luc Flanders. On the night of February eleventh, when Luc Flanders came to you, what was the gist of your conversation with him?"

"About the break-in at the farm. That's what he comes to know. I don't give him much information, again because of policy."

"Was he . . . bothered?"

"Not after I tell him the provost calls his mother about it." She pauses. Jenkins is finding her mixing of past and present tense truly curious. "And then he checks his phone to see if there is a message. He said he would wait to hear from his mother. And that's it. He left. And I know nothing more than that."

The problem with questioning foreign speakers of English, particularly those who'd pretty much mastered the language, was that you couldn't really analyze syntax or word choice in any sort of forensic way. While still with the FBI, Jenkins had spearheaded a course in analyzing the diction as well as the writing style and substance of anybody the bureau questioned. It was a particular interest of his; he'd been keen to hire more linguistics experts such as the one now studying Luc's diary and his emails to Sam Solomon. A subset of linguistics geared at forensics is now taught at a minute number of universities and criminal justice colleges. One thing he's learned: a word that might set off alarms with a native speaker of English could very well be insignificant when uttered by a foreigner such as this woman, who clearly came to the language much later in life. Around fiftyish, she probably emigrated to the U.S. in her twenties. And while—ironically—her English has more dimension than the vast majority of native speakers, the text of what she says will, because of the natural influence of her mother tongue, be more difficult to break down.

As he walks back toward the conference room, Jenkins takes out his phone and sends Kennedy a text. *Ask Randy James about Greta Thornhill at campus security. I think she is sitting on something.*

A text comes back almost immediately. *Do you want me to try her myself?*

Yeah, why not?

Portia is done speaking to her father by the time Jenkins returns to the conference room. There is a fury of wind belting the side of the building and the clapboards are crackling in submission to its force. Jenkins looks out the window at the frenzied weather. "Crappy out there," he says. "And warm and . . . pretty cramped in here, isn't it?"

She looks around, her face wrinkling. "Kind of."

"Everything okay with your dad?" Jenkins says.

"Everything is fine," Portia replies curtly.

"So before we go back to Elizabeth, I need to speak to you about something else," Jenkins tells her.

"Me?" Portia says, startled.

"Yes," Jenkins says. "Having to do with the incident back in October when . . ." He pauses, wanting to frame his question with some delicacy. "When your garments were stolen," Jenkins clarifies. "Greta Thornhill from campus security spoke briefly to Luc Flanders." Out of his peripheral vision he can spy Elizabeth Squires shifting uncomfortably in her chair. "Was he actually in your dorm room?"

"Yeah, he was there. But he dropped in to see . . . Liz . . . Elizabeth, not me."

Pivoting quickly toward Elizabeth, Jenkins says, "So you were good friends with Luc back before you got involved with him?"

"I've known him since freshman year."

"She's always had a thing for him," Portia says. Elizabeth clucks her tongue as though in protest and Portia insists, "Well, you told me you did."

Jenkins says, "So, Elizabeth, when did you start to suspect that Luc might be gay?"

"I think any woman these days wonders . . . if a guy isn't really into it."

"And Luc wasn't into it?"

Elizabeth ponders this for a moment. "While we were dating, he was always preoccupied with something, not quite completely with me in the moment. That's what I mean."

He turns to Portia. "What about you?"

"Oh, I thought he was gay, gay, gay from the moment I saw him. Or pretty close to it."

"And why is that?"

"Because when he looked at me, he didn't really look at me the same way most guys look at me."

"What way is that?"

"He looked . . . let's put it this way: I never saw his eyes anywhere but on my face. He never checked me out, let's say."

"Did you share this opinion of him with Elizabeth?" Jenkins asks.

"From the very beginning." Portia looks over at Elizabeth. "But you didn't believe me."

"No, I didn't," Elizabeth says with baleful exasperation. She now seems—oddly—more tolerant of her overbearing roommate.

"I don't think Luc is even into women," Portia continues. "I think any interest he has is all show. I think he just went through the motions of being with a woman. You know, he wanted to save face among all the jocks."

"That's so wrong!" Elizabeth disagrees. "He's not like that. He wasn't your boyfriend, so you don't know!"

Portia looks warily at Jenkins. "Okay, so I don't know. Don't listen to me." Then she says to Elizabeth, "Why am I here anyway?"

"Ask him!" Elizabeth snaps." But Jenkins wouldn't dream of interrupting the exchange. Tears are glossing her eyes, and she bows her head for a moment. "Portia," she says at last, "can you lighten up on me a little? Don't forget you're on the outside of this."

"Well, not really if I'm here with you being asked questions. But all right. I'm sorry, Elizabeth." Portia now sounds sincere, notably using the name her roommate prefers. And then to Jenkins, "*Cosmo* recently did a survey of women and seventy percent of them said they would never date a man who even one time slept with another man."

Jenkins uses the opportunity to take two business cards out

of his billfold and gives one to each woman. "That's my contact info if you happen to think of anything else, or just to be in touch for any reason."

His card threaded between her fingers, Elizabeth is looking up at him. "Do you think Luc might be hurt, or maybe even . . . dead?"

"I'm not at liberty to speculate," Jenkins says, watching her carefully.

"But if he didn't take his car, how far could he have gone?"

"Could somebody have given him a ride somewhere?" Jenkins asks her.

Elizabeth frowns at this.

"Somebody could've helped him and, then, maybe not helped him."

"So what are you saying?" Portia asks. "That he could have been, like, kidnapped and taken somewhere?"

Jenkins doesn't answer for a moment. At last, he comments, "Hard to say."

Elizabeth says, "Or like the last time: living someplace where he doesn't even remember who he is?"

"Possibly."

Then her voice goes high-pitched. "Or that somebody . . ." She convulses into tears. Portia moves to comfort her with an arm loosely placed around her neck.

Waiting for Elizabeth to collect herself, Jenkins vaguely wonders what kind of father he would've been. Probably because he has seen so much, too many families devastated by gratuitous violence and death, he would be neurotically overprotective. Then Jenkins wonders: *Would it be easier for this young woman if she knew Luc were dead?* He'd already ended the relationship; she'd become his inadvertent casualty and by now she knew things would never resume. So if he were to die or be killed, then she could assume his barely articulated troubles somehow led him to someplace where he otherwise shouldn't have been. Perhaps from Elizabeth's point of view, if she couldn't have Luc Flanders, neither should anybody else.

Kennedy is waiting for him outside, maintaining a discreet distance from campus security. She nods at the two women as they walk away, watching their backs until she's sure they are out of earshot.

"You talk to Thornhill?" Jenkins asks.

"Yup."

"And?"

Kennedy glances at the building. "She's Charlie Taft's aunt."

"Oh really? And I specifically asked her how she knew Luc Flanders," Jenkins carps.

"But you didn't ask her how she knew Charlie Taft," Kennedy points out.

"True," Jenkins admits.

"When I asked her how she knew Luc and his roommates, she presented her connection to Taft like it was no big revelation."

"Of course. She's not going to lie if she knows you're zeroing in on her." Jenkins reflects for a moment. "And you didn't find her a little strange?"

"Maybe a little."

"My gut is there is something she doesn't want us to know."

"Like what?"

"McKinnon does too much of the talking. We have to get Taft alone and see what we come up with. Maybe one of us should take a trip up to his hometown. Poke around."

"I actually don't mind going up to Newport," Kennedy offers. "I need to discover the Northeast Kingdom anyway."

"I'd do that in the summer, if I were you."

"But I like bleak. I like bleak winter landscapes."

"You really do sound like you're from New Jersey."

She glances at him sharply. "Hey, I'm proud of my humble beginnings."

"I know you are. But it's different up there . . . in the Kingdom," Jenkins remarks. "It's insular and folks aren't so forthcoming."

"I have my ways of getting people to talk," Kennedy assures him.

FEBRUARY 21; SOUTH WOODSTOCK, VERMONT; 10 DEGREES, SNOW SQUALLS

Sam dreams he has driven up to a car service station attached to a junk store that he recognizes from an earlier time in his life. Somehow he knows he's traveled back in time and sees the confirmation of this when he catches a glimpse of himself in the rearview mirror: a much younger, contented, cleanly shaven man is staring back at him. Overjoyed, he jumps out of the car and runs inside the building to find out what year he's gone back to. But the people manning the counter are Hasidic Jews with top hats and peyot, and when Sam asks them, they tell him in severely broken English that they go by Jewish years, 5770, which he cannot translate. Frantic to find out in which Western year he has ended up, Sam thinks to look at an expiration date on some food item, and opens a freezer to find a pound of frozen hamburger meat stamped: "June 17 1999." Fourteen years in the past. He's only thirty-four years old, and immediately he thinks: *Now only eleven years older than Luc makes me more age appropriate.* Until he realizes: wherever he is, Luc Flanders is only ten.

He awakens to a familiar, desperate desire to be a decade younger, to the quixotic belief that a smaller age gap—say, between men of twenty-three and thirty-nine—would make the relationship more attainable, that if he were thirty-nine, the idea of his getting older, transiting middle age, would be still comfortably in the distance. Winter light is glinting off a foot of new snow, which normally would have him in "powder panic," up at dawn and packing his car with gear and heading to Killington to get "freshies," as he and all his ski buddies call them. Soft skeins of it fathom the rolling land in drifts and swales. But waking is also remembering that Luc is missing. Gone. Disappeared. He sees the monolithic obstruction of his severely broken leg, the mound of fiberglass pushing up belligerently through the bed sheets. Sam glances out his bedroom window at the new quilting of snow. He is hit with an intense flash of misery. He can't quite bring himself to believe that Luc might be dead and yet recognizes there is a part of him that is beginning to wrap itself around the staggering idea of it.

He hears a thump and then clicking of toenails against the soft pine floors downstairs. He listens to Panda ascending the stairs with a bit of hesitation. Sam grimaces. "She's getting old. Soon I'll have to put a runner on those stairs to make it easier for her to get up and down." *Don't leave me yet, dog of mine*, he thinks. One departure at a time.

Stocky, longish-haired Panda trots into the room, looks hard and penetratingly at him. "There she is," he coaxes his dog, and suddenly feels guilty about a certain lack of affection that he showed Panda after he dropped into a chasm of depression over Luc pulling away. Panda is presently gazing out a large low window at the dark shape of an animal that looks like a porcupine moving steadily along the perimeter of the land where the white blanket ends at a mass of snow-laden trees. She whimpers and barks wildly for ten seconds and then goes quiet and still.

Sometimes after Luc would leave to go back to Carleton, Sam would say to her, "Where's Luc, Panda? Where is he?" And she'd start to whine. Didn't go and look for him because she knew he was gone, but just cried. He could say, "Where's Mom, Panda, where's Mike, where's anybody else," and she wouldn't peep. But Luc's name? She'd weep.

It was a late November afternoon, cold and gray and the

wind whistling through the barren trees. Luc was glancing over Sam's shoulder at the markups on the paper he wrote for his Greek and Roman history course. "Wow, you're all over it."

"I taught expository writing," Sam reminded him and then looked at Luc askance. "Did you get any help writing your essays when you applied to Carleton?"

Luc's face crimsoned. "No! Why?"

"I'm sorry," Sam said and returned to his markings on the paper. "You just make some . . . mistakes here."

"You mean elementary mistakes?"

Sam stroked Luc's arm. "Don't worry. I'll help you."

"I'm not a natural writer. I'm more of a visual person."

Sam could tell that Luc was still simmering over his question about getting help writing his college essays. "What's wrong?" he asked gently. Luc didn't respond at first. "Did I hit a sensitive nerve?"

"Kind of," Luc said and avoided meeting Sam's gaze.

"Do you want me to give you some basic pointers about style?"

"Sure."

"Keep it simple. If possible, try not to use words like 'currently,' 'additionally,' or phrases like 'very unique.' The word 'unique' doesn't need a modifier."

Luc brightened a little. "That makes sense."

"And then there's the 'gerund.' The gerund can be used in a powerful way. You don't always use it . . . effectively. "

Luc studied his sentences. "Okay, I see what you're saying."

Sam waited a few moments and then asked, "Didn't your parents give you any help at all?"

Luc looks up at him, disconcerted. "The few times my father helped me with my papers, he was kind of dismissive of my writing ability."

"Really?"

"Really! And honestly, because he's an academic, it bugged me."

"But he teaches fine art," Sam clarified. "Not writing."

"He's still very well educated. And much as I hate to say it, he writes beautifully."

"That's the first complimentary thing you've said about him. Whenever you talk about your father, you tend to dismiss him."

"That's because he always has been too critical of all of us. He's also having a shit time getting older."

"So am I, for that matter, having a shit time getting older," Sam said with a sad smile.

"But I think he envies the fact that I'm young." Luc looked at Sam quizzically. "You don't, do you? Envy me my youth?"

Sam shook his head. "Not the last time I checked with myself." And they both laughed. "Although, naturally, I've just wished we were closer in age."

Luc now pointed to the marked-up essay that lay between them on the desk. "My father had the ability to help me but never bothered. My father discouraged me from pursuing the things I was good at like painting and drawing. My entire life he has said how hard it is to make it as an artist and how he's afraid of what failure would do to me. Because of what failure did to him."

Sam said, "I mean, you can understand that, his fear of you failing? Then again, if you really wanted to be an artist, your father would be unable to discourage you."

"I suppose that's true."

"You told me your parents never held a gun to your head when you were choosing your college courses."

"Obviously, your parents never discouraged you," Luc muttered.

"That's probably because being an architect is . . . respectable, not to mention quantifiable."

"Exactly!"

"Hey, it's not too late. You could go to college for another year and study art and other electives if you wanted."

"You always go back to that. And it's just not going to happen," Luc said gently but emphatically.

Sam is stirred from his reverie by the ringing telephone. He picks up to hear the voice of Heather Finlayson, the dog-sitter.

"Sorry I couldn't talk to you much when you cane to pick up Panda," she tells him. "I've been wondering—I just want to know—how you're doing?" she says.

"I wish I knew how I was doing," he replies.

FEBRUARY 21; READING, VERMONT; 13 DEGREES, HEAVY SNOW

Jenkins stands on the front porch of Heather Finlayson's house in six inches of new snow. It is late afternoon and his knock has driven the league of dogs inside into apoplectic barking. "Shut up!" he hears someone shouting. "Everybody in your crate! Pronto!" And when she answers the door a few minutes later, the barking has miraculously died down. He enters a living room with bare old pine floors covered by a traditional, mauve-colored cable knit rug. Dog crates are positioned all around the room and, looking from one crate to the other, Jenkins feels watched by many pairs of eager, curious eyes. "How much time do they spend in confinement?" he asks after they greet each other.

"Only at mealtimes and at night and when people come over to leave or pick up a dog," Heather says. "I don't have a lot of company. Or, I suppose I should say, human company."

She is a large-boned woman of around sixty with short dark hair that has a pink streak running down the middle of her head. Her movements are quick and spry, and she looks at Jenkins with wry discernment. "Have a seat," she says. Jenkins complies.

"I thought it would be better to see you in person this time rather than speak to you on the phone."

"That's fine," she says.

One of the dogs begins to yip and Heather snaps: "Give it up, Crosby!" The dog quickly obeys and goes silent.

"You certainly have them under control," Jenkins remarks.

Heather stabs a finger into her own chest. "I'm the alpha in this house." She gazes at him with narrowed eyes. "So what's going on? Why are you here?"

"I'm here because of my conversation with Sam Solomon last night."

"What about it?" Heather asks.

"Well, if you recall, when I was first trying to locate Sam and called you, we discussed the fact that on February eleventh, after Sam Solomon left his dog here, you subsequently telephoned him at home."

"That's correct."

"And he dropped his dog off at?"

"Just before five o'clock. Sam is punctual. If anything, he comes early. If he's even three minutes late, I start worrying."

Jenkins nods. "And you spent some time chatting with him?"

"A little bit, yes."

"How long was he here, would you say?"

"You've asked me this before."

"Then I apologize for the repetition."

"Did you not believe me when you asked me the first time?"

"I want to make sure I am clear about what happened."

She looks at him with skepticism and then says, "He was here, at the most, five minutes."

"Do you happen to remember what you talked about?"

Heather considers this for a moment and then says, "I told him I thought it was good he was getting away. I told him I'd been worrying about him ever since he broke up with that kid."

"Anything else?"

Heather looks up at the ceiling and then shrugs. "I don't know. I probably told him I inherited three hundred thousand dollars from my mother and because of that I was going to cut back on dog care. But that I would always have room for Panda. She's easy as pie. She's a real love."

"And then you called him at home?"

"Yeah."

"Why did you call him at home?"

"Because I didn't think he'd left enough dog food."

"And what time did you call him?"

"Like I told Sam when I called him yesterday, six twenty-eight on my clock," Heather says.

Jenkins hesitates, carefully framing his next question, and then decides to be blunt. "When we spoke originally, you told me you called him at five fifteen."

"No, Sam told you I called him at five fifteen."

"He did tell me that."

"Well, then you've gotten us confused. When you called me, I told you I called him. My memory is you didn't ask me what time I called him."

Jenkins believes this is untrue, but says, "Then that's a mistake on my part. Not asking you what time. And if so, I apologize."

"Says Mr. ex-FBI."

And he carefully watches Heather Finlayson's face for a wrinkle of tension. Because, as Kennedy points out, Heather could now be trying to help Sam out by insisting she hadn't been asked what time she'd called Sam and now claiming she'd called him at 6:28 p.m. on the evening of February eleventh. If this were true, he could not have driven to Carleton, met up with Luc and then driven down to Boston and arrived at Logan Park and Ride by 10:03 in the evening. But this will be easily verified by checking the phone records.

"So you called him at six twenty-eight?"

"Correct."

"It's a very specific time. Not six twenty, or six forty, but six twenty-eight."

"I called him right before the six thirty news went on. And it's a good thing I did because look what happened, he got injured and was away a lot longer than he planned. So I did need to get her more dog food. By the way, I didn't charge him for the extra days Panda was with me."

"That was generous of you." Jenkins hesitates and then says, "I don't suppose you remember the kind of dog food Panda eats?"

Heather glares at him. "Mister, are you testing my memory?"

"Not really. Just curious if you recall."

They hear the tinny-sounding yapping of a dog coming from the far-off kitchen. "Hey, Serena, give it up!" Heather cries. Then to Jenkins she explains, "That's my dachshund bitch. If you really want to know, she's the real alpha queen around here. Even I kowtow to her."

Jenkins resumes. "So why did you call Sam yesterday?"

Heather Finlayson explains that she didn't have a chance to talk to Sam when he picked up Panda. "I just wanted to know how Sam's doing. With all that's been going on."

"I see. So that was your first contact with him since he picked up his dog?"

"That's right." There is an awkward lull and then she asks, "Do you think he has anything to do with this kid's disappearance?"

"It doesn't matter what I think. I'd like to know what you think," Jenkins tells her.

"Me? What I think?" Heather Finlayson intones. "How would I know? The only thing I know is he's completely obsessed."

"Completely obsessed?" Jenkins repeats.

"With that kid."

"Okay. And so if he's obsessed—"

"Now let me ask you a question," Heather interrupts. "If my calling Sam means that he couldn't have driven up to Carleton . . ."

"Did I say that?"

"No, I'm saying it. But couldn't they have met somewhere?"

"Luc's car never left the street outside his apartment."

"What about Luc hitchhiking?"

"In the middle of winter? Why would he do that? If he has a car."

Heather shrugs. "He's hitchhiked down here before. Sam told me he did."

FEBRUARY 22; CARLETON, MONTPELIER, WOODSTOCK, VERMONT; 21 DEGREES, GRAY SKIES

Kennedy is driving an unmarked official car, and they are halfway up College Hill. It is one of those dark, saturnine winter days when the sky remains dreary and the air promises snow that is never delivered. They are heading to a symposium on cyber attacks that is being sponsored by the computer science department at the University of Vermont. Glancing in the side view mirror, Jenkins gains a glimpse of the harbor front of Lake Champlain, a place that becomes so much more alive and vibrant when the weather is warmer. Now, the watery plain that separates Vermont from New York State unfolds toward the horizon; it's a sullen, monotonous pewter.

Kennedy is saying, "Anyway, despite what Sam claims, we have to consider that Luc may have hitchhiked down to South Woodstock on February eleventh."

"Goes without saying," Jenkins replies.

The previous evening, subsequent to his conversation with Heather Finlayson, Jenkins asked Sam about Luc hitchhiking down to South Woodstock. Sam explained that Luc had stopped hitchhiking down to see him in October when it got colder.

"And you believe Sam's explanation that Luc hitchhiked because he didn't want his roommates to know where he was driving?"

"He was paranoid that they'd find out."

"Why would it matter so much if and what they knew?"

Jenkins looks over at her. "How many college jocks do you know who are struggling with their sexuality?"

"I don't know many college athletes, period."

"Right. So here we have a twenty-two-year-old athlete who breaks off a heavy affair with an older man and starts dating a woman his own age. For me, that says a lot."

There is an edgy silence and then Kennedy says, "Okay, I hear you. But I am still not going to close myself off to the idea that, at the very least, Sam and Luc may have met up somehow."

"Okay, met up somehow. And then?"

"Something could have happened between them that really set Luc Flanders off. Set him off on a . . . tangent where he could have ended up somewhere else and maybe have been harmed. And Sam is sitting on it, the fact that they met."

Jenkins ponders this as Kennedy makes the turn into a long driveway that proceeds behind several of the university's tall, nineteenth-century brick Victorian buildings. At last, he says, "Okay, I'll press that with him," as she pulls into a faculty parking area behind the new science hall. "And who says we can leave the car here?"

"I do." She reaches over him, opens the glove compartment and extracts a University of Vermont campus security pass.

"Where did you get that?"

"I have my ways," Kennedy says with a smirk.

During the seminar, Jenkins feels his phone vibrate and sees a text from Barbara Kessler, the state police lieutenant down in Bethel. *Call me ASAP.*

Gently elbowing Kennedy, Jenkins shows her the text. Kennedy whispers, "Wonder why she didn't message me." Bending down to avoid attracting attention, he makes his way out of the lecture hall, strolls quickly through a throng of students waiting in front of another seminar room, and hurries down the hallway where there is suitable quiet. "Kessler!" She picks up after the first ring.

"Hey, it's Jenkins," he says.

"Hello, Nick."

"Kennedy's pissed that you didn't text her."

"I couldn't find her number. Apologize for me."

"So what do you have?"

"What do I have? I have Sam Solomon in custody."

Jenkins laughs despite himself. "Come on."

"Get this story. Early this morning, a woman named Heather Finlayson, who told me you went to see her last night, was driving one of her dog sittees back to its bed-ridden owner when a pickup truck went into her at a higher speed and ran her off the road. She was pretty reluctant to ID the offending car. But it was Sam Solomon's."

"Did she see him?"

"She believes so but isn't sure."

"It makes no sense." Jenkins goes on to say that an article in that day's *Valley News* reported Heather's testimony to Jenkins had made Solomon's presence in Carleton on the night of February twelfth all but impossible.

"Yeah, I know. I saw it," Kessler says.

"So where did you arrest him?"

"At home. Swears up and down he's been there all day and that somebody must've stolen his car."

"Without him knowing it?"

"That's what he says."

Jenkins goes quiet, trying to piece it all together. "So where are we?"

"How about I hold him until you get here?"

"Okay. We'll head down there now."

Kennedy is driving again, and they are on the interstate just passing Montpelier, Vermont's capital city. The weather seems—at least momentarily—much improved. The sun, at intervals, is breaking through the heavy clouds to strike the gold capitol dome, which responds with a Byzantine glint.

"Ever spend time here?" Jenkins asks.

"Can't say I have," Kennedy answers. "Apparently, Mont-pelier's got more liberals per capita than Burlington."

Knowing Kennedy's politics skew toward the conservative, Jenkins glances over at her. "Got a problem with that?"

"Obviously not. I mean, I do live in Vermont—voluntarily."

There is an uncomfortable pause. At last, Kennedy glances over at Jenkins. "Admit it, this little development is . . . Why would somebody take the risk of going to Sam's house to steal his car? Especially when he has a dog that could bark and alert him. And why didn't Sam hear his own car driving off?"

Jenkins says, "It's winter? It's windy? Maybe the dog recognized the person who came up and took the car?"

"In that case, Luc Flanders would be the most likely person."

"If only."

"Well, we'll see if he's telling the truth."

"And if he is?" Jenkins asks. "If somebody actually did steal his car?"

"Then they must not be too happy that he now has an alibi," Kennedy says.

They finally arrive at the state barracks in Bethel. Sam has been sitting with Barbara Kessler, a svelte, exceptionally pretty state police lieutenant whose appearance completely belies her capabilities. From Kennedy, Jenkins knows that Kessler has a black belt in karate and is the one who teaches the state police trainees how to subdue rowdy and recalcitrant male citizens who fall under the stupid delusion that they can intimidate law enforcement, or motorists who fume and sputter at the three hundred dollar-plus speeding tickets that the state of Vermont loves to hand out. Sam's crutches are nowhere to be seen.

"You didn't really take his sticks away from him, did you?" Kennedy says to Kessler.

The lieutenant grins broadly. "Of course not. They're behind the door. They were taking up space, so I parked them. Sorry I didn't text you, Helen."

"I'm over it. But can you please program me into your phone?" She nudges Jenkins. "I'm not his gopher."

Jenkins turns to Sam. "So what's new?"

Looking distraught, Sam says, "I have no clue. You tell me."

Glancing at Kessler, Jenkins says, "Hey, come around the corner with me for a second?" He glances at Kennedy as if to ask permission.

"It's okay. I'll get to know Sam a little bit. Go on."

The lieutenant gets up from her chair, carefully straightens her pant legs and follows him. Once they are out of earshot, Jenkins says, "So what did Heather Finlayson say exactly?"

"She was very reluctant, but she said she saw him."

"She saw Solomon behind the wheel of his own car?"

"Saw the back of his head when he drove away."

"So that's not quite a positive ID. Would you agree?"

Kessler shrugs. "I guess I'd have to agree. I decided to bring him in because we were able to match the blue paint on her car to his truck."

"I think it's a good call. I would have brought him in."

"But by the way, Heather Finlayson ranted a little bit about how you originally neglected to ask her what time she called Solomon."

"That's her claim. But not my distinct recollection." Jenkins sighs. "And quite honestly, I worry how reliable a witness she actually is."

"Well, in this case, she is because of the paint match. So if anybody is lying, it's Sam Solomon."

When Jenkins and Kessler return to the examining room,

he looks over at Kennedy, who says to Sam, "So now give us your version."

Sam's face is a mask of distress. "Not much to say except I was not driving my car."

"Any idea who might have been driving it?" Jenkins asks.

"I've been racking my brain. I mean, what would be my motivation for running Heather Finlayson off the road? She just gave you concrete proof that before I went to Boston, I couldn't get to Carleton on February eleventh. So I should be thanking her, not antagonizing her."

Kennedy says, "But leaving that aside, you did neglect to tell us that Luc sometimes hitchhiked down to see you."

Sam faces her squarely. "Doesn't matter if he hitchhiked. As I've said all along, I have not seen him since the end of December. And I did not rear-end Heather Finlayson this morning."

Kennedy continues, "Then let's get down to logistics. The person who stole your car had to get hold of your keys—"

"I leave them in the car. As do most people in Vermont."

Kennedy turns to Jenkins. "I told him I was from New Jersey. Now he's patronizing me." And then to Sam, "But you have a dog who presumably barks."

"Yes. All the time whenever somebody comes to the house."

"And yet she didn't this time," Lieutenant Kessler says.

"I honestly don't know why she didn't this time."

Kennedy says, "Would she bark if she recognized the person?"

Sam considers this. "Sometimes yes, sometimes no. She never barked when Luc arrived, for example."

There is knock on the door and a stout, non-uniformed woman opens it. "Lieutenant, just a moment."

"Can it wait?" Kessler asks.

The woman shakes her head. "No, it can't."

Turning to them, the lieutenant says, "My apologies for the intrusion. Just keep going. I'll be right back."

Kennedy continues, "I want you to consider our point of view, despite your assertions. On one hand, Heather Finlayson clears you from being able to get up to Carleton on the night of February eleventh. But on the other hand, she doesn't clear you because she tells us that Luc Flanders often hitchhiked down here to see you. Combine all this with the bizarre circumstance of somebody coming to your house this morning, stealing your car, and then running her off the road. If you had to, how could you explain that?"

"My only explanation is the *Valley News* article. Somebody must have read it this morning and got angry enough to do what they did."

Agreeing with Sam's assessment, Jenkins remarks, "That's plenty angry. The question is: why?"

"I don't know why."

Kennedy goes on, "Luc told you he liked to hitchhike because he didn't want his roommates to know he was driving down here. But how would they even know where he was going?"

Sam turns to Jenkins. "I actually remember a conversation Luc and I had that might help explain this better."

"When was this conversation?" Jenkins asks.

"Early last December, a few weeks before Luc broke it off."

They had their coats on and were headed for the snowmobile trails that wind through the fields across the road from Sam's house. The temperature was down around ten, there was a stiff, punishing wind, and they were winding scarves around their faces when Luc, who was jamming his phone in his pocket, received a text. From Taft, who wanted to know where he was. And Luc complained that Taft was always keeping track of him. And Sam joked with him and said, "I thought your roommates were straight."

Luc turned toward him with his disarmingly pale eyes and said, "I don't know if it has anything to do with that. Anyway, when you and I first met, you thought I was straight."

Bewildered by this remark, Sam replied, "I never thought you were straight. How could I think that?"

"No, I mean . . . all the women I've been with and . . . will be with." Luc said the last bit without real conviction.

Discouraged by Luc's persistent self-delusion, Sam led the way outside into a terrific wintry wind. That first week of December the mantle of snow had already arrived. Mid-afternoon winter skies were often striated with a plumage of pink and purple bands, noticeably different from the more orange and red eventide of summer. They crossed the street and picked up one of the Vermont Association of Snowmobile Trails that snaked across the fields and meadows of South Woodstock. Because the thoroughfare went narrow for a hundred yards, they were forced to walk single file. Luc was wearing his goofy, thigh-length coat, which looked vaguely like some military knockoff. He was whistling. But then he pivoted around and faced Sam with a baffled look on his face, his longish hair sticking out of the sides of his khaki-colored woolen cap. "Taft treats women pretty shabbily. He mainly has had physical relationships with them, and he always seems to end them without warning."

"He sounds like a player," Sam said.

"Maybe he is a player," Luc replied.

"Why didn't you mention this when I first questioned you?" Jenkins asks.

"Because, for me, that conversation was about Luc telling me he still might want to be with a woman. Not about Taft. Taft was incidental. I only just remembered that part of it."

"Okay. I get that," Kennedy says and turns to Jenkins. "I'm done here. How about you? Any more questions?"

"Not at the moment."

Kennedy opens the door, walks down a corridor and finds Lieutenant Kessler standing next to a water cooler, reading a printout. She looks up. "I need you folks out here. Can you grab Nick?"

Once the three of them are in an adjacent office, Kessler shuts the door. "We just got this." She pauses. "One of my guys just spoke to the young woman who comes by every day to help Solomon. She arrived at his house, saw his car wasn't there and kept going. Presumably, when his car was out ramming into Heather Finlayson. But she happened to notice a Jeep Wrangler . . ."

"Camo?" says Kennedy.

"Yup."

Both Jenkins and Kennedy stare blankly at Lieutenant Kessler.

"How much bail did those knuckleheads pay?" she asks.

"Around fifty k," Kennedy says.

"You'd think they'd lie low," Kessler says. "And not kick up any more dust."

"You'd think," Kennedy agrees. Then to Jenkins, "Well, we're in the neighborhood. Why don't we go tackle the boys about their Jeep?"

Cradling the phone to his ear while he swipes crumbs of toast into the kitchen sink, Sam tells Mike about his car being stolen and Heather Finlayson being run off the road.

Mike goes suspiciously silent. After a lengthy interval, he says, "So I guess really the question I have for you, Sam, is: was Heather lying? On your behalf? Did she actually call when she said she did?"

"Like I told you, I remember her calling me earlier. But a lot has happened since then. So my memory could be skewed."

"So you defer judgment to her," Mike says.

"Wouldn't you if you were me?"

"So how did it get into the paper so quickly?"

Sam had known that the interview he did with Pete Skalski was about to run. "I called Pete to say Heather cleared me. And he verified it with her before the paper went to press."

At this very moment, Panda rounds the corner and clicks into the kitchen, and without hesitation, comes over and puts her head in Sam's lap. Nervously stroking her head, he says, "It sounds like you've had doubts about my story all along."

Mike hesitates. "I didn't at first. Then Detective Jenkins asked me if I thought you were deliberately reckless when you skied down Black Diamond. I started to rethink what happened. I told him that, from my vantage point, you looked fine when you were heading down that first headwall. That your turns were consistent, that you chose a great line, but then suddenly you were somersaulting down. You must know, Sam, you're alive only because you're unbelievably lucky.

Look what happened to Billy Poole. He tried to recover while he was falling and he didn't make it."

"But Billy Poole went down a different chute, didn't he? Wasn't his descent more extreme?"

"Not really—it was pretty much the same degree of vert. And I'll be totally honest with you now, Sam. From where I was below, it almost seemed like you were being deliberately reckless."

"We both skied the same chute!" Sam cries.

There is a brief, perturbing silence. "Not exactly," Mike says at last. "You made a turn and went off a cornice that we said we'd avoid."

"I honestly don't remember doing that."

"Well, I do. And you took it. You got air. Too much air."

Sam is stunned into silence. His only recollection of the Fall is being down, skis broken, his limbs radiating the agony of the injury. The most pain he'd ever felt in his life, so much that he actually forgot his constant grieving ache over losing Luc Flanders—that sorrow passed from his body like his soul leaving him. There were a few moments before a certain numbness gave way to the deeper agony, when he was glad to feel a vacant peace inside him where the hurt and rejection had been constantly churning; it was a fragile yet precious relief. A mini death of the love that had only resurrected itself later when he was in the hospital.

Mike comments, "I told Jenkins that before the accident, Gina and I were really worrying about you." He pauses. "Worrying that you'd lost your will to live."

"Well, I didn't!" Sam insists, and then more quietly, "I fought my way back."

"After you got injured."

But now, Sam's confusion hardens into raw anger. "But I still don't understand why my accident in Utah would have anything to do with Luc going missing."

Mike tells him, "Well, if you saw Luc Flanders the night you left and something bad happened between the two of you, maybe that would cause you to be really reckless out there."

"Like what could have happened between us?" Sam cries. "Like I did something to him?"

"I have no idea. I don't know," Mike says.

FEBRUARY 22; RANDOLPH, VERMONT; 29 DEGREES, WIND GUSTS UP TO 25 MILES PER HOUR, OVERCAST

Their less viable option would have been confronting Mark and Howard Newcombe at their downtown Bethel home, which is cheek by jowl with a row of other homes. From having arrested them once before, however, Barb Kessler knows the twins spend around four hours every day at the gym at Vermont Technical College.

Once they pull into the parking lot, Kennedy spots the camouflage vehicle immediately. "Is that their rig?" she asks Jenkins.

"Looks like it. Have to check the license plate. Last time I saw that baby, it was clean, spanking shiny in Portsmouth. Doesn't even look like the same car."

Kennedy looks out the window toward the entrance of V-tech's gymnasium and two ledges of plowed snow on either side of a walkway that leads to a drab, one-story building hewn of institutional red brick. "Lemme go inside to make sure they're here. They don't know me."

She is absent longer than Jenkins would expect.

At last, Kennedy exits the building and is soon back in the car, her cheeks red from the spiteful cold and a delighted look on her face.

"You know, you really should cover your head," Jenkins says, affectionately rubbing his knuckles against her brush-cut scalp.

"Didn't realize it was so frigging freezing out there."

"Anyway, what took you?"

She turns to him with delight. "Pure and utter fascination is what took me," she says, shivering and chafing her hands against the blasting car heater.

"How so?"

"These guys are total, bat-shit freaks. You should see how they work out. They're all over the place, grunting and throwing weights like two orangutans. There is no rhyme or reason to what they do."

"Well, they look pretty jacked so they must be doing something right."

Kennedy dismisses this. "Hello . . . it's all drugs, steroids, HGH. Like the pro athletes did before they all started getting caught." She goes on to say that one of the twins right now is on the elliptical machine, going at a frantic pace. "The guy has this glaze on his face. Like he's getting himself off."

At last, the two men emerge dressed head to toe in matching tan Carhartt coats and trousers, and black woolen fisherman's caps, looking like tradesmen—which Jenkins and Kennedy know they are anything but. "Talk about workman drag," she remarks.

"They claim not to be gay," Jenkins says.

"You don't have to be gay to be in drag," Kennedy says. "If a farmer went around town wearing an Armani business suit, that would be considered 'urban drag.'"

"Is that what it says in the urban dictionary?"

"In my urban dictionary, that's what it says."

They watch the twins crossing the parking lot. At one point, both men stop to have a short conversation.

Jenkins turns to Kennedy. "Okay, so surprise them."

Exiting the car once again, Kennedy begins strolling toward the twins, who are just about to climb into their Jeep. Sensing her progress toward them, they stop and look at her warily.

"How's it going, boys?" she says to them both. "Good workout today?"

"Who the hell are you?" says the twin about to climb in the passenger side. His eyes, glittering beneath the band of his fisherman's cap, are a penetrating, walleyed blue.

"I'm about to tell you, Marko," she says. "If you'll come back inside where it's a little warmer."

"How do you know who we are?" asks Howard, standing at the driver's side.

"How do I know who you are? You're the famous New-combe twins of Bethel, Vermont. Everybody knows who you are." Kennedy swipes her glove along the army fatigue flank of the Jeep and looks at the dirt on it. "Wow, you let this get dirty."

"Come on! Who are you?"

"Detective Kennedy from Carleton. I work with Detective Jenkins, who is right over there in that car and whom you've already met."

"So you're a cop?" Howard asks.

Kennedy reaches inside her coat, grabs her badge and flashes it.

"Okay, so then why are you here?"

"Detective Jenkins and I drove down here to remind you that one of the conditions of your bail is that you cooperate with us." Kennedy glances back toward where Jenkins is waiting and flicks her head upward. Both twins look furtively in that direction.

Jenkins leaves the car and heads over to them. Both twins go motionless and stare. "Fuck!" Mark Newcombe says.

"Shut up!" says his brother.

"We'll explain it all to you," Kennedy assures them. "Let's go on into the gym." And without waiting for Jenkins to catch up, the twins dutifully pivot and head back into the building.

They all pass a room in which two scruffy-faced students are playing a fast game of Ping-Pong. Noticing the twins, one of the students says, "I thought you guys split."

"So did we," the twins say in unison.

For a moment the students stare after them, and then put their paddles on the table and start following.

"Go back and finish your game, boys," Kennedy orders them with an admonishing wave of her arm.

Sensing the gravitas of the situation, the students advance no farther.

In a room sparsely occupied with students drinking coffee and eating bags of chips and candy bars dispensed by a snack station at one end, there are a few empty and flimsy sofas made of cheap foam. Jenkins invites everyone to grab a seat, and, removing their overcoats but not their fisherman's hats, the twins perch next to each other facing the tall floor-to-ceiling windows which look out onto forests and rolling hills that graduate to snow-capped mountains.

"So what do you need?" Mark asks impatiently.

Jenkins replies, "We've been wondering about those books of poetry that were found in your black duffle bag."

"We loooove poetry," Kennedy adds. "We're both Robert Frostniks."

"Is this some kind of joke?" asks Howard.

"Why would it be a joke?" Kennedy says. "We found it very interesting, the contents in your black duffle bag. A combo of highbrow poetry, workout shorts, skimpy underwear, tank tops, and let's not forget those hypodermic needles." She pauses and then says, "Were those rare poetry first editions going up for sale, too? Were you offering a two for one poetry/steroid special?"

Howard says, "Like we told him, they belonged to our dad."

"But they have Frost's signature in them," Kennedy points out.

"Frost stole them," Mark says.

"So Robert Frost put his signature in books that weren't his?" Jenkins says.

"Right," Howard says.

"Why would he do something like that?"

"Why? Because he was a tool!" Mark Newcombe says.

"Anyway, can you just tell us what you want?" says Howard.

"It's very simple," Kennedy begins. "A camo Jeep Wrangler matching yours was seen early this morning down in South Woodstock."

"At nine o'clock a.m.," Jenkins clarifies.

"That's early for us," Mark says. His gaze is unsettling, menacing. "We're late sleepers. So it's somebody else's Jeep."

"Can you prove it? That you were at home?" Kennedy asks.

"Do we have to?"

"Would make things a lot easier," Jenkins says.

"And how would that be?" asks Howard.

Kennedy and Jenkins glance keenly at each other. She turns back to them. "How far a drive is it to South Woodstock from Bethel?"

"Thirty minutes maybe, why?"

"That's probably about right," Kennedy agrees with their assessment.

"We told you. We didn't drive to Woodstock!" Mark suddenly rages, and Jenkins wonders if this is an example of what is commonly known as 'roid rage.

She takes advantage of the opportunity. "When my partner was questioning the two of you up in Carleton, you happened to mention that you know the student who's missing."

"No, we don't know him. We know of him," says Howard Newcombe.

Raising his hand to catch Kennedy's attention, Jenkins waits until she acknowledges him with a nod. Then he turns to the twins. "The night after the vandalism occurred, the night this Carleton College student disappeared, somebody claims to have spotted a Jeep Wrangler that matches the description of yours in the general area of where he vanished."

This statement transparently unnerves both men. "Really? So what?" Howard says.

Mark says, "Check the DMV. You'll probably find lots of camo Jeep Wranglers driving around the state of Vermont."

"Lieutenant Kessler gave us the count."

"Oh, Lieutenant Kessler, I'm quaking in my boots," Mark says.

"You should be. She probably could kick your ass," Kennedy tells him quietly.

"How many are there?" Howard challenges her. "Camo Jeeps."

"Let us ask the questions, okay?" Jenkins says. "What time did you leave your house this morning?"

"At eleven thirty. And there are plenty of students who saw us here and can vouch for us being here," Howard says.

Jenkins suddenly stands up. "No need. Okay, you guys can get a move on now."

The twins look alarmed at the abrupt way Jenkins has ended the discussion. "So that's it?" Mark says.

"You want more questions?" Jenkins asks.

Kennedy says, "Don't worry—we'll be in touch very soon."

After they watch the two men file out of the gymnasium, Kennedy turns to Jenkins. "That was brilliant about seeing the Jeep near Skylight Pond."

"You think it worked?"

"Perfectly," Kennedy says.

Eleanor is reading about snowy white orchards and early blossoms felled and scattered by a freak spring freeze; birch trees as objects of ornamental beauty; black alders dying out at the edge of a forest from lack of light. It seems that Frost believes in God, but Eleanor has never been sure. *For this is love and nothing else is love, That which it is reserved for God above.* The poet's mother was a devout Christian, but it's hard to tell, beyond the physical spirituality of his intimacy with the outside word, if Frost was actually a believer.

She marks the volume with a dried sprig of calendula, stands up, walks over to the stove and turns the flame down on a boiling pot of sycamore bark, the water now stained a deep vermillion. She will use the solution for itchy rashes: for eczema, for poison ivy. In the sink there is a crystal high-ball glass, the sign that Giles has slipped back into steady drinking. These days he rarely emerges from his side of the house, except to fulfill his teaching obligations at Dartmouth. Leaving his study, he will make an effort to walk upright and correctly, and Eleanor figures he has the presence of mind to at least remain sober while tending to his art classes. Then again, in view of what has happened to them, the dean's warning about the attrition of enrollment is probably all but forgotten.

I dwell in a lonely house I know
That vanished many a summer ago
And left no trace but the cellar walls
And a cellar in which the daylight falls.

This, her state of being—her life a vanishing point beyond

the day-to-day grinding movements of survival. She has dropped ten pounds from barely eating. She can no longer look at herself in the mirror; her face sags, drawn from lack of sleep, from acute uncertainty. Friends have told her about salutary books written by brave mothers whose children vanished or died, but she can't bring herself to read them. Her life feels as desolate as a wartime city bombed from the height of its grandeur into a crater of specters and ashes. All alone in the house where her inebriate husbands sleeps narcotically in another wing, she wonders how she'll get through yet another day. Luckily, today will be different. Eleanor glances at her watch. Janine will be disembarking from a bus in Hanover in just under an hour, her arrival only a faint promise of some sort of mainstay.

Her daughter has insisted upon taking a two-week emergency leave from her job, and her arrival from New York City coincides with today's article in the *Valley News*—SOLOMON PROVES WHEREABOUTS IN CARLETON STUDENT'S DISAPPEARANCE—with a photograph of Sam in his study looking bewildered, his faithful black-and-white dog at his feet. Sam is a handsome, rugged-looking man, more or less the same age as Giles but far fitter and younger-looking. At least the newspaper has been sensitive enough not to publish any more pictures of her son. Eleanor had known the article was coming; they'd received a phone call from a fact-checker.

The interview, reiterating everything Jenkins already has told them, is filler around a spanking new fact: that on February eleventh, Sam Solomon received a phone call from his dog-sitter at 6:28 p.m. This left him without enough time to drive northward to Carleton from his home in South Woodstock and then head down to the Boston airport, where he arrived at ten o'clock that evening. Eleanor can't believe that Sam played absolutely no crucial part in her son's disappearance.

The bus stop is next to the Hanover Inn, and Eleanor

and Giles meet Janine at the drop-off point. Their daughter descends the steps of the Dartmouth Coach with a bit of a head-tossing feminine swagger, totting a small rollaway suitcase and wearing a sleek urban-looking backpack. Eleanor, with a shock, can see her own drawn features re-etched in the taut, lineless face of her tall, rangy, athletic-looking child, who approaches them with tears freezing on her reddened cheeks as she wipes them away with the back of her mittened hand. They all embrace for a moment, and out of the corner of her eye, Eleanor can spy bystanders looking on.

The fifteen-minute drive home along the Connecticut River is ruminatively quiet. Each of them is reflecting that the space in the backseat next to Janine is where Luc should be — as he was for all the road trips they took up to Prince Edward Island and out to Jasper National Park. Their family, reduced to three, has been crippled into a lopsided formation. Most of the river is snowed in, encrypted in a grayish craze, but there are welters of dark wet spots where the currents prevent ice crystals from forming—a reminder of the unstable state of the ice on Skylight Pond before the unexplained events that pulled Luc away from everyone. At one point, Eleanor turns around to find Janine staring out the window, perhaps making similar connections.

"I have the *Valley News* article for you," Eleanor says.

"I saw it." Janine is still gazing out the window. "I was sent a link and read it on the bus." She hesitates. "Pete Skalski called me in New York to ask me for clarifications."

"Why didn't you mention it?" Giles asks sharply.

"I made the decision not to, Dad, okay? And I think I was right. It was difficult enough to know that the piece was appearing. And I have to say I'm actually glad it was by him."

Eleanor turns around in her seat to meet her daughter's calculating gaze. "So you don't think a college friend of Sam's would be biased?"

"Sympathetic, yes. Biased, no. I mean, Sam is going through a lot, too. I think he needs a bit of a break."

Eleanor turns back around and looks ahead into the monochromatic winter landscape. "I wanted to write to him. But I didn't."

"Mom," Janine says, "you know I believe Sam is innocent. That if Luc has come to any harm, Sam has nothing to do with it. It's got to be somebody else and that's the hardest part, because nobody has any idea of who it might be."

Eleanor can see Giles nodding. Their elder child always seems to have the final word on things. And she concedes— momentarily—that usually, when Janine is certain, Janine is rarely wrong.

FEBRUARY 23; BURLINGTON, VERMONT; 9 DEGREES, SLEET

A somewhat assiduous chef, Jenkins has concocted a Cassoulet confection of white beans, Vermont pork sausage, and duck confit and has left it smoldering in a ceramic Crock-Pot. "Would never peg a cop for a gourmet cook," Connie had ribbed him when they first met. But soon discovered—by her own admission—that he was generally more cultured than she was. Knew two other languages, for example.

They sit silently at the dining table, a bottle of Chianti in its festive straw basket marking the distance between them.

At last, she says, "It's been a while since I've seen a case preoccupy you to such a degree."

Somewhat surprised at her observation, Jenkins sits there considering all the disparate pieces that don't make sense, not just Luc Flanders's disappearance, but the bizarre car theft that seemed orchestrated to frame Sam Solomon, the Carleton College security guard concealing her connection to one of Luc's roommates, the possible involvement of the bodybuilder twins in Luc's disappearance as well as in the vandalism. "I feel like I'm falling down on this one," he says at last

Rolling her nearly empty wineglass between her fingers, Connie says with a frown, "You've said that before. You don't seem to realize that being in a state of . . .well, near despair is the way you work, the way you grope toward a solution. But you don't usually let work creep this far into your life." Wondering if he welcomes the distraction of work now more than ever, Jenkins grabs the wine bottle and pours the rest of it into

176 • • • JOSEPH OLSHAN

her glass. "No, have some of it," she says, stubbornly pouring half into his glass. "I won't sleep well if I have more."

"Okay." He takes a sip.

"So what is it about this one in particular?"

"I don't know precisely. Kennedy and I don't quite agree. She thinks that the two lovers met up the night Flanders disappeared. And that Solomon might be lying."

"But you believe him?"

"I do."

"Because?"

"My gut. Kennedy thinks I've been easy on him because . . .maybe I see myself in him."

"Do you?"

Jenkins hesitates. He doesn't say what troubles him most of all is that Sam, a reasonable, middle-aged man who loves the outdoors, a man — despite his sexual preference — not altogether different from himself, is mourning the loss of his great love, while he, Jenkins, is married to this woman who sits across from him, looking at him with polite interest and whose love for him, he believes, has changed into something like fond tolerance.

"I could be. But I've been in this game long enough to know my own prejudice." He pauses. "The one I really want to talk to is Luc Flanders. But the only way I could do that is if he weren't missing. And if he weren't missing, then *Je n'existe pas.*"

"Ah, a Pascalian concept," Connie says with a dry, appreciative smile. She reflects for a moment. "So what would you ask this kid if you could talk to him? What would you say?"

"I'd mentioned the letters he wrote to Sam Solomon. Tell him how beautiful they are. I'd encourage him to be honest with the people close to him. And then I would ask how he lost his way." What he doesn't say is that the letters Luc wrote to Sam could be letters that Jenkins once might have written to Connie if he'd had more guts.

Connie taps her fingers against her wineglass. "And you're absolutely sure Sam never got those emails?"

"He claims not to have, even though it says they'd been read and deleted. I just don't believe if he'd seen them, if he'd read them, that he'd be able to deny knowledge of them."

"Which means you don't think he did something in a fit of passionate rage and then regretted it later."

"No, I don't."

"So can you at least give him—Sam—the letters?" she asks.

"I will soon. They're still with our linguist."

"Because?"

"There have been some discrepancies in the speech patterns. We're trying to be certain Luc wrote them."

"Maybe somebody got into them and deleted words?"

"More difficult, but not impossible to trace."

"Maybe one of the cookie-cutter macho roommates?"

"Possibly. Kennedy is up in the Northeast Kingdom doing some digging on one of them."

At this, they hear the ring tone of a text message that could be from either of their cell phones, both of which are in the kitchen.

"That could be her."

"Mine's in there, too. It could be for me," Connie says in an abrupt manner that Jenkins finds a bit odd.

Both get up and head into the kitchen. Jenkins grabs his phone and sees the text message is from Kennedy. *Just back from the Kingdom. Give a call when you can.*

Jenkins can't help noticing that, as if aware she's going to get a message, Connie grabs her phone, lying on the kitchen counter next to some cucumber parings, and as she's walking back into the dining room, Jenkins hears the ring tone of her text messaging. He reenters to find Connie staring at her phone. When she looks at him, he holds his up. "It's Kennedy."

Connie, however, doesn't identify the person who has texted her.

Jenkins tries to put this out of his mind as he walks into the front parlor. A streetlamp beams through the stained glass once fitted in a high transom by some distant hippie relative of Connie's who occupied the house in the late sixties before heading off to live in a commune in Oregon. One of the panels is the color of blood.

"Well, I know why Greta Thornhill was so guarded about her connection to Taft," Kennedy tells him when she answers his call. "Up in Newport, Taft wasted somebody. The guy can only see out of one eye. She probably knows all about it."

"Why didn't this come up when we did the check on him?"

"Because nobody was charged. Because the locals like keeping some things hushed. You'll be pleased to know that I didn't have to dig too hard to find this out. I went to the local garage. Hung out a little bit, showed the guys I know how to take apart and put together engines. Got some respect and then started asking questions. It was a fight that, apparently, was mutual. The guy called Taft a fag. Taft apparently just kept going, wailing on him. "

"Can we find this other guy?"

"Lives in Michigan. But I got his name."

"Good."

"Worth noting is the slur that started it."

"Yes, indeed," Jenkins says.

"And I haven't even gotten to the best part."

"Oh?"

"I asked the guys at the garage why all the rage and they told me, point blank. 'Roid rage."

Jenkins is stunned.

"You seeing what I'm seeing?"

"Oh yeah."

"I'm thinking about the way the twins reacted when you

mentioned Skylight Pond." Each falls silent. At last, Kennedy says, "It's after nine. How long will it take you to get down here?"

"I can be there probably by ten fifteen. "

"I'll be waiting for you outside the apartment," she tells him.

FEBRUARY 23; SOUTH WOODSTOCK, VERMONT; 10 DEGREES, LATE AFTERNOON SNOW EXPECTED

Sam, on his crutches, is maneuvering out his front door en route to his pickup truck, when he notices, parked across the road from his house, a fresh-faced news reporter from WCAX television in Burlington. The kid vaults out of his car clutching a microphone.

"Mr. Solomon, I would love to talk to you," the man says tentatively.

"I have nothing to say. Please just leave me alone."

The guy stubbornly remains on the street, staring at him with a furtive hope as if he might change his mind. And in the momentary standoff, Sam realizes he's forgotten a collection of renderings, turns around and hobbles back inside. As he begins combing through his desk drawer, he hears the reporter's car start and the sound of it driving away. He takes a deep breath just as he sees something, a manila folder, and opens it.

He recognizes the drawing Luc did of him while he was suffering his episode of Afib, but then several other drawings of him as well. Sam is stunned to see himself in various unconscious attitudes: his arms wrapped around Panda; leaning against the brick chimney that occupies the center of his old farmhouse; outside on a pair of cross-country skies. The drawings are executed with confident precision. And Luc has been able to capture the deep setting of Sam's eyes. Except for the one during his atrial fibrillation episode, remarkably, Sam never sat for any of these drawings; clearly, Luc had done them from memory. But why had he left them in Sam's drawer? In the top-right-hand corner of each sketch, there's a date: 10/19/13; 11/3/13; 12/5/13; 12/21/13. The last date was on the drawing of Sam on cross-country skis when he and Luc had gone for a quick tour. It's as if Luc somehow knew that one day Sam would stumble upon them. The thought is oppressive.

Today, for the first time since his injury, Sam is headed out to a client meeting; having the cast on his left leg luckily doesn't impinge on his driving. On the way to the interstate, en route to a late afternoon appointment in Concord, New Hampshire, he realizes he's thirsty and decides to stop at a country store on Route 4 that has easy access for somebody on crutches. It's a store he rarely visits, and as Sam propels himself in the door, he recognizes a few of the locals sitting around a wood stove, drinking coffee and eating homemade muffins and sugary donuts. Their murmuring conversation dies to a hush, and the door shutting firmly behind him sounds as loud as a firecracker. A forbidding silence follows, and pairs of eyes lock on him as he swings his way toward a row of glassed-in refrigerators holding all kinds of craft iced teas and beer and exotically flavored waters. He's grown used to these quizzical silences when he makes a public appearance, his romantic connection to Luc Flanders a broad topic of discussion in the Upper Valley of New Hampshire and Vermont.

At the glass gates of the coolers stands a young, strapping guy in a denim coat and painters jeans who can't be more than thirty-five years old. He has a neatly trimmed black beard and, in Sam's opinion, a rough-hewn, rural beauty. The man has just chosen his alcohol for the evening, perhaps soon to head home and polish off every single can in the twelve-pack of Budweiser. Recognizing Sam's incapacitation, he opens the glass door so that Sam can grab a bottle of spring water. "Thanks, man," he says and pivots toward the cashier's counter. As he stops in one of the aisles to grab a few cans of tuna fish, the guy breezes past him, swinging his twelve-pack. Looking after him, Sam remarks to himself on the habit of nightly beer drinking to excess. He sees tradespeople just like this guy throughout New England and Upstate New York buying large quantities of beer that they'll consume at home quietly embedded with family, polishing off one can after another until they reach a state of nocturnal numbness that leaves many of them a bit bleary in the daytime. Sam joins the cashier line right behind the fellow when he hears the snap of the words "Faggot murderer!"

Sam knows that sometimes the word "faggot" is trotted out for stupid, belligerent mudslinging, not necessarily slurring sexual preference, just an ill-chosen jibe of ignorance. But "murderer" is something altogether different. Sam assumes the person has read the article in the *Valley News* and is refusing to believe he is innocent of wrongdoing.

Meanwhile, the guy standing in front of him has turned around with a questioning, almost hurt expression. Even he assumes they are talking about Sam.

Knuckling the bottle of water, Sam pivots and deftly hobbles his way over to the group of men, a collection of mostly grizzled fellows in their forties and older—and maybe one in his thirties. "Who said that?" he demands aggressively.

The group looks shocked by the force of his arrival and confrontation. Nobody answers at first.

"Look," Sam persists, "if somebody is going to call me that, then he needs to own up to it."

Silence for several moments more and then all the eyes focus on a gray-haired portly man, probably in his mid-forties, slightly taller and admittedly bigger than Sam.

"You don't belong here . . ." The man speaks up at last.

"Here?" Sam repeats. "You mean Vermont?"

"You know what I mean," the guy says, bolder now and with characteristic New England flatness. "You belong in jail."

"Okay, that's quite enough," Sam hears somebody say, but not quite loud enough for everybody else to hear. Now some of the other men tamp down the accuser's rant by telling him, "Come on, Doug. Lay off."

"You guys just won't say how you really feel," says the man named Doug.

"You are not bringing us into this!" exclaims the original dissenting voice, much louder now. A wiry older man with clear eyes has just spoken. Turning to Sam with a shrug and a kind, apologetic look, he then says, "I read the paper and I know you've been cleared. So I don't know what this fool is on about. Don't lump me with him, please."

Sam is both surprised and grateful. He says to the man, "I won't. Thank you, sir."

"My name is Ad." The man stands up and then turns to the man called Doug. "Don't you say another word. Got that? I will never sit at any table with you again."

Ad holds the door for him so that he can hobble outside. He sees the guy who bought the twelve-pack of beer getting into a shiny new black rig and who makes a point of nodding to him.

"Looks like you did a number on your leg." Ad is examining Sam's ankle-to-knee cast.

As Sam explains about the skiing accident, it occurs to him that the event—reported in the *Valley News*—probably needs no explanation. Then again, the *New York Times* is tucked under the man's arm, so maybe he doesn't read the *Valley News*.

"Thank you for saying that . . . in my defense." Sam is leaning heavily on his right crutch, trying to stretch away an ache in his lower back, the result of having been on his feet for longer than usual.

"I should be apologizing to you for being in bad company," Ad says. "Where I come from in Wisconsin, there are bigots, too, but in the Midwest, people tend to think before they open their mouths."

Sam feels quite rattled as he drives south on Interstate 89 to Concord. It occurs to him there probably are very few places in the U.S. where an incident involving a possibly murdered gay student could have happened without rousing some acid reflux of bigotry and suspicion. Still, to be vilified like this in his own town, in a state he grew up in . . . Sam's parents are both dead, and while he misses them, he's glad they don't have to bear the burden that their son has ever been a suspect for murder.

He misses Luc with an intensity that almost makes it impossible to drive.

Luc said to him one Sunday night, "If something happened to you, I wouldn't even know it. Who would even tell me?" It was early December and Luc was preparing to drive back to Carleton. Snow was forecast for later in the evening; however, when Sam glanced out the window, it was already flurrying heavily. He suggested that Luc spend the night and leave early in the morning, and Luc argued that, since it was supposed to snow at least six inches, the roads could be more treacherous close to dawn.

"You're always worrying about me," Sam told him, "but here you are about to go out in the beginning of a snowstorm. What happens if that little car of yours doesn't make it over the Carleton Gap?"

Luc smiled confidently. "It'll make it. I've never not made it."

And then Luc pointed out that if, for example, Sam got into a motorcycle wreck, it could be weeks before he'd hear anything. Sam explained that he'd given Luc's number to his friend, Lynn, in New York City, and that Lynn's is the top name on his contact list with doctors and health insurance and even with the alarm company that monitors his house for cold and excessive heat and smoke. "She would let you know. I told her to. Meanwhile, I have nothing, no contact info for you."

"I'm almost twenty-three years old, what's going to happen to me?" Luc said with the typical self-assurance of someone whose life ahead probably appears like an endless ribbon of dry roadway.

Nevertheless, Sam reasoned that if anything were to happen to Luc, he'd probably never find out until months later, or maybe not even at all. Sam doesn't read the local paper, and even if he contacted Carleton, the college would refuse to give information to a stranger.

"Then you'd call my parents," Luc said. "I told you where they live. I told you their number is listed."

Not an easy conversation.

On the spur of the moment, they ended up making love. And in the depths of their hunger for one another, it occurred to Sam that what seemed like a heightened eroticism was rather something more primal. Maybe like life wanting to perpetuate itself in the midst of preoccupation with death.

And afterward, amid a static silence, watching Luc gathering his clothing strewn around the bedroom, methodically folding what still needed to go in his overnight bag, Sam said, "Why don't you just tell them? I'm sure you're imagining worse than it actually will be."

Luc turned his pale, penetrating gaze on Sam. "But if I'm not sure about myself, about what I want, why should I tell them?"

"But you do know what you want, Luc! Come on. You've said so."

"I want you, yes . . ." Luc admitted. Then with a short shrug said, "But I also want to get married."

Sam grabbed a towel lying on the floor. "You told me you couldn't and wouldn't get married."

Luc shook his head and glanced down at his overnight bag. "I did . . . I do say that. And then I get confused."

A dead-end conversation. Desolate, Sam glanced out the bedroom window. The spot lamps outlined a silver eddy of snow swirling down more heavily than before. "The weather has gotten worse."

Luc approached him from behind and fit his chin on Sam's shoulder, something he always did whenever Sam got upset. "It doesn't matter because I'm going to stay until tomorrow. And if the roads are really bad, I won't go back to school."

Sam turned around to find Luc grinning widely. In the beginning of their relationship, Luc would never even have wanted to spend the night. But now with the departure postponed until tomorrow, Sam, mired in a sad realization of Luc still being conflicted, was able to rise into the momentary embrace of happiness.

The snow has begun to fall fairly steadily, and the highway quickly accumulates a white lacquer that is slick with motor oil. Suddenly there is a large animal standing in the middle of the highway and Sam realizes at once it's a moose. His first thought: *Good thing I'm not going fast because of the weather.* His second thought: *Good thing I broke my left leg instead of my right one.* Gut instinct dictates that he must do what he can to avoid the creature. He knows he can't slam on the brakes; he gives them a few quick frantic taps to decelerate; however, the massive animal has remained stationary. The car begins fishtailing dangerously from side to side. He manages to swerve around the moose and soon is farther down the highway, his frantic breathing calming down, his rocketing heart slowly sloughing off the effects of adrenaline. All at once he feels a sudden flash of heat in the car and then strongly aware of Luc, of Luc's smell: fresh laundry soap and slightly sweet sweat. He could swear that some presence has invaded the car with him; maybe it is Luc—from wherever he might be. Could he somehow be asking for Sam's intervention . . . in order to . . . save his life?

PART 3

When some beloved voice that was to you
Both sound and sweetness, faileth suddenly,
And silence, against which you dare not cry,
Aches round you like a strong disease and new—
What hope? What help? What music will undo
That silence?

—Elizabeth Barrett Browning

FEBRUARY 23; NORWICH, VERMONT; 4 DEGREES, SNOW AND GUSTING WINDS

The children have always loved macaroni and Vermont cheddar—well into adulthood—and Eleanor, who has cooked hardly anything in weeks, loses herself for a hour or so, making the meal for her daughter's arrival. The house fills with the smells of melted cheese and organic semolina pasta, and at some point, Janine wanders into the kitchen, smiles weakly at her mother and nods with appreciation.

But Janine finds herself unable to eat much when they sit down to an early dinner. Giles has taken out a bottle of Chianti from the old wooden card catalog where they store wine, but one look of disdain from his daughter makes him reconsider. Eleanor watches him open the drawer and carefully replace the wine from where he'd prized it. If only she could have the same effect on her husband! But they often say the oldest child can evolve into the parent feared by all.

The table is set for three, not four—once again, Luc is conspicuously absent.

With a glance at his empty spot, Janine says, "It's become more and more of a reality as I've been here."

"Now you know what . . . well, what we've been living with," her father says.

"I guess I just figured because, you know, he was at school . . . it wouldn't be all that much different."

"Except, of course, we don't know when he's coming home . . . from school," Eleanor says.

"Or from anywhere," Giles mutters.

"Of course," Janine says. "Foolish of me to think otherwise. Denial, I suppose."

He'll come home, Eleanor grimly thinks, *one way or another*. Because they'll find him eventually. Whether it's living or dead.

Janine sighs and puts down her fork, ruminative. Her eyes are the same shape as Luc's, only not as pale in color. Yes, he did always have a wraith-like look in his eye—could that have been the portent of something? First, the alarming head injury, now the second unfathomable disappearance. Despite herself, Eleanor is reading anything into everything, and what she might find faintly reassuring—seeing her son's gestures, expressions, all genetically linked to her daughter's gestures and expressions—she also finds disturbing, reminders of his fuller being, extant or not. She can't imagine how a mother of an only child can go on after losing them. Even before this, when she heard such stories, she would switch off. Because to feel the reality of their pain would be unbearable. Wouldn't most of these mothers want to, yearn to, die themselves? Wouldn't they cease to fear death and long for it? To put an end to the unrelenting misery?

"You all right, Mom?" Janine has reached across the table and has been tightly holding her hand. And Eleanor realizes this is because she's been crying, emotions all run together, indistinguishable from one another.

"I'm sorry."

"Don't apologize."

Eleanor glances at Giles, who looks inconsolable; she knows by now that he's blaming himself for his own failures to reach his son, his casual cruelty, and that her bitter criticism of him has at last wormed its way into his heart. She regrets making him suffer more than he needs to. It's hard to speak, but she manages, "Just gotten used to . . . the fact that it's Dad and me here. You're . . . well, proof there's more to it. And it brings me back to him. To Luc."

Janine gently releases her hand and slowly sits back in

her chair, the still steaming square of mac and cheese barely touched. "But do eat something, Jan," Giles coaxes.

She glances at him with a frown. "I'm not really hungry, Dad."

"Make your mother happy."

Janine shoots Eleanor a guarded look of questioning.

"Eat what you want or what you can," Eleanor amends, and Janine delicately consumes a forkful and says with false brightness, "Good as always."

When she was a child, Janine often picked at her food, whereas Luc would be ravenous, and if he were here now, he would certainly be polishing off every morsel and then heaping his plate with one or two helpings more. Eleanor can't believe this is happening not to anybody else, but to her. It seems so wrong and obviously so unfair. *Can't I trade this in for something else?* she asks the dark façade of Providence when the phone rings. Grabbing the cordless handset that she placed on the floor next to her, Eleanor identifies the caller. "It's the cop, Jenkins," she says, glancing at her watch and panicking. "I had a feeling it was going to be tonight. I can't bear answering it. I can't bear to hear it."

"I'll take the call," Giles offers with an unsteady voice.

Somehow, in the midst of her desperation, Eleanor realizes that the last thing she wants is to get the bad news from her husband; she will associate the moment she hears of her son's fate to her husband's wretched lips uttering the words. And so she picks up finally, light-headed and breathless.

Jenkins says immediately, "Good evening, Mrs. Flanders. Glad you're in."

"We're all here," she says, glancing at Janine and Giles, needing them to help her face the news.

"It's not about Luc," Jenkins says. And once again a reprieve comes, the instant relief almost narcotic.

She meets the terrified eyes of her husband and daughter and repeats, "It's not Luc."

Jenkins continues, "Detective Kennedy and I are outside your son's apartment. And we're watching an altercation between Elizabeth Squires and Charlie Taft."

"An altercation," Eleanor repeats automatically.

"We're parked a bit down the street."

"Hang on," Eleanor hears Kennedy say. "Looks like they're splitting apart now."

A few beats of silence and then Jenkins contradicts, "No, they're not." And then, "Mrs. Flanders, do you happen to know how well Charlie Taft and Elizabeth Squires know each other?"

"Unfortunately, I can't comment on that. I've met Charlie Taft only once. And Elizabeth Squires only twice." Then something occurs to her. "Wouldn't this whole ordeal with Luc have brought them closer together?"

"Possibly," Jenkins says.

Janine, in the meantime, has grown agitated, rubbing her hands nervously together. Reaching across the table, she says, "Mom, let me speak to him?" Eleanor reflexively resents her daughter's involvement in the conversation. But Janine is persistent and trills her fingers impatiently. "Mom, I really need to talk to him."

Afraid of what her daughter might say, Eleanor glances helplessly at Giles, who says, "Go ahead, Elle."

"I will give it to her!" Eleanor says testily. "But I want to listen to both sides of the conversation. So just hang on." She hands the phone to Janine and hurries into the hallway, where another cordless handset is standing upright on a small wooden table. Grabbing it, she returns to the kitchen, hits the talk button and says, "Go ahead."

Leaning her head to the side and tossing her fine mane of hair away from her ear, Janine says with great composure, "Hello, Mr. Jenkins, I'm Janine, Luc's sister. Sorry to barge in."

"Not a problem," Jenkins says.

"I'm on the other extension," Eleanor announces.

Janine continues, "I do know Taft and Squires a bit more than my mom."

"Okay," Jenkins says. "Please tell me everything you know."

"Taft is a player and Elizabeth used to give Luc grief about it. Like Taft was . . . let's call it a bad influence on him. And something else: Taft dated somebody I know who now goes to NYU. According to her, he's sadistic. One of these guys who can find a woman's weakness and exploit it to his own advantage."

"I understand," Jenkins says. "Wait, so are you suggesting they might be having an . . .intimate relationship of some kind? And he—Taft—is somehow exploiting her?"

"No, I'm pretty sure she has no use for him. And I certainly don't think they'd bond over Luc's disappearance."

"Well, they are together tonight. And they're arguing. Like they know one another pretty well."

"Well, they're probably arguing about my brother."

"Really? How so?"

"Maybe Taft somehow came between Luc and Elizabeth."

"I see. So what is your take on your brother's relationship with Elizabeth Squires?" Jenkins asks her.

"I don't have a take. All I know is she's always been kind of stalkerish."

Even though Eleanor has thought the same thing herself, she finds herself once again defending Elizabeth. "But can that really be true?" she interjects.

Janine looks over at her with stark sadness. "Mom, you don't know enough about this, I'm sorry." Eleanor is unable to determine if Janine is commenting on her current understanding of what is going on or her capacity for understanding what is going on.

Jenkins is saying, "Stalkerish? How so?"

"Luc told me she went through his things, his drawers, his papers. That one night he woke up and she was reading his diary. She was holding her phone and was going to use the screen light to read it. After that, he just kept the diary hidden. In my opinion, that kind of behavior can drive people away."

"This is very helpful, thank you, Janine, " Jenkins says. "I may want to ask you some follow-up questions."

"Anytime."

Once the phone call has ended, the two women stare at each other. Giles says, "Why didn't you tell us what Elizabeth did?"

"That she went through Luc's shit?"

"Yes, exactly," Eleanor chimes in.

"It's really not so unusual, Mom," Janine says sadly. "People in relationships do these sorts of things when they start to question how devoted the other person is."

"She probably felt that way because Luc has always been so secretive and shut down," Giles points out.

"What you don't know is he confided in me about her," Janine points out. "And his impression was Elizabeth defines her life according to the guy she's with."

"Many women do," says her father.

"Well, I'd rather be alone than have to mold myself to a guy."

And then Giles asks, "Janine, are you trying to tell us something about . . . your relationship to other women?"

Eleanor and Janine look at one another in surprise and actually burst out laughing. Then Janine says with deliberate gentleness, "Oh, Dad. That question . . . I want to say it's dumb of you, but . . . shit, we're all in a bad way here, aren't we?"

Giles foolishly tries to defend his remark. "Well, I don't know any other women who obsess over hockey the way you do. Who, when they watch the Bruins, wear not one, but two jerseys, Bergeron and Marchand."

"Yeah? Well, I love those guys. However, if either of them were my boyfriend, I'd whip him into shape." Then, more philosophical, Janine says, "But no. I'm not gay. However, men are definitely wary of me."

It occurs to Eleanor that perhaps a few of Elizabeth's softer qualities might help her own daughter find men suitable for dating. "Does anybody want more of this?" She points to the glass casserole dish of perfectly baked macaroni and cheese.

"I'm good," Janine says, looking down appraisingly at the substantial leftovers clinging to her plate.

Eleanor doesn't even wait for Giles's response; she assumes he is finished eating. She grabs his plate, reaches for the nearby potholder, picks up the casserole and pushes back from the table. She takes out a box of foil wrap and prepares the hardly touched meal for the refrigerator. It occurs to Eleanor that putting the meal away is like preparing a body for burial, and like so many of her activities these days, this one seem final, like last rites. Just the other day, believing that viewing slides of her son might somehow precipitate his return to her, Eleanor scrolled through several carousels of family holidays and summer sojourns, lazy days of balmy weather around their cabin on Lake Fairlee. She'd projected the pictures on the living room wall and kept a cardboard box next to her into which she dropped the slides. Hearing the sound of the slides hitting the bottom of the box reminded her of the sound of dirt being thrown onto a coffin. Yes, her sense of mourning is aching, pervasive. Two days ago, she broke down and wept over a little big-eared mouse that had gotten stuck in the children's bathtub and couldn't climb out and slowly perished, its body desiccated from starvation and thirst.

"I mean, maybe it's the amnesia again," Janine says once they've moved into the family room and are sitting in front of a blazing fire. "Maybe he just hitched a ride, went somewhere else like he did the last time, and . . . I don't know, is flying under the radar now? Maybe flipping burgers someplace?"

"He didn't have his wallet with him," Eleanor says. "No ID."

"Exactly! So once again living without a name."

"Yes, and maybe he's become somebody's slave!" Giles says angrily. Both women stare at him. "Look, I'm sorry, but how can that be: he's living somewhere without his name?"

"Because he did it once before," Janine says.

Giles refutes, "He was fifteen then and fresh off that injury. He's responsible now. He's a man. I think it's ridiculous to speculate that he's gone anywhere." Glancing at Eleanor, Giles says softly, "I just don't think he's alive anymore, Elle," his words like rock salt subsuming the fire roaring up before them. "The snow is deep this time of year. He could be in it anywhere and we won't know until spring. Until he thaws."

As she watches the flames in the fireplace flicker and crackle, a now familiar weariness comes over Eleanor, the fatigue of having to live every waking moment with the tangible possibility of catastrophe. She wants to get up and go straight to her bedroom and take a Xanax; she wants to wait for the gently falling curtain of chemical relief, her nocturnal escort away from the reality of Luc being gone but which, she knows, will once again break upon her as predictably as daylight.

Janine says, "Too long to wait. We can't live like this."

"We have to," Giles says. "We have no other choice."

Taft is wearing a heavy sweatshirt emblazoned with *Newport*. Standing a foot away from him wearing a pair of white earmuffs is Elizabeth Squires, her vehement words punching the air in frosted plumes. At last, Taft pulls the hood of his sweatshirt down over his face and, looking druid-like in the bitter darkness, stalks away from the building. Elizabeth stands there watching him leave and then hurries in the opposite direction, arms crossed against the severe, windy cold. She walks right by the unmarked car, and her aqua ski parka looks momentarily iridescent beneath the nearby streetlamp. Jenkins and Kennedy watch this unfold from inside the vehicle.

"Stalkerish," Kennedy remarks, "interesting. Let's try on the fact that something else went down on the night of February eleventh, that they know more than they're saying."

"Agreed."

"Any gut reaction?" she asks him.

"Yeah. Either one or the other or both followed him back to the pond."

Kennedy smiles. "I think that's right on the money. Let's go on that assumption and see where it gets us."

Peering up at the dimly lit apartment, they figure McKinnon is probably at home. Kennedy gets out of the car, climbs the stairs and knocks on the door. Nobody responds. It's going on ten thirty. She returns to the car. "Absolutely frigid out there." They continue waiting. At last, somebody wearing a long dark wool coat crosses the street, approaches the ground-level door, opens it and heads inside. "McKinnon. So that's one down," Kennedy remarks. Five minutes later, Taft returns. "I guess it's now or never."

Jenkins says, "So I'll mosey Taft to Maplefields?"

The plan: When Kennedy is done questioning McKinnon, she will text Jenkins and then head over to find Elizabeth, who will either be in her dorm or in the library. Whether or not Jenkins is through questioning Taft, he'll keep him tightly under watch to make sure he doesn't try to contact either of the other two. The detectives glance at each other and each gives a final nod to say they are in agreement about strategy. They then venture out into the unforgiving, blustering night. "Jesus, it's deeper than the grave," Kennedy says with a slight Irish lilt as they head toward the apartment stairs.

"I'd rather this than roasting in a D.C. summer," Jenkins says.

"Right now that roasting sounds pretty fine to me."

Jenkins climbs ahead this time and knocks. A moment later, Taft opens and looks miffed, a line of apprehension knitting itself across his dusky features.

"We need a quick word, can we come in?" Jenkins says.

"Do we have a choice?" they hear McKinnon say from somewhere in the near background.

Taft says nothing in reply, shrugs, and admits them into the kitchen, which smells of frying and oil. McKinnon, shirtless at the stove, is cooking what appears to be scrambled eggs and generously adding hot sauce from a pencil-thin bottle. His pale, freckled body is muscled and pumped up and defined; he looks particularly powerful. There is a rash of acne on his broad shoulders—according to Kennedy, a telltale sign of steroid use.

"A little late for dinner, isn't it?" Jenkins asks.

"Dinner number two." McKinnon greets them with a wave of a spatula. *Increased appetite, another sign of steroid use,* Jenkins thinks.

"Looks like you spice your eggs."

McKinnon gulps and nods his head and says, "Yeah, sometimes."

"So what's going on?" Taft asks them.

"I thought you were done asking us questions," McKinnon says.

"We thought we were but we have some things to clarify and thought you could help us," Kennedy says.

"Okay, so what are they?" Taft says nervously.

"I'd like you to get your coat and come with me," Jenkins says to him.

"Can't we talk here?"

"We'd prefer to speak to each of you separately," Helen says.

Both men stare at them, as though stunned. Then McKinnon says, "Not without a lawyer."

"Absolutely within your right," Kennedy says. "You can each call a lawyer, but we'd like Mr. Taft to go with Detective Jenkins and Mr. McKinnon to stay here with me. If neither of you have a lawyer on tap, we'll help find you one."

Taft grabs his heavy sweatshirt and begins jabbing his arms into the sleeves.

Jenkins follows him down the stairs. "Make a left," he orders as Taft opens the outer door and a forbidding blast of sleet hits them, "and keep going until you hit that Ford."

"It's too dark to see the make of these cars," Taft complains.

"Then just keep walking until I tell you to stop."

The air inside the car is still warm from Kennedy's and his vigil, and sleet is slamming softly against the windshield. Jenkins sits there, waiting.

"Are we going to just hang here?" Taft asks.

Jenkins starts the car and maneuvers out of the parking space.

"Where we headed?" Taft asks.

"To the police station. Where you can call a lawyer."

"I don't want to go to the police station."

Jenkins explains this is necessary to get the name and contact information for a public defender.

"I'd rather find one on my phone."

"How about a cup of coffee?" Jenkins suggests.

"How about one," Taft says.

Jenkins drives down Weybridge Road, continues onto the Pulp Mill Bridge Road and drives slowly across the covered bridge. By now the sleet has evolved into snow, and he notices what looks like a group of college students staggering out of Flatbread into a vortex of flakes. Eyeing them, Taft grunts with disdain and perhaps, Jenkins wonders, maybe even with a bit of envy.

When they come to Greg's Market, which is a minute's drive from Maplefields, Jenkins decides he needs a few more minutes to strategize and takes a longer route. Glancing at Taft, he makes a left onto Exchange Street and drives them along a curving road with tall, silo-like structures that almost look as though they might conceal nuclear warheads but are actually state-of-the-art microbreweries of beer and hard cider. Deep in a silence of his own, Taft doesn't even seem to register the detour. They pass a do-it-yourself carwash and then an Agway parking lot, where two pickup trucks with headlights blazing are facing each other in an automotive showdown, a slanting curtain of snow illuminated between them. Jenkins hangs a right on Route 7 and they proceed a quarter mile to the parking lot of Maplefields.

"There are a few seats in the back," he says once they are inside.

On a winter night full of uncertain precipitation, the gas-and-convenience store is nearly empty of customers. A bored-looking cashier with tattoos and piercings in her eyebrows, nose and mouth watches them with a scowl. Rap music is blaring. Jenkins fishes out his wallet. "Get yourself a coffee," he tells Taft.

Taft walks stiffly over to the line of cylinders supplied by Vermont Coffee and pumps himself a tall hot drink but doesn't put anything in it. He goes and stands at the counter while Jenkins, now filling a small cup and adding half-and-half, calls, "Just got snag us a table and sit down."

Taft sits in one of the vinyl booths in the back. Jenkins arrives at the table to find him staring worriedly into his coffee and sits down opposite him.

Taft looks up, dark eyes flashing. "So?"

"Let's just talk."

"Okay."

Leaning toward Taft, Jenkins says, "Why don't you tell me about the soccer team."

Taft looks miffed. "The soccer team?"

"You're at Carleton on a soccer scholarship, right?"

Taft nods.

"So you must be pretty good to get a scholarship."

"I'd like to think so. My family can't afford this place." He guardedly looks around the chain convenience store as if it were a proxy of the Carleton campus. "I guess the college wanted me enough to help out."

It strikes Jenkins again that Taft, thickly muscled, swarthy and dark-eyed like a Latino, probably stuck out in his small Vermont border town. Pointing to the bold lettering on Taft's sweatshirt, he says, "Carleton's a far cry from Newport, isn't it?"

Taft looks at him warily. "Oh, for sure."

"Anyway, you consider yourself to be pretty good friends with Luc Flanders, right?"

Taft colors. "Well, he's my roommate."

"Roommates aren't always good friends, though, are they?"

"I guess not always." And then well before Jenkins expects

it, the opening comes. "Why do you want to keep questioning me?"

"Like I said. To make sense out of some unrelated facts we have. And we think talking to you will help us."

"But what unrelated facts?"

"Well, for starters, your aunt, Greta Thornhill, seems to have hidden her connection to you."

"But if you'd asked me if I was related to her to begin with, I would have told you, no problem." Taft was obviously prepared for this.

"I can appreciate that. By the way, Detective Kennedy, who is back at your apartment taking to your roommate . . ." Jenkins waits a moment. "She went up to Newport."

"Why?"

"Let's call it a fact-finding mission."

"Facts about what?"

Jenkins says, "Facts about you."

"Facts about me," Taft says slowly.

"Because we found out you wasted somebody up there in Newport and we wanted to learn more about it." Jenkins inverts the truth.

Taft, who has been sitting up straight, suddenly deflates in his chair. Then he glares at Jenkins. "I didn't go around wasting anybody. It was a fight."

"What was the fight about?"

"Why else do guys fight? Somebody rubs somebody else the wrong way."

Jenkins pauses for effect. "He must've made you really angry. I understand he only has one good eye left."

Taft spits out, "Fucking Christ!"

"I am amazed you weren't arrested for that."

"It started mutually. It wasn't anybody's fault. So no arrests, okay?"

"But usually, somebody starts a fight," Jenkins points out reasonably.

"Somebody swings first. But the other person says something that makes them swing."

"So, in this case, who said something first? And who swung first?"

"I actually don't remember. It wasn't a good thing. I don't like to think about it."

"I don't blame you." Jenkins knows it's time to move on. "So let me ask: how well does your aunt, Greta Thornhill, know Elizabeth Squires?"

Taft says, "Her roommate got stalked. They met then. Other than that, my aunt doesn't know her."

Jenkins hesitates and then asks, "So what do you think of Elizabeth Squires?"

Taft shifts uneasily in his chair. "What do I think? She was Luc's girlfriend. They kept to themselves. She's seems okay."

"Ever run into her on campus?"

"It's a small school. You run into everybody you know."

"So you don't hang out?"

Now Taft realizes where it's going and stops, pondering his next move. "Sometimes we'll see each other and talk. Mainly about Luc."

"Have you talked with her about Luc recently?"

Taft is glaring at him. "She tell you that?" His voice croaks.

Jenkins lets several moments pass, watching carefully how Taft hunches nervously forward, one of his legs pumping up and down. "She was outside your apartment tonight. You two seemed pretty upset. What were you talking about?"

Taft manages to say, "I was just giving her a pep talk. She's been really depressed."

"Didn't look like that to us. Looked like you guys were having an argument."

Taft remains silent.

"When I asked you about her a few minutes ago, why didn't you tell me you saw her tonight?"

Taft looks perplexed and stares at Jenkins for a moment. "I

think I need to have that lawyer."

"Okay, then let's finish our coffee, head to the police station, and I'll get you a list of public defenders."

"I told you I don't want to go to the police station. I—"

There is a sharp clattering and both turn to see that the young woman with the nose piercings has accidentally dropped a glass coffeepot, which has shattered on the floor. A few of the shards bounce up close to where they're sitting. Lackadaisical, she hunches her shoulders and bends down to start picking up the pieces. Turning back to Taft, Jenkins continues, "I can't call you a lawyer here. You'll just have to come with me."

"Why can't you lay off me?" Taft says softly.

Jenkins ignores him. "But before we go, can you tell me: how long have you been on the juice?" Jenkins is satisfied by Taft's expression of pained recognition, and then adds, "McKinnon's on it, too. I saw tonight he's all broken out in acne on his back."

Taft doesn't respond.

"Detective Kennedy is pretty good with questioning. I wonder what he'll say when she asks him about the juice. There won't be any reason for him to lie. He doesn't really have anything to worry about. Detective Kennedy will assure him she's not looking to bust him for steroids and that he's not a suspect in the disappearance of Luc Flanders."

"But I am?"

"Did I say that?"

Taft is now shifting uncomfortably in his chair.

"You bought the steroids from the Newcombe twins. Who were up in Carleton the night Luc disappeared."

"If you say so." "Did you and McKinnon buy steroids from them that night?"

"I can't. No more. I demand a lawyer."

"Fine." Jenkins stands up. "Come on, let's go."

FEBRUARY 23; CARLETON, VERMONT; 1 DEGREE, SNOW, WIND GUSTS

"You're a smart guy," Kennedy says to McKinnon. "Lots of your friends look up to you."

He looks at her strangely. "Yeah, so?"

"So, we have a bunch of gaps. And I have a feeling you can help me fill them." She leans back in the chair that is pulled up to the kitchen table, the chair Taft had been sitting in before Jenkins whisked him away.

"So we found out that your roommate, Mr. Taft, wasn't at home at six p.m. on the night of February eleventh. So why did you lie and say he was?"

McKinnon's hand shoots up. "I'd like a lawyer."

Kennedy stands up. "Okay, then let's go to the station and we'll find you one."

"Okay, okay," McKinnon decides to go on. "I lied because he—Taft— asked me to."

"Why did he ask you to?"

"Because he was afraid of being a suspect."

"Ah, I see."

McKinnon has put on a pale green T-shirt for this interview. They are sitting at the table, facing each other. The pan of eggs is on the stove, still uneaten.

Kennedy decides to move on for the moment. "Did you know that your roommate and Elizabeth Squires had a dispute tonight outside this apartment?"

Kennedy carefully watches the flicker of skepticism on McKinnon's face; with her experience, she believes she can identify unalloyed surprise.

He says, "I didn't know they were even hanging out."

A text pings on her phone and it's Jenkins. *He asked for a lawyer. Headed to the station.* She types back, *Keep me posted.*

And then another text from Jenkins arrives and it makes Kennedy smile to herself. She turns her palms up toward the ceiling. "What would you say if I told you that the night Luc Flanders disappeared, Squires and Taft followed him back to Skylight pond?"

"I think Taft would have told me if they had."

"Well, according to this text, he just told my partner," she says, holding up her phone. "He did go back to the pond. As did she. I wonder why didn't he tell you."

McKinnon recoils. "What are you implying? That he did something to Luc?"

"I don't know," Kennedy says and notices that McKinnon looks perturbed. "Do you know anything about Taft's past?"

"Like what?"

"Like that he has violent tendencies."

McKinnon blinks and frowns. "You mean he attacked people?"

"Yes. Seriously hurt people. Sending them to the hospital."

"No, I didn't know that," McKinnon says, looking spooked.

"Any idea why, if both Squires and Taft were at Skylight Pond on the night of February eleventh, they never told you or anybody else?"

"Like I said before, he was probably worried about being suspected."

"So let's do a timeline of the evening of February eleventh, shall we?"

"Okay."

"When did you guys get home from playing pond hockey?"

"Just before six."

"And contrary to what you stated previously, Taft actually did go out again."

"Yeah, he did."

"Did he say where he was going?" McKinnon shakes his head. "That's not a very convincing 'no.' Look, I'm not here to arrest you for illegal purchase of a banned substance—the steroids."

McKinnon looks astonished.

"I could give a shit about what you inject into your body," Kennedy persists. "Steroids are not my jam." She deliberately uses a millennial expression. "So he went out to score. But do you have any idea why he went back to the pond?"

"No."

"How long would you say he was gone for in total?"

"Maybe an hour or so."

Kennedy feels the table vibrate. Another text from Jenkins. *See if Taft's computer is there. Trying to get a warrant.*

She looks up at McKinnon. "Is Taft's computer in his room?"

"I assume so. Why?"

"I just need to check if it is."

"Go all the way down the hall. It's the last room on the right."

Kennedy pushes back from the table, stands up, and walks down the dim hallway, glancing up at a naked, anemic-looking light bulb haloed by a cobweb whose pendent mesh contains a scattering of dead flies. She passes Luc Flanders's room, shut and secured by a police locksmith, with a bar across the door, and then another room, which is quite messy with gym shorts and T-shirts and fleeces strewn everywhere, thick college textbooks in piles on the floor—obviously McKinnon's room. Taft's door is closed, and she opens it to a space meticulously in order, scrupulously clean, redolent of cheap drugstore cologne, which she notices all the young guys seem to wear these days. The walls are bare, except for a relief map of the Northeast Kingdom—with a red dot pinpointing Newport—and a poster of a soccer scrum with the block lettering REAL MADRID. There is very little furniture: a simple metal writing table and chair and a tensor lamp arcing over the table. In the midst of this Spartan order is the titanium rectangle of a Mac Book Pro. Glancing around the room, Kennedy divines that this is the sort of person who'd carefully cover his tracks.

She texts Jenkins. *The computer is here.*

She migrates back to the kitchen, where McKinnon has decided to eat his cold scrambled eggs. Pointing the fork at her, he says, "Was it—his computer—there?"

"Yes, it was."

McKinnon shrugs and says, "Okay," with an air that signals he is beginning to detach from the fate of his roommate. Sensing this, Kennedy says, "Back to what you and I were discussing before. Let me ask you this. If you had to come up with a reason, why would Taft go back to Skylight Pond on the night of February eleventh?"

McKinnon grabs a tall glass of whole milk and drains it. She watches his prominent Adam's apple bobbing. "He probably had something to talk to Flanders about."

"Like what?"

"Let's put it this way: Charlie was really revved that night."

"Revved?"

In a burst of frustration, McKinnon says, "I don't mean that. I don't know what I'm saying here."

Kennedy scrutinizes him. "You don't mean what you're saying? So what are you saying? He wasn't revved up that night?"

Pausing for a moment, McKinnon is considering something and finally blurts out, "Taft's in love with Flanders, okay? So now you know!"

"In love with Flanders," Kennedy repeats.

"Yeah, and I think Taft despises himself for it."

"Why would he despise himself?" Kennedy asks, reflecting on the brutality of what went on up in Newport.

"Because Taft just can't admit it to anybody, let alone to himself."

"And how about to you?"

"Not to me. He probably thinks I'd hate him for it."

"Would you?" Kennedy asks.

"Of course I wouldn't. I'm not a homophobe."

"You're not?" Kennedy says, thinking: *Not so fast, buddy.* "Okay, so did Luke ever mention he was involved with another man?"

"No."

"Any reason why you think he didn't mention it?"

"Because no matter what anybody says, more often than not, it makes you 'less than' when you admit to being gay."

"Okay, then how would you know about Taft?"

"Way easy if you saw Taft's face whenever he was looking at Flanders. It was all there. He loves Luc. But, of course, Taft will never admit it. Just like Flanders will never admit to being in love with his older guy."

"Won't he?"

"I don't think so."

"So Taft might have been jealous of . . . that relationship?"

"Yes. I think he was."

"Other than pure observation, do you happen to have any proof . . . of Taft's romantic interest in Flanders?"

"I don't think anything ever happened between them. But I did see something . . ." McKinnon hesitates and then divulges. "Back in the fall. I believe Charlie followed Luc down to Woodstock, at least once."

"And you know this how?"

"Because around the same time, Charlie and I went to have dinner at Prohibition Pig in Waterbury. We took his car, and I noticed a gas receipt on the floor of the passenger side.

From a Sunoco station in Woodstock, Vermont."

"So you think he might have followed Luc down to Woodstock."

"Yeah."

"And yet you don't think he had anything to do with Luc's disappearance."

"I don't think so. But I guess I honestly don't know."

"But do you think Taft might be capable of doing something to Luc?"

"Like you just said, he's got a side to him, a side full of anger. Sometimes he explodes."

"Maybe it's 'roid rage?" Kennedy says.

McKinnon smiles grimly. "Maybe."

"Well, let me ask you this. Do you happen to know why Luc went back to Skylight Pond?"

McKinnon nods. "He asked to borrow a flashlight, so I assumed he lost something."

"Any idea what he might have lost?"

"No."

Kennedy now sends a text to Jenkins.

Taft followed Flanders down to Woodstock. Back in the fall. McKinnon found a gas receipt from Woodstock Sunoco.

The reply: *Good to know.*

When Kennedy looks up at him, McKinnon, of his own volition, says, "There's something else you should probably know."

"What else should I know?"

"Late this afternoon, I saw Taft get into his car. He was gone four hours. Didn't get back until nine. He seemed in a weird frame of mind when he came home. But then maybe it was because . . . you said he had the argument with Elizabeth."

Kennedy grabs her phone. *Taft went MIA today for four hours.*

Kennedy is considering her next question when another text comes in. *Okay, warrant is signed, sealed, and delivered: take the computer AND check the car.*

"I've been cleared to take the computer," she says to McKinnon.

McKinnon nods. "Okay." He hesitates a moment and then asks, "So I'm being cooperative?"

"Yes. You'll get a star for your cooperation." She smiles at him. "Now where are Taft's car keys?"

"On that hook next to the front door." He beckons Kennedy to a window looking down on the lamp-lighted street. "You can see his car from here. It's that gray Subaru right under the light pole."

The first place Kennedy looks is the trunk of the car. Nothing there. Then she goes directly to the driver's seat, reaches under it, and feels a small nylon drawstring bag shaped around something heavy and hard and cold and metallic. She pulls out a .38 caliber revolver. And just as she does, another text comes from Jenkins. *Shit has hit the fan.*

The house is strangely quiet when Sam gets home, and yet outside the wind is bellowing. He calls out to Panda. At first, there is no response, not so unusual. Sometimes she jumps up on his bed and waits for him to come upstairs, where he'll find her, looking at him whimsically, tail thumping on the sheet he spreads over the bed to collect any hair she might shed. But because of his bum leg, he doesn't climb the stairs right away. He goes into the kitchen and puts the kettle on for tea.

As he listens to the heating water beginning to stir, he finds it odd that Panda hasn't come downstairs to find him. He walks out into the hallway and, listening to the silence, decides to go back into the kitchen, turn the flame down beneath the kettle and make his way upstairs. Using his crutches, he climbs slowly to his room, where he finds the bed vacant. He calls out, "Panda? Panda!" But the only response is the shuddering old farmhouse windows lashed by frightening blasts of wind.

And then it happens again, the sudden breathlessness, the flash of heat on his face, the ionic presence of someone or something brushing against him, simultaneously urging him on, trying to soothe him just by being there.

But Sam throws off this feeling. As well as he can, with the impediment of his cast, he makes his way downstairs again, pushing himself to get to ground level as quickly as possible. She's got to be somewhere. Maybe she went to sleep on the downstairs bathroom floor and got shut in, something that has happened a few times before. Sam limps there, flips the light switch, and checks, but no Panda. The white tiles on the shower backsplash and the tub gleam with menacing emptiness. He calls everywhere for her and then a terrible shattering presentiment comes over him, that despite the fact that the house was locked and secure, Panda somehow ended up outside. But then she'd have been waiting near the door or somewhere close and surely would've come running when he pulled up in the driveway.

Opening the door, he calls out into the vortex of cold, assaulting wind, and then he ventures out into the bitter elements, yelling for her. But the hostile gusts and the freezing slant of snow drown out his summoning, and he knows that even if she's farther out there, she won't be able to hear him. Maybe she's gotten outside and, drawn by the scent of a nocturnal animal, has gone too far and got somehow hurt or temporarily lamed and stranded in the deep, accumulating snow. But there is no way that he can go through the drifts on crutches to look for her. Whom can he call? The only person that comes to mind is Heather Finlayson.

They've spoken only once since she was run off the road, when he'd reassured her that his car was stolen and he wasn't behind the wheel. When she answers the phone now, her voice is chilly, no doubt having recognized his caller ID. In his frantic state of mind, it briefly dawns on Sam that she might be at the very least displeased to have been run off the road and now involved in his personal nightmare. But when he tells her about Panda missing, reminding her that he has difficulty moving around, she is soon on her way over to his house to help.

So many possible grim scenarios flutter through his thoughts: Panda being stolen; Panda being hit by a car and thrown where it might be difficult to find her; Panda perhaps marooned in the farmer's field across the road; or perhaps most distressing, Panda harmed by somebody who presumes

Sam has harmed Luc Flanders. It's an interminable twenty minutes of waiting, every possibility of misfortune flitting through his mind. Sam's world seems to be caving in, he's losing purchase on everyone and everything he loves, made all the worse by having to hobble around inept and unable to move easily from place to place. His febrile thoughts revert back to Panda, bewildered how this usually sensible dog could have wandered outside.

"She's way too smart to do anything like go trekking around in the snow," opines Heather when she arrives with a grave face in an oversized Army-issue peacoat, knee-high muck books with snow pants gripping the tops of them tightly. "Especially tonight. It's crazy out there. Wind chill way below zero. I just hope somebody didn't come in here and take her."

The gruesome possibility of abduction certainly can't be ruled out.

"Just stay here and let me go check," Heather says, moving back toward the front door. "You can't drag that leg through the snow."

Sam sits down, overcome with a worry that somehow transmutes into fatigue. It's as though he loses consciousness for a minute or so, because Heather is now standing before him weeping quietly and managing to articulate, "She's barely alive, Sam. She's at the bottom of the driveway. I couldn't lift her. I tried to."

"Oh my God!" Sam cries. "Bottom of the driveway. Did . . . could I have run her over?"

"No, she's off to the right. Doesn't appear injured. But I don't know what's happened to her."

"Then how did she get out there?"

He hardly hears what Heather says, her admonitions as he launches himself out of the chair and limps toward the door. He doesn't bother to grab his crutches; they will only get in the way. And then outside in shirtsleeves, zero temperature and the flailing wind. He doesn't feel the cold, unaware it's snowing harder, and his eyes focused ahead of him where the orb of the motion detector spotlights illuminate a dark welter against the floury white. Hobbling desperately with Heather behind him, Sam hears her saying something he doesn't understand, almost in another language. Nothing will derail his purpose. Moving inexorably forward, he loses his balance at one point and slams down on the driveway, his face hitting the snow, which softens the impact of the fall. He feels pain rocketing through his injured leg and cries out in surprise and rage. And Heather is there, helping him up and ordering him to let her take care of Panda, to go back inside, but he shrugs her off and forges ahead. This is his ritual, his rite. Finally, he reaches his dog.

She is very still, her slight graying brow furrowed in worry, her eyes weakly scanning the darkness until they fix on him. And then he sees the soulful reflection, the purity of emotion, the dubious, pained trust as she looks up at him, as though to say *How could this have happened?and how could you have let it happen?* Tears are streaming down Sam's face as he holds her head in his hands and softly kisses her snout. He feels a rattle in her throat as though she's trying to speak. The wind is animating her fur, her eyebrows, snow feathering through her tail, and he gains an inkling of the agony a parent must feel when holding a dying child. Panda quivers violently. He can feel her letting go of him, of her life, and that moment of passing is anything but a relief. It is a torment, a slice deep into his heart. He cries out and then weeps unabatedly.

Tapping into an instinct deeper than thought, he bends down and lifts her up as all the living do with their dead. Her body is remarkably heavy and slack as it settles into his arms. He knows he probably won't be able to carry her all the way back to the house, and yet he begins his own little cortège. He just wants her inside, where it's warm. Her limp body somehow becomes the weight of her life. And before his complete and utter abandonment to grief, he comes to understand why there are death marches and why mourning is very much part of surviving.

FEBRUARY 24; CARLETON, VERMONT; 19 DEGREES, OVERCAST

At 3 a.m., Charlie Taft is sitting opposite Kennedy and Jenkins at Carleton police headquarters. Taft grabs the paper cup of coffee brought to him and, drinking it like water, clears his throat. Kennedy says, "So you can't pinpoint exactly when Elizabeth got to the pond herself but you say you arrived pretty much the same time."

"Yes."

"And your purpose in going back to the pond?" Jenkins asks.

"I was going to" — Taft swallows — "talk to Luc. But then I saw him — Sam — walking away from the pond."

The statement would contradict Heather Finlayson's assurance that she spoke to Sam Solomon at his house at 6:28 p.m. on the night of February eleventh. However, upon their return to the police station, Jenkins and Kennedy were given a report from Fairpoint Communications, the local telephone company, that Sam Solomon, in fact, received a single call from Heather Finlayson's landline number at 5:15 p.m. on the night of February eleventh. Jenkins and Kennedy have decided, for the moment, not to go back to Heather Finlayson and ask her to amend her testimony, the lie she may have told to protect her friend. They certainly cannot accuse Sam of lying since the phone record matches his original statement. Now, of course, the time frame does make it possible for him to have driven up to Carleton before heading to Logan Airport.

"How clearly could you have seen Sam if it was so dark?" Jenkins says.

"He had a flashlight. But the moon was out." Taft looks up at the ceiling, squinting at it as though gauging something in the light fixture not quite identifiable to the other two.

"Moon or not, you'd still have to be pretty close to him," Kennedy points out.

Now Taft stares at them. "At first I thought I was seeing Luc. Then when I got closer—"

"How much closer?" Jenkins asks.

"I don't know, twenty-five yards away. But then I realized the person was shorter. And that it wasn't Luc."

Jenkins is thinking to himself, *We will have to examine a pair of Taft's shoes.* "What size shoe do you wear?" he asks.

Pushing back in his chair, which scrapes loudly against the floor, Taft shows them the underside of one of his feet and says, "Ten and a half."

"You know," Kennedy says, "there's a whole wide world of men shorter and stockier than Luc Flanders. There is something called Craigslist, where shorter and stockier men put up ads."

The arrow hits its desired mark. Taft's face flushes and he suddenly rants, "I know that happens on Craigslist. That's how they met!"

Kennedy replies, "And my point is he could have been meeting somebody else at the pond that night. And maybe it just didn't work out. Or maybe that unknown person ended up having an altercation with him."

Taft almost says something but then clamps down.

Jenkins nods to Kennedy, who says, "Our forensic computer guy just told us that there is a folder on your computer called 'Luc.' And in the folder are two passwords—which correspond to both of his email accounts."

Taft nods his head. "Yeah."

"You also hacked into Sam's account. You read Luc's emails to him and then deleted them after you read them."

Taft looks at them blankly.

"Did you tamper with those emails?" Kennedy says.

"Okay, yeah, I did."

"Why?" Kennedy asks.

"Because it was gross."

"What was gross?"

"I mean, come on, the guy was way old. Almost thirty years older."

"And it made you upset enough to commit computer fraud?"

"Well, they broke it off so, obviously, they didn't care that much. It made Luc miserable."

Jenkins and Kennedy look at one another.

"When did you start hacking into their computers?" Kennedy persists.

Taft runs his fingers through his hair and then rubs his scalp. "Around November."

"And after it ended between them in December, you made sure Sam Solomon never got Luc Flanders's messages," Kennedy says.

Taft nods his head but doesn't answer.

"So why exactly did you go back to the pond?" Jenkins says. "On the night of February eleventh."

"Because I wanted to talk to Luc."

"About?"

"To tell him that I read and deleted the emails."

Jenkins's cell phone rings, and he digs into his pocket and harshly silences it.

Kennedy continues, "So why didn't you say what you had to say after the pickup hockey game?"

"Because she showed up. At the time, I took that as a . . . I don't know, a sign."

"A sign?" Kennedy sounds dubious. "I have trouble believing that there was to be a sudden confession after months of snooping. Why that night in particular?"

"Why not?" Taft says, surprising both Jenkins and Kennedy with what seems to be a momentary gush of sincerity.

Jenkins picks up. "Okay, so you say you saw Sam Solomon walking away from the pond. Do you have any idea of what time that was?"

"Like I said before, somewhere around six thirty."

"And what did you tell Elizabeth?"

"Nothing then. Later on, after Luc disappeared, I told her I thought I saw Sam."

"So she'll corroborate this . . . telling," Kennedy says.

"She will," Taft says.

Jenkins nods to Kennedy, who now says, "So you've driven down to Woodstock a few times?"

Taft looks at them both questioningly.

Kennedy says, "On the floorboard of your car, McKinnon found a receipt from the local Sunoco station in Woodstock. Your family lives in Newport, in the Northeast Kingdom. Even a flatlander like myself knows that Woodstock is not exactly on your route home."

With a gloomy expression, Taft looks down at the table. "Yeah, I went down there."

"To spy on them," Kennedy says.

He looks up at her. "I'm not that fucking desperate."

"So why, then?"

"I just wanted to see where Luc was going all those weekends and coming back so fucking happy."

"I thought you said he was miserable," says Kennedy.

"Later he was. In December, he was happy."

Jenkins asks, "How many times did you drive down to Woodstock?"

Taft holds up two hooked fingers. "Twice last fall."

"And did you drive down there recently?"

Taft leans forward and shakes his head miserably.

Kennedy nods to Jenkins, who says, "A woman who works

for Sam happened to see your friends, the twins' Jeep parked down the street from his house."

Taft looks up now, first at one detective and then the other.

Kennedy says, "Do you want to tell us why you drove to Mark and Howard Newcombe's house and borrowed their Jeep?"

Taft exhales forcefully. "I didn't drive to their house to borrow their car. They live a mile from the Route 12 turnoff. My car kept stalling out. On bad gas. I didn't think I'd make it, so I just stopped at their place and asked to borrow theirs."

"Hell-bent to get to South Woodstock," Kennedy intones.

"Did the Newcombe twins know where you were going when you borrowed their car?" Jenkins asks.

"No."

"You didn't tell them where you were going?" Kennedy asks.

"No."

"So they just let you borrow it?" Jenkins says.

"They like me. They like hanging with college kids and giving them workout advice."

Jenkins says, "So you borrowed the Newcombes' car. Drove to Sam Solomon's, stole his car, and then drove to the house of his dog-sitter. And waited. Why?"

"Because she helped get him off. Because I knew exactly where he was at 6:28 p.m. on February eleventh."

"But why did you steal Sam's car?"

"Why did you let him off because of what a fucking dog-sitter says?" Taft fumes.

"You thought that if you ran her off the road with Sam Solomon's car, she would change her story and take back what she said," Kennedy says, incredulous.

"Would have done it with my own car if I'd had it."

"Oh, so you didn't want to bring any heat on your drug dealer friends."

"Right."

"Their car was still spotted," Jenkins says.

"Got to say, your thinking here makes no sense," Kennedy says.

Taft shrugs. "It is what it is. I don't care anymore."

"So let's get back to the Newcombes," Jenkins says. "They met you in Carleton the night Luc went missing."

"Right."

"You went to them directly from going back to the pond?" Kennedy says.

"Yes."

"Where did you meet them?"

"Just a bit south on Route 7."

"More specifically?"

"There's a pullover spot."

"What if we told you that somebody spotted their camo Jeep driving on the road Luc took after he left the pond."

Taft goes still and then shakes his head resolutely. "Look, I borrowed their car. I met up with them. But they have no connection to the rest of this."

"How can you be so sure?" Kennedy asks.

"Because I told you that I saw him—Sam—leaving the pond."

"But you're not completely positive you saw him," Jenkins says.

"Okay, then I saw somebody who looked just like him."

"Then all the more reason to have reported it earlier," Kennedy says. "The fact that you never told us you went back to the pond undermines your credibility."

Taft doesn't respond. Kennedy nods to Jenkins, who says, "Did you drive down to Sam Solomon's house last night?"

Taft hesitates.

"Did you drive—in your own car—down to Sam Solomon's house last night?" Kennedy repeats.

Taft looks at each of them with bewilderment before saying, "Yes."

"Did you go inside his house?" Jenkins asks.

"Yes."

"Why?"

Taft flares up. "To tell him that I was on to him. That I knew he was there. At the pond."

"But you didn't tell him?"

"I waited two hours for him, and then I just couldn't stand being there anymore."

Jenkins says, "And the gun we found in your car. What were you going to do with that gun?"

"Because if he killed Luc, maybe he'd try and kill me, too."

Both detectives let this statement settle into the charged atmosphere of the room. Then, after several beats of silence, Kennedy says, "Look at me right here." She points to both of her eyes with her middle and index fingers. "Did you put his dog outside?"

Taft looks bewildered. "No. Why?"

"Did you see the dog?" Jenkins asks.

"Of course I saw the dog."

"You've seen the dog before," Kennedy says.

"Yes."

"When you drove up in the Jeep and stole Sam's car."

Taft nods.

"She didn't bark at you then. Why is that?"

"Because I gave her meat treats."

"And yesterday?"

"She barked at me, she was playful, and then she ran away in the house. I didn't see her after that."

Jenkins says quietly, "Sam Solomon came home and found her dead."

Both are watching Taft. "What do you mean?" he says, looking appalled.

Kennedy says, "He found his dog outside. Dead."

"Somebody killed her?"

"We think you killed her," Kennedy says.

"You think I shot her?"

"No, we think you left her outside, where she froze to death," Jenkins says.

Taft is distraught. "Look, I did stuff, okay? I creeped into Luc's computer. I went into his boyfriend's house. I looked for shit. 'Cause I fucking hate that guy. But I didn't do anything to his dog. I swear to God!" he screams. Tears are flooding Taft's eyes. "I would never do something like that. I love animals. I grew up with dogs like her. I love mutts." He breaks down completely and they allow him a minute to collect himself.

"You think maybe you didn't close the door properly?" Kennedy says with a bit more sympathy.

Taft covers his eyes with his hands. "I closed it," he agonizes. "But I don't know for sure."

They watch Taft carefully, and his reaction, his claim of innocence regarding Sam's dog, strikes Jenkins as credible. "The wind," Kennedy says at last. "I suppose the wind could have opened it."

They wait until Taft has somewhat recovered from the news of Sam's dog. Then Jenkins resumes, "If Sam had come home, what exactly did you plan on saying to him?"

There is no trace of anger left on Taft's face, just misery and hopelessness. He's barely able to articulate, "To tell him I know he did it."

"Did what?"

"Murdered Luc."

Both detectives stare at Taft and say no more.

"I don't understand why you're just letting him off!" Taft cries out at last. "I don't understand why you aren't questioning him again."

"Well," Jenkins says. "If what you say is true, we will be questioning him again."

FEBRUARY 24; ROUTE 89 SOUTH TO WOODSTOCK, VERMONT; 21 DEGREES, FREEZING RAIN

"We'd like to come and see you," Jenkins tells Sam. "Detective Kennedy and I. Can you make yourself available?" There is a dire yet flat tone to Jenkins's voice, and Sam, in the midst of studying the depths and dimensions of a sunroom in a set of mechanical drawings of a house he is redesigning, watches the indigo lines of his carefully written specifications blur before his eyes. He manages to ask when and Jenkins says, "We're ready to drive down there right now if that can work for you."

There is a stunned pause. "Did you find Luc?"

"We have not found him."

"Then can you tell me what's going on?"

"We'll be there soon, in an hour or so."

"Can't this be done now, on the phone?"

There is a lull before Jenkins replies, "I'd rather meet face-to-face."

"Okay," Sam says reluctantly. "I'm here."

Looking ahead of them on Route 89 through the sheets of freezing rain that strike the windshield with a hollow popping sound, Jenkins says, "It's well below freezing. I don't understand, why aren't we getting snow?"

"Inversion layer," Kennedy remarks. "Happens more often now because of global warming. The guy who plows my driveway said fifteen years ago, they sanded driveways maybe once or twice a winter for ice. Now they're up to seven or eight times."

"And yet we still get plenty of below zero weather?"

"I think the flip side of global warming is polar vortex," Kennedy says.

Jenkins snorts.

A small green Mazda Miata convertible that passes their unmarked car on the left momentarily diverts their attention. The top is down and they can clearly see the driver is a young-ish guy, probably in his twenties. His longish hair is flapping in the freezing wind. He seems impervious to the weather.

"What the hell," Kennedy says. "It's twenty-one degrees. Why is he driving with the top down? Did he just get out of the mental ward?"

Jenkins says, "Maybe he's an athlete training for some cold weather event."

Kennedy says, "I think it's reckless. I think that kind of thing should be illegal."

Jenkins says, "We've got enough going on."

Kennedy flips her hand in a dismissive gesture.

"I don't think I've ever told you this. But the more time I spend in the state of Vermont, the more it reminds me of when I lived in California," Jenkins says.

"How so?"

"Higher volume of wingnuts in Vermont than I ever thought."

A few moments elapse and then Kennedy says, "Yeah, wingnuts." Jenkins can feel her eyes carefully surveying him. "So where are you now, Nick?"

"Where am I now? Sam never got those emails is where I am right now."

"You can't accuse me of lying to you," Sam says quietly to Jenkins. "I told you when you first questioned me that Heather called me around five fifteen. I never tried to make it seem that I couldn't get up to Carleton." Panda's strange, inexplicable death is weighing heavily on him, and he's just plain weary of worrying. Right now, he feels curiously detached from it all.

"But why did she lie on your behalf?" Kennedy says.

"Why? I think she really believes she called me right before the evening news."

Kennedy says, "Have you known her to have . . . cognitive problems remembering?"

"Not at all. She always seems to be pretty on top of everything. I mean, just the fact that she thought to call me because she was afraid I hadn't brought enough food for . . . my dog," he says, struck by a pang of desolation.

Jenkins ponders this for a moment and then says, "Speaking of your dog, I don't think Taft is lying about that."

"Oh?"

"Taft claims to loves dogs. I believe him."

Sam now admits, "That door has always been a problem. I've come home a few times to find it flung open." Then again, it's a lot easier for him to believe that no malice had ever been directed toward his dog.

They are all situated in the living room, Sam sitting stiffly upright on a distressed leather loveseat, Jenkins occupying a wingback chair. Kennedy, who has taken a wooden ice cream parlor chair away from the kitchen table, is sitting right next to Jenkins, so that Sam can speak to both of them simultaneously without having to look from one to the other.

"So Taft believes he saw you leaving the pond," Jenkins announces quietly.

The real reason why they've driven down there, Sam concludes miserably. He stares at the blue fiberglass encasement of his broken leg, feeling imprisoned by it, wishing he could release himself from it and pace the room in a frenzy. "Then why did he wait until now to say something?"

"Because we already suspected you," Kennedy says. "That it was only a matter of time before we'd find proof. And that if he'd admitted to going back to the pond, he'd end up being a suspect himself. And that would only take the pressure off you."

"And you don't think that sounds suspicious?" Sam says with disgust.

"Of course it does," Kennedy says. "But sometimes people who are innocent have more trouble trying to explain—or even extricate—themselves than people who are guilty and know they have to concoct lies."

Sam takes this in for a moment and then says, "Then I guess you have a choice. To believe him or to believe me."

At this, they hear a car pull into the driveway.

"That must be Mike," Sam says, catching a look of annoyance on Jenkins's face. "He called me right after you did—he calls me every day to check in—and I told him you were coming and he said he wanted to talk to you. He has a light day at work," he explains just as Mike bursts into the room.

"I need to say. . ." he announces to them all as he shrugs off his leather bomber jacket and throws it on a spindled wooden bench chair next to the door. "And I probably should've said it way earlier."

With a severe look on his face, Jenkins turns both his hands over. "You need to say?"

"I was at the pond on the night Luc Flanders disappeared. I didn't do anything to him. But I was there."

He didn't do anything to him. Sam's vision narrows with

a rush of blood while the light in the room begins pulsing in strobe-like syncopation. He's suddenly dizzy, even a bit nauseous, and can't quite believe what has just been said. The confession, meanwhile, has caused a general commotion.

"Sit down," Jenkins orders Mike.

"How could you have been there?" Sam demands.

"Just wait a second." Pointing to an empty club chair that is some distance away from the gathering of other chairs, Kennedy says, "Bring that one over here."

Mike complies.

"Okay," Jenkins says. "So let's have it."

Mike begins, "It was literally a five-minute conversation between Luc and me."

"A conversation," Kennedy repeats.

"About someone we both really cared about." He glances worriedly at Sam.

"What do you mean by 'cared about'?" Kennedy asks.

"I mean like . . . best-friend-cared-about, at least from my end. I guess from Luc's perspective, romantic-love-cared-about."

"So wait, you drove up to Carleton from Boston and back to Boston in time to meet me at the airport?" Sam says.

"Yes."

"Three hours both ways just to have a five-minute conversation with Luc?"

"Sam," Jenkins warns. "You need to stop talking. This is not your investigation."

Sam ignores him. "Why didn't you say anything about this before, Mike?" He slams his fist down on the arm of his chair. "You know what's been going on!"

Mike glances at Jenkins and then at Kennedy, who says, "Go ahead and answer him."

"Wait," Jenkins says.

"Nick." Kennedy surprises Sam with a tone of pleading in her voice. "Just let him talk."

"Fine," Jenkins agrees at last.

Mike resumes, "I didn't say anything because I truly believed that what happened to Luc had nothing to do with my talking to him. And I also thought that if I said something, it would've made things worse for you," he tells Sam.

"Worse for me? How? That's ludicrous!" Looking at Jenkins, Sam says, "I can't believe I'm hearing this."

Jenkins says to Mike, "Tell us why you think it would have made things worse."

Tears are flooding Mike's different-colored eyes. "Okay."

On February eleventh, he had impulsively driven up to Carleton from Boston. "I just felt that I had to talk to Luc, to try and get through to him. When I was able to find his address from the campus directory, I left Boston convinced that I'd find him. I drove right to his apartment. And bingo, he was leaving just as I got there." He recognized Luc—from the photographs Sam had shown him—in his funky military overcoat and his hat with its two Slavic-looking earflaps. Luc was headed toward the pack of Carleton college students who were trekking up and down the lanes of the institution in the early darkness.

Mike quickly parked and followed. The moon paved the way on the path to Skylight Pond, and both men were able to walk in concert with each other, Mike significantly behind. As he followed Luc, Mike rehearsed what he would say. He would tell Luc how much Sam was suffering, that it was more than just depression over the breakup. That it was a crisis of faith in love itself. He believed that Sam, hitting fifty, felt doomed to be alone for the rest of his life and just might be tempted to do something reckless.

When they reached the pond, Mike saw Luc beaming his flashlight against the snow and the ice that had been sheared for the miniature, makeshift hockey rink. Luc was beginning to cross the frozen plane when Mike called out, "Hey, Luc," and watched him stiffen and hunch over, giving the impression of being caught in the act of doing something covert.

Luc whirled around, shining his flashlight in Mike's eyes. "Who are you?"

"I'm Mike, Sam's friend from Boston. You've probably seen photos of me. I've seen photos of you."

Luc collected himself and slowly walked toward Mike until they were a foot away from each other, their nervous breath accumulating in frosty pillows around them, the cold air burning their lungs. Holding the illuminated flashlight in one hand like some Norse deity, six-foot-two Luc was towering over him, a sad, pained, quizzical look on his face. "What are you doing here? How did you find me?"

"I saw you walking away from your apartment. I came up here because I need to talk to you."

Luc crossed his free arm over his chest. "Talk to me about?"

"About Sam."

Luc's voice softened. "About Sam? Is he okay?"

"No, he's not okay. He's not sick or anything . . . but then again, he's really gutted over this breakup."

"He's not the only one," Luc said. "Gutted over the breakup. I don't know how I can help him if I can't even help myself. And it's pretty douchy of you to drive up here and expect to just talk to me like this. I don't suppose he knows you're here."

"He doesn't."

"Are you going to tell him?"

"Probably. He'll probably be angry."

"Knowing Sam, he'll be fucking furious!" Luc said. "So what do you want from me?"

Struck by Luc's palpable distress, Mike said, "Communicate with him. Don't let him twist in the wind. He's about to go out to Utah with me. I know he'd love to hear from you before he leaves tonight. Just pick up your phone and call him tonight is all I ask."

"I've already reached out to him," Luc flared with hostility. "He never responds to my emails. Except for a few stupid text messages."

"But then why haven't you replied . . . to the texts?"

"Did you hear me? He hasn't even answered my emails!"

"Your emails?" Mike repeated. "Sam never said anything about getting your emails."

"Maybe he's done with me and just doesn't want to talk to you about it, his straight buddy from Boston who drove all the way up here to creep after his ex," Luc said with noticeable irony. "You're probably about as straight as I am."

"Well, everybody thinks you are—straight—don't they?"

"That's my problem, thank you. I've been lying to nearly everybody. And I'm sick of lying, to be honest." It got windy suddenly, and granules of snow stung their eyes. Luc wiped his and looked down at Mike. "So maybe I can detect lies from other people."

"Look, I love Sam like a brother," Mike told him, "like family. But I am not in love with him. You don't have to be into guys to love another guy—a dear friend—to love him enough to want to do anything you can to help him."

"Wait, wait, wait. Hang on one second," Jenkins interrupts, and then to Kennedy, "Luc had a flashlight."

Kennedy says, "McKinnon says he never came by to get it."

"So then where did he get a flashlight?"

Kennedy says, "I'll verify this once again with McKinnon." Turning to Mike, "Do you recall what kind of flashlight it was?"

"It was a small one. I think it was an LED."

"Go on with your story," Kennedy says.

"I thought Luc was bold-faced lying about the emails and was just doing it to shut down the conversation, to get rid of me," Mike says. Then to Sam, "Do you remember when we were flying out to Utah, when I asked if you'd heard from him?"

Sam nods.

"I felt there was something weird and evasive about the way you said you hadn't heard." Now facing Jenkins and Kennedy, Mike says, "After everything happened in Utah, after Sam's accident, I started to wonder if Luc was actually telling the truth and"—he turns to Sam again—"that maybe you had read the emails and just didn't want me to know you'd read them. And then later on, when the emails were discovered to have been read and deleted, you claimed not to have been the one who read and deleted them. Because at the pond Luc told me—he insisted—that in those emails he'd begged you for a meeting. And ever since then I've kept wondering how three emails could possibly have failed to reach you. Or perhaps I should say somebody read them but you never did."

"I don't know how!" Sam cries.

Mike hesitates, his two-colored eyes darting like a cornered animal. "So I eventually decided that the emails did get to you. That you had read them. And I didn't want to bring that up against you."

Sam says, "I swear on everything that is sacred to me. I swear on the life of Luc Flanders, I did not get them!" He stops, realizing that swearing on the life of Luc Flanders is probably the worst thing he can possibly say.

Looking even more distressed, Mike shakes his head and mutters something unintelligible. "Just need to finish." He glances at Kennedy and Jenkins. "So I started to believe that Sam denied receiving those emails because he didn't want anyone to think he actually had a pressing reason, an agreement to meet up with Luc in Carleton the night we left for Utah." Now he can't even look at Sam.

It's supremely difficult but Sam knows he has to remain embedded reasonably in the conversation. "But, Mike, don't you think that would be a desperate denial if I were lying, if I actually had read the emails? How could I have faked something like that? How could I have hidden that from you, my best friend in the world?"

Mike shrugs and says, "I thought the same thing. But then I thought maybe you had to lie."

Sam happens to notice Kennedy throwing Jenkins a quizzical look. Jenkins shakes his head slowly and then says to Mike, "Okay, so let's move on. What happened next between you and Luc?"

"He took a step toward me and said, 'Get the hell out of here! Leave me alone! Tell Sam have a great time!' He was sarcastic." Mike remembers seeing a vague expression on the younger man's face, a look that oddly was not in keeping with his angry outburst. "So I walked away. I was off the pond and heading along the path when I heard some commotion and turned around. It was dark, obviously, but from where I was, it looked like he'd slipped and fallen on the ice again and was lying on his stomach. I started back toward him, but then I stopped because I saw him getting up. He looked shaky. And then he noticed that I hadn't left. 'I told you to leave me alone,' he yelled at me. And then I walked back to the campus. I walked back to my car."

Everything is crashing down: the terrible demise of Panda; the endless two-week vigil for news of Luc; and now this confirmation of the suspicion harbored by his best friend, who, at last, is staring at him unrelentingly, his mismatched eyes flickering nervously. Sam says, "So all this time you were covering for me. All this time you believed that I went up to Carleton, that I saw Luc on February eleventh, and that I've been lying about it."

Pondering this for a moment, Mike says, "All I can say is when I left Carleton to drive back to Boston, there was still time for you to have driven up there yourself."

Nobody speaks for several moments. At last, Jenkins says, "Mike, about those emails." Glancing meaningfully at Sam, he says, "Sam never got them. We now know somebody else intercepted those emails and read them. So Sam is not lying about this."

"Why the hell didn't you say this earlier?" Sam cries out.

"Because, once again, you need to let me handle this," Jenkins tells him quietly but forcefully.

Kennedy asks Mike, "So when Sam told you we were on the way, you just dropped everything to drive up here?"

"I figured you'd finally found evidence against him and maybe were going to arrest him. I wanted . . . to be here. I wanted to make sure all the facts were in."

Jenkins says, "Well, the facts are in. But we could also construe that you hid your trip up to Carleton because you were afraid of being suspected."

Mike shrugs. "You're certainly welcome to suspect me."

"I need to ask Mike something," Sam says.

"Go on," Jenkins says, lackadaisically waving a hand.

"Why drive all the way up to Carleton the very night we're supposed to go out west? Why not another time? Why in such a tight time frame?"

Shaking his head, Mike says, "Like I told you, Sam, it was because of Black Diamond Fall. It came to me that Luc would have been constantly on your mind before we skied it, while we skied it. That thinking about him could have been a distraction. I was hoping that if I could get him to contact you the same night we were leaving, you'd feel better. That you'd be able to focus on hiking up onto the ridge and making the descent. That you'd be able to ski free. Ski free of him. But then, just like I feared, you pushed it too hard. You fell and you almost died. And like I've told you before, I began to wonder if your fall was deliberate, like it was some kind of death wish. Maybe because he was already dead? Maybe because . . . well, because maybe you'd done something to him yourself?"

There is a long, wretched silence following this. At last, Mike says, "But there is another thing. When Sam called and told me you were on your way, I remembered . . . a flash of something that I, for some reason . . . hadn't considered. Or maybe, maybe I just didn't want to think about it because I didn't really understand it. I don't know, I . . . don't blank me, Sam, please!" Mike cries. "Look at me!" And Sam does. "When I was leaving the pond, when I was walking along the path, I think I saw somebody else walking away."

"Who was that?" Jenkins demands.

FEBRUARY 25; CARLETON, VERMONT; 40 DEGREES, UNSEASONABLY WARM

In the campus police conference room sits a young lawyer with fashionable scruff, dressed in a slim-fitting tailored suit. The guy has long hair pulled back and twined into a bun, and he wears expensive-looking tortoiseshell glasses.

"Did you see that hipster with the hair bun who arrived from Jersey?" Kennedy remarks to Jenkins out in the hall.

"That's what all upwardly mobile youth look like in the metro areas," Jenkins comments.

As they file into the cramped, book-lined room, Jenkins looks up at the small crosshatched windows viewing the monotonous gray afternoon. Remembering the last time he was there with Elizabeth and Portia Dominic, he feels a bit of transitory claustrophobia. Introductions are made, necessary pleasantries exchanged, and once everyone is seated around the large cherry wood conference table, the young lawyer presents Kennedy and Jenkins with a sheaf of interrogatory guidelines. Perusing them, Jenkins has difficulty hiding his skepticism. "We've never spoken before, have we?"

"We have not," the guy says with ridiculous-sounding formality.

"How come Thompson didn't come up?"

"He was called away to California."

"You're an associate?"

"Correct."

Jenkins looks hard at him, refraining from saying "junior associate." "Okay, well, some of this is just plain wrong. The restrictions. They can't be met. Because we have proof that . . ." He glances at Elizabeth. "Let's just say that we demand leeway if someone we've questioned hasn't been forthcoming." He regards Elizabeth, who looks surprisingly calm. "Besides, we only want to question Ms. Squires about a few things that she neglected to mention to us. Shouldn't take very long. Let's see how far we can get without you trying to shut this whole thing down."

The lawyer noticeably stiffens but agrees.

"I am going to turn the questioning over to my colleague, Detective Kennedy. Detective?" Jenkins says.

Seated opposite him, Kennedy is dressed casually in a black untucked shirt and black trousers. "Hello, Elizabeth," she says, "thanks for coming in again."

"It's fine," Elizabeth replies nervously.

Glancing at her yellow legal notepad, Kennedy cogitates for a moment and then looks up. "So let's begin with the fact that when we questioned you, you kept to yourself the fact that you walked back toward Skylight Pond the night Luc Flanders went missing."

Brushing wings of hair out of her eyes, Elizabeth says in a hoarse voice, "Charlie and I decided it was no big deal. Because we never ended up running into Luc."

They've decided that it's best—at least at first—to soft-pedal the fact that Elizabeth Squires lied. "So you never saw him, Luc, the second time you were there?"

Elizabeth shakes her head. "No, we didn't."

Kennedy looks meaningfully at Jenkins, who nods slightly. And then to Elizabeth, "When we asked you what you did that night, you easily could have told us. By not telling us, you were obstructing our investigation."

"She's aware of that, Detective," says the attorney briskly.

Elizabeth speaks up, "Like I said, Charlie described it like going for a walk anywhere else around campus. And not running into a person we expected to see. I went along with that. That's why we didn't say anything."

"So you didn't have a mind of your own on this?"

"No, I didn't."

"And Charlie Taft just happened to arrive at the same place at the same time you did, but coming from a different direction?"

"Correct."

"And he told you he came to look for Luc?"

"Yes."

"Did he tell you why?" Jenkins asks.

"To help Luc find whatever he lost."

Kennedy says, "How did he know Luc lost something?"

"Because Luc . . . was upset and said he lost something."

"Did he say what he lost?"

"To me he did."

"And you told Charlie Taft what Luc said he lost?"

"Yes."

Slightly raising her eyebrows, Kennedy glances at Jenkins, who nods. "Did Taft ask you why you'd come there?" she continues.

Glancing at her lawyer, Elizabeth sighs and says, "I told him why."

"Okay, why? Tell us again, why."

"I just wanted to talk to him, to Luc, again. I thought it would make me feel better."

"I see. So was it a difficult conversation that you had with Luc?" Kennedy momentarily looks sad herself. Jenkins is actually stumped by this unforeseen reaction in his tough-minded colleague.

"It wasn't really. But I still felt bad."

"Because the breakup was recent?"

Elizabeth nervously exhales. "Yes."

Despite her words to the contrary, it dawns on Jenkins that Elizabeth Squires has a cooler, more detached demeanor than when he'd previously questioned her several days before.

It's as if she's already moving beyond Luc Flanders; yes, he's observed that some people develop an automatic revulsion to the demise of a person who never really loved them. But then, too, kids of twenty-two pick up and go on more quickly than somebody such as himself, mired in love with a woman whose feelings for him, disconcerting as it is, seem to have faded over time.

Jenkins interjects, "Did you ever get a sense from Charlie Taft that he had feelings for Luc?"

"Not at first."

"Had you figured it out when you two met up the night Luc disappeared?"

"No. Not yet."

"So when did you figure it out?" Kennedy asks.

"I suspected. But then, two nights ago . . ." she says.

"He admitted it to you," Jenkins fills in the gap.

"Well, not exactly."

"Tell us," says Kennedy.

"He was going on about how Sam got off and how he was sure Sam did it. And then I just said, 'You're in love with Luc yourself, aren't you, Charlie?' And then he just flipped out."

"Where did this conversation occur?" Jenkins asks.

"In front of his apartment."

Kennedy says, "What was your reaction?"

"I was mad, too."

"Why were you mad?"

"Because he'd made mean comments about Luc being gay. And then he seemed to be in love with Luc himself."

"Did Taft actually admit to being in love with Luc Flanders?"

"No, I guess not really."

When Jenkins glances at Kennedy again, she tilts her head to the left, prodding him to ask the follow-up question they both have rehearsed. He shakes his head slightly. He still wants to wait. Squires needs to soften up just a bit more.

"Let's just keep going," he tells Kennedy. "So Charlie Taft told you he was going back to the pond to help Luc find what he lost. Did you wonder if he was going back to the pond for another reason?" Jenkins asks.

"No."

Kennedy continues, "Did you get the sense that Taft was deliberately escorting you away from the pond?"

"Yes, I did."

"As if he perhaps didn't want you to see something."

"Pretty much."

"And you didn't wonder what it was that he didn't want you to see or why he was escorting you away?"

"Not then, no. But I did later on."

Twirling her pencil with one hand, Kennedy leans back in her chair, her eyes narrowing with inner calculation. "Do you think you'd have gotten an inkling if Charlie and Luc had had some kind of altercation?"

Elizabeth shakes her head with a look of bafflement that makes it seem as though she's already wrestled with this idea. "Hard to say. I don't know. Charlie did seem agitated."

"Charlie said you seemed pretty agitated, " Kennedy points out.

"I was."

Jenkins interjects, "When, as you say, Charlie Taft called you a few days after Luc went back to the pond and then disappeared and suggested that you both deny being anywhere near him, didn't you wonder if maybe Charlie had another reason for suggesting you both keep quiet?"

"No, not then." Glancing sharply at her attorney, Elizabeth adds, "And I mean, really, if I thought something had happened between them, I would've spoken up about it."

"Would you have?" Jenkins says quietly but emphatically.

"Even though you promised Taft you wouldn't?" Kennedy adds.

Elizabeth falters. "I would have spoken up if I thought he'd done something wrong to Luc."

Kennedy now looks intently at Jenkins, who picks up.

"Elizabeth, as you know, we're trying to figure out whom Luc Flanders might have encountered once he left you at your dorm and went back to Skylight Pond. We have one person that you don't know about, somebody—and not Sam Solomon—that Luc actually did meet up with while he was at the pond."

Elizabeth looks frightened. "Really?" she says in a hoarse voice. "Was it a woman?"

"Do you think it might have been a woman?" Kennedy asks.

Now observing that Elizabeth seems to be rattled, Jenkins poses the question that he and Kennedy have decided he would ask. "Anyway, we began this . . . discussion by asking why you neglected to tell us you'd decided to go back toward the pond. Is there anything else that you haven't told us?"

Not even glancing at the attorney, Elizabeth says, "No."

Jenkins continues, "You indicate that Charlie Taft said 'he just knew' Sam did something to Luc, but did he actually ever say that he saw Sam walking toward Skylight Pond?"

"He said he thought he saw him."

"So Charlie didn't seem sure he saw him?" Kennedy says softly.

"No, he didn't seem sure."

"Elizabeth," Kennedy says and waits until the young woman's eyes are trained on her. "Like I said before, we know of somebody else who did meet up with Luc. At the pond."

Jenkins says, "We questioned this man yesterday. However, we don't have any reason to believe he harmed Luc Flanders. But when this man was leaving, he happened to see someone heading toward the pond, somebody just about to arrive there." Jenkins looks down on a single page of a lined notepad that contains the words that he reads aloud. "'It was almost at the lip of the ice. The moon was bright enough for me to see that her parka was light blue.'" He now glances up.

Elizabeth's face is suffused with a crimson flush; her lawyer is glaring at them.

Kennedy says quietly but sternly, "According to this man, Luc had a flashlight. This flashlight." She pulls a plastic bag out of her pocket and shoves it across the table toward Elizabeth, who gives the small, square LED a frozen glance. "I spoke to your roommate, Portia Dominic, who told me that on the night of February eleventh, you gave this to Luc Flanders right in front of her. I'm assuming that after you did whatever you did to him, you decided to take the flashlight you lent him back home with you. So now, Elizabeth, you need to tell us the entire truth." Kennedy throws the lawyer a withering glance and tells him, "Either way, we're taking her into custody."

FEBRUARY 25; DONNER'S FIELD, THE HAY BALE, WEYBRIDGE, VERMONT; 25 DEGREES, SNOW

Luc's body is slowly shutting down, his organs slowly giving up. The languor of dreaming stays with him. He vaguely remembers an uncle with kidney disease who'd asked a physician about stopping dialysis and what would happen to his body. And the answer: that he'd slowly fade away, overcome by fatigue, eat and drink less and less, and eventually just slip into sleep. Not so bad, his uncle had said. Not so bad.

Luc has consumed most of the snow around him and now desperately needs water. He's too weak to leave where he is and take in what will sustain him. And then admits there is part of him that would let go. After all, he believes he has put Sam off forever, and what's left if that possibility has perished?

Hard to believe that Sam received none of his emails. Mike surely was lying. Or maybe Sam was lying to Mike about having received them. Then again, Luc knows that Sam just got tired of the pain. Understandable. Especially since Luc was the one who ended it, and ended it because he was losing control, his fear of rejection getting the better of him. He thinks of his parents, no longer in love but forced to live together. How they're dead and numb to each other. How it's safer not to feel anything. And yet he can't imagine not having any feeling for Sam.

It was humiliating to be cut down by somebody half his size. First feeling the gentle breath grazing the back of his exposed neck. Then the blur of a body coming from behind him. The rage of the rejected. The missile of the small woman tackling him, her small fists beating on his back, shoving him

as hard as she could. Falling forward. Her hands on the back
of his head, slamming his forehead against the ice. "What are
you doing?" he managed to cry out. She didn't answer except
with grunts and gasps as she exploded against him. And then
one word escaped her breathily. "Fag!" He just let her flail at
him because he knew he deserved her anger. But when his
forehead smashed against the ice, he was propelled back into
disconnection.

She was gone when he woke up to the wind and to the
frozen kiss of the ice that seemed as harsh and brittle as a
blade. What possessed him to muster the strength to stand
up? What compelled him to drag himself over the ice until
he regained his sense of balance?

A long, arduous, zombie-like march of mile after mile
until out of nowhere came those guys in the Jeep, the guys
Taft and McKinnon get their drugs from.

Recognizing him, the one with the weird-looking, unfo-
cused eyes rolled down his window and asked where he was
going. "To my car, down the road," he lied to them. Then
accepting a ride and climbing in with those whack jobs that
rambled on about bodybuilding and teenage girls. And telling
him that Taft has to watch his intake, that Taft has 'roid rage.
And remembering the day before when Taft had actually
complained that he was getting too big and that his balls had
shrunk and how he'd laughed about it with McKinnon. "No,
I'm not interested," he told the Newcombe twins when they
offered him something they called a "stack." "I don't have the
money. And why don't you lay off selling to my roommates!
If Taft has 'roid rage, then maybe what you're selling to him is
fucking him up!" And then the twins went quiet and Luc got
nervous and asked to be dropped off.

And just walked until light was no longer cloistered and
flames began to curl at the edge of the sky, and the smell of
wood smoke from the chimney of a farmhouse. Faint frissons

of music and the droning tones of public radio personalities. Cars in their early morning cortège beginning to drive by and inquiring faces peering at him. He decided he really wanted to be lying in a place where he couldn't be found. He had dreams of leaving, of being somewhere with his eyes open and empty of everything except the deepest shadows.

Dry snowflakes falling on the pasture. The undulate furrows filling with snow and glyphs on the surface hewn by the unforgiving wind. His body generating surprising warmth in this makeshift straw cave.

The warmth of Sam's body, the heat of making love, the difference between the body of a man and a woman. The shock and excitement of a face that needs to be shaved, and no matter how close, the shave will never be as soft as Elizabeth's face looking up at him with that certain tenderness he sees only in women.

The tenderness he saw even when they were completely consumed in their own pleasure. The softness of their bodies that he was penetrating with the hardness of his own. If only that could have sustained him. But hunger was ignited inside him when he was the one being entered. And he even—foolishly—thought that hunger would make him a better lover to Elizabeth. Knowing what it was like to want that and to get it, wouldn't that lend him a better understanding of how to give it? But it just didn't work that way; once he'd gone through the crucible of being passive and wanting passivity, he suddenly no longer felt as complete in being active. And knew that he was lying to himself and to her, but how would he have known this if he hadn't tried being with a woman again? How could he have been sure about his desire? And that was what he'd told Sam in his first letter, what he'd tried to explain, that the last time they made love, he took that risk because he wanted—at least once in his life—to feel that he couldn't be closer to another human being than he was the night he begged Sam to keep going and not stop for any reason, to do what would have been the most natural act in the first order of the world. And maybe even then he was in some way already aware there wasn't much time left for him.

And even though Luc worried, he carefully hid this worry from Sam, who foolishly believed that Luc was unconcerned because he was too young to have context on a fatal illness transmitted by sex; that much younger people never felt the same impulse to be careful. And yet even then, even though Luc knew he wanted to break off the relationship, he felt that if a virus had passed between them, it didn't and somehow just wouldn't matter in the end, and lying in Sam's bed, their legs intertwined, the talk turned to other things, to skiing, to the world cup, to hiking up Moosilauke.

As sleep comes on again, like a heavy elixir, like release, a vision is scrolling before his tired eyes like celluloid: the sharp peaks of a western mountain range, a bluebird day, he and Sam with skis strapped to their back ascending, stopping to collect their breath, which is noticeably shallow at ten thousand feet, crossing a narrow divide between steep slopes that cannot be descended because of sheer cliffs that would fling someone into oblivion. And then the entrance to the headwall off a five-foot cornice, Sam hesitating but Luc launching himself and a soft landing and then making those first fresh turns on a blanket of snow that nobody has touched, quick turns down a chute that is only slightly wider than the length of his skis, but caught up in the rhythm and sheer delight of mastering a slope whose difficulty is so extreme and remote that you need avalanche gear. But then he sees something, a shadow crossing over the sun, over the steel glint of the ice, and wonders for the first time if Sam made it all the way down Black Diamond Fall.

Dear Sam:

I hope this reaches you before you leave for Utah. I hope you have a great trip. I will think of you out there and will wish it was me skiing Black Diamond Fall with you like we said we might. Didn't we say we might one day? I know I really let you down. But I got scared, not so much of people knowing or anything like that, but scared that it would only be you, and nobody else but you, for the rest of my life. How could I have known this so soon? And what if something happens to you and I have to live for a long time without you? But now I realize I made a mistake. You are everything to me, and I just have to go with it.

I don't think I ever really explained it to you, how even though the injury did all kinds of weird shit to me, the fact that I heard music when we made love made me believe that you and I had something. And even when I said goodbye to you that day when I felt I had to, I knew I probably would never hear that music again when I made love to anyone else or have the feeling that making love could be like finding God.

There isn't a moment when I don't think about you. There isn't a moment when I don't need you. I tried being with Elizabeth, but she quickly figured things out and couldn't bear me as I was, and I had to let her go. I really can't blame her for hating me. Now I know it's better this way because, like I said, the day we were watching U.S. women's soccer against Japan, I can't get married with this sort of feeling for another man burning a hole inside of me. It would be unfair. And you agreed. I was resigned to it, but I still was afraid of staying with you. But now I'm no longer afraid. Now I want you.

I'm sorry for breaking us apart, Sam. I'm sorry about breaking you. I'm sorry I'm not older. I'm sorry I ran away. I realize that you might not be able to forgive this and might go on without me. And of course I will try and understand.

All my love,
Luc

The bodybuilder twins, Howard and Mark Newcombe, have been told that their cooperation with the search for Luc Flanders will be factored into the length of their sentencing for vandalizing the Frost farm. They have no idea that Elizabeth Squires has been arrested and charged with assault.

"Right here. We dropped him right here," says Mark, the walleyed twin, just as the patrol car reaches the end of London's Field, a long pasture in Weybridge, just outside of the boundaries of Carleton. Jenkins brakes and a cloud of salty dust rises off the dry, winter-beaten dirt road.

Beyond them a long expanse of snowfield, in bare patches, shows the stubble of straw. A line of carefully planted larch trees limns the far perimeter. It's a cold, bleak place, like some end-of-the-earth place and yet located in one of the smallest states of America. Vast for Vermont, anyway, it's a field big enough for a jumbo airplane to land. Out of the contemplative silence that is wrought by such a broad vista, Jenkins asks, "So you saw him walking down the road."

"Walking, yes," says Mark.

"Walking real slowly," Howard interjects, and then does the rest of the talking.

"And you stopped and offered him a ride," Kennedy says.

"Yes."

"Did he say where he was going?" Jenkins asks.

"We asked him and he said he was on his way home."

"Did you ask him where he lived?" Kennedy asks.

"He told us he lived near Dartmouth and we told him we

could give him a ride part of the way south. To Bethel."

"But then he asked to get out of the car?" Jenkins says.

"Right," says Mark.

"He asked to get out in the middle of nowhere."

"In the middle of nowhere," repeats Howard.

"Why the middle of nowhere?" Kennedy asks.

There is an odd pause and then from Howard comes the hoarse, accusatory, "He probably would've stayed in the car if my brother hadn't weirded him out with stupid talk."

"Stupid talk?" asks Kennedy.

"Bodybuilder bullshit," explains Howard.

"Did you try and sell him steroids?" Kennedy asks.

There is a brief pause and then Howard says, "Look, we saw him. We offered him a ride and then he wanted to get out."

"Doesn't answer my question," Kennedy says.

"Yeah, we did, okay?" Mark says.

"But he didn't want them," Howard says.

"Anyway, he wasn't going to stay in the car forever," Mark says.

"Oh?" Kennedy asks. "Why wouldn't he just take the ride and go the distance you offered him?"

"He got jumpy, what can we say?" says Mark. "Maybe he had figured out a destination. Maybe he's somewhere like San Francisco by now."

Pointing at the pasture and the distant looming shadow of Snake Mountain, Kennedy says to Howard, "And did you note which way he walked?"

"No, not really."

"You didn't watch him out of the rearview mirror when you were driving away?" Jenkins asks.

"No," Howard says. Indicating his brother with his beefy shoulder, "Because he kept opening his big trap!"

Jenkins waits a few moments and then proceeds. "And

once again, how did he seem?"

"He seemed out of it," says Mark.

"Like on drugs out of it?" Kennedy asks.

"No, more like . . . depressed out of it," says Howard.

Kennedy and Jenkins glance at one another. "Okay, let's head back into town," Jenkins says.

MAY 16; CARLETON, VERMONT; 65 DEGREES, SUN AND HIGH CLOUDS, BREEZY

In early May, with the last traces of ice still plaguing the slowly awakening land, a hay bale is found by a farmer at a place called Donner's Field in Weybridge. Inside the bale is an entombment large enough to accommodate a person of six feet two inches who seemed to have dug themselves in with their fingernails. The arrival of spring could have allowed the body to plunge into the swollen river.

When the DNA samples are extracted from the crusty remnants of straw and matched to the DNA of Luc Flanders, a river search begins. A helicopter team from Maine flies over the Millstone Creek, snapping photos with a special camera able to plumb turbulent river depths, scanning for human remains.

Then, on the sixteenth of May, a young mother with a toddler on her back is walking along the riverbank and sees a raft-like pallet protruding from a crest of the turbulent water. The wood—yellow pine—is soaked dark and gelatinous and crosshatched in a grid and, she imagines, once sustained the weight of some heavy piece of machinery. Maybe last summer the pallet had been appropriated by a wood-worker for plea-sure-river-riding with family and friends but then abandoned like a boat to nowhere—perhaps at the end of September when the days cooled off and the temperature was no longer warm enough for swimming.

The tall body, hewn and muscled from years of sport, is caught in the interstices of the wood, born up from the depths, still quite intact because it had frozen solid during the winter and slowly thawed in the river that for many weeks couldn't have been more than forty degrees. Photos have shown her that Luc Flanders always wore his hair fairly long, and she can see the strands undulating like tendrils of aqueous plants near the surface. The angelic white face angled up toward her and those remarkable arctic eyes — wide open and milky pale under water — shocks her.

Kennedy is the one who calls Sam. She listens to him break down, the gasping, the high-pitched sobbing. She thinks deeply: *What can I possibly say to comfort him?* And then words come. "The winter preserved him, Sam. He still looks beautiful. Like a god under water."

Sam drives up to Carleton. To a parking place along the Millstone Creek and begins walking toward the cluster of police vehicles. At one point he stops, arrested by a conviction that he's not alone. He glances out toward the perimeter of the just greening fields that roll up to the river and can see a rash of snowdrops in the wild. There is sense of a presence, of someone or something in possession of him, and the air becomes difficult to breathe. He puts his hand on his chest and tries to calm down. He's thinking of the afternoon back in December when Luc arrived at his house wearing a funny-looking Christmas sweater and standing nervously by the broad kitchen window. Flicking his finger at the imperfections of the rolled glass that bent the light and warped the view of the snowbound landscape, Luc said he was too afraid and too conflicted to go on. Hearing the words, Sam's heart turned over and felt squeezed and he had a similar difficulty in breathing. Interminable silence followed Luc's declaration and Sam's tacit acceptance, a silence most wretched because Sam knew it could be filled with words or tenderness or even an embrace that lasted a lot longer than the one that Luc used to say goodbye.

But surely there is some other memory to conjure up that's more positive than this one. And looking at the river silvered in the sun, Sam remembers the time they visited Walden Pond as Luc sat next to him without his shirt, reading Thoreau's lyrical passage about water being like an unbreakable mirror and watching Luc's lips move and his eyes flitting over the page and thinking this young man is so incredibly alive and feeling such an abiding and tender love for him.

But there are no more thoughts in Luc's head, no more regrets. He's as sentient as a stone. And now he's just downstream.

Sam pictures the sodden ankle-length coat undulating in the current. Himself walking into the water without thinking, entering the same deep and primal rhythm that made him hobble down his snowy driveway to find Panda and carry her in his arms back to the house: the arms of the living cradling the limbs of the dead. If only he could enter the river, if only he could feel the freezing onslaught of its shallows and very methodically untangle the fabric that lashes Luc's body to the entrapment of the raft. If only he could set him free, if only he could lift out of the water, the man he loves like a newborn child, and the body, limp in his arms, as heavy as the world. Luc's eyes would be open and still be that pale supernatural blue, staring at him relentlessly as though, even in death, they can look deep inside him and miraculously find their own reflection.

FEBRUARY 11, 2015; BLACK DIAMOND FALL, UTAH; 20 DEGREES, BRILLIANT SUNSHINE

"You first this time," Mike tells Sam.

"Okay."

"It'll be good enough the way it is."

"I know. I'm not going for anything more. I know my own limitations," Sam assures him.

Mike grins. "Consider yourself even lucky to be on a pair of skis."

And yet reclaiming this very moment is what single-mindedly propelled Sam through rehab, made him work tirelessly at his own recovery. "Yes, I'm damn lucky," he agrees.

"Not to mention, crazy." Clearly on edge now, Mike grabs hold of Sam's arm. "You have to promise me. This time you're not going to do anything out of range. You're not going to push . . . your own envelope."

Annoyed, Sam gently wrenches himself out of Mike's grasp and says, "Of course I won't."

Mike looks at him steadfast with his one gold eye and one blue eye. An always-unsettling gaze. "If anything happens out here . . ."

"Nothing is going to happen out there!"

Mike hesitates as though debating whether or not to say, "Gina said she'd throw me out."

"She wouldn't throw you out."

"You don't know her." Mike now mentions the huge row he had had with Gina the night before he and Sam flew out to Utah. Gina had accused Mike of encouraging Sam's continuing delusions and having a midlife crisis of his own.

"Well, I've been through my own midlife crisis," Sam says. "I know what I can do. And what I can't." *And whom I can and cannot love,* he thinks but does not say.

Giles Flanders had staunchly opposed Sam attending the memorial services. He argued that such events are supposed to be comfort for the living, and that Sam's presence would cause him pain. While Sam understood this, he felt the need for his own private memorial and requested—via Janine Flanders—a small quantity of Luc's ashes. Luc's mother naturally wanted to hold on to every last molecule of her son. But by then Sam had consented to the parents reading Luc's sabotaged, penitent emails that professed the depth of his devotion, emails that begged reconciliation. And when Eleanor read them, she knew she could hardly deny the proof of how deeply her son had cared for the older man. She made a decision and kept this decision from her husband.

Eleanor and Sam finally met in Hanover, New Hampshire, at a café largely populated by Dartmouth undergrads. When Sam arrived a few minutes early, he wondered if perhaps they should have gotten together elsewhere. Surely these students streaming in and out of the coffee shop, talking about trivialities as much as the demands of their classes, would be sore reminders of Eleanor's loss. When, at last, she came in the door, and before she spotted him at a table toward the back of the café, Sam watched her taking in the young people, her face tightening slightly. He caught her attention with a gentle wave, and, seeing him, she started a little. And as Eleanor moved toward him, the first thing he noticed was that she had Luc's pale, spectral, unsettling eyes. Only at first was this oddly comforting rather than disturbing. As though perhaps some part of his life was still captured, was not yet given away. But then the sadness invaded.

When he stood up, she gave him a quick, impulsive hug,

sat down opposite him, and muttered something about having trouble finding a parking space. He commiserated and said that it was always difficult to find parking in the middle of the academic year. "Do you come to Hanover much?" she asked a bit nervously as she placed her handbag carefully down next to her, the handbag that surely contained the measure of Luc's ashes that she'd brought with her.

"I don't. I'm not a big fan of Hanover," Sam confessed. "But it may be because I'm not a big fan of Dartmouth College."

"How so?"

"For one thing, they approached me about teaching a course, the history of architecture. I came in for the interview and was treated dismissively. But then I happen to have a friend who was about to be hired for a professorship in the English department. He was suddenly turned down because of one person's objection. He's a minority and also gay."

"Oh yes, I do know about that," Eleanor said. "My husband was actually on the hiring committee. And Giles was very angry about that, too. What amazed me was that it was a woman who got in the way of the hiring. Rather than some homophobic man," she said as though wanting Sam to know she was and would have been accepting of Luc's sexual preference. And that her husband certainly was.

"But Giles is no longer with the college," Eleanor informed him. "I don't know if my son ever mentioned . . ."

"You mean, the drinking?" Sam filled in.

Eleanor nodded with noticeable embarrassment. "Giles has never been able to get a handle on it. It affected his teaching. He'd had several warnings before they let him go. And then, of course . . . losing his son."

"I'm sorry to hear he lost his job."

Eleanor shrugged. "It was meant to happen, I guess." Then she looked at Sam intently. "I suppose you also know how Giles was as a father. I suppose my son told you about that, too?"

My son. The use of the phrase sounded deliberate and Sam figured she had difficulty saying the name aloud. "We spoke a fair amount about . . . his father."

"They never really were very close."

At a sudden loss for what to say, Sam glanced out the window. Then, turning his attention to Eleanor, he said, "Just so you know . . . between us, it wasn't really like father and son."

"I understand," Eleanor said simply, and Sam wondered if she really did. But then her eyes filled, and while he felt he should reach forward and grasp her hand, he didn't. She wept quietly, unnoticed by the students, in a private, acute moment of grief, and Sam found himself remembering the narcotic daydream he'd had on the plane home from Utah: about meeting Eleanor Flanders at the art opening and lying about the loss of his own son. And now here they were. This conversation didn't seem all that different from the one he'd imagined. Maybe that narcotic daydream had been some kind of premonition. Because, after all, part of the great loss he was feeling was a bit like that of a parent mourning the death of a child.

He said, "Maybe I should've kept the father and son bit to myself. I can see that it upsets you."

"No," she said, managing to collect herself. "It's not that. If anything, I'm glad to know some of what it was like between you and Luc." The spear of pain now brought on by hearing Luc's name passing her lips was stunning. She continued. "It's just that I was thinking . . . well, two things I was thinking. The first is: I am looking at you like the last landmark of his life . . . I know Luc was probably thinking about you at the very end. And then I'm also thinking, maybe even regretting, that I didn't tell Giles that I was meeting you today and why I was meeting you."

Sam nodded. He understood the implication: that Luc's father might have stepped in and tried to prevent the meeting. He couldn't help glancing nervously at her handbag.

"I'll not be telling him what I'm giving you," Eleanor admitted at last, her eyes glassy with tears. And then, looking at him with Luc's unsettling gaze, she reached down to the floor and closed her fingers around the leather straps of the bag.

The cloudless weather, the quicksilver sparkling of far-flung Black Diamond Fall, mirrors the bluebird conditions of two years before, but the snow is better now, deeper, safer, hopefully, but they can't really know for sure. It amazes Sam how everything around him, the mountains, the icy crevasses, look exactly as they did when he last saw them as he was ascending into the rescue helicopter. These rock formations have born witnesses to many lifetimes of snow travelers and skiers whose attempts to master these descents were perhaps fugitive ways to prove to themselves that they were spirited and skillful, strengths that over time will prove to be more and more fleeting. He's doing this run against the advice of nearly everyone he knows.

"So are you ready?" Mike asks.

He's referring to the ritual that Sam has insisted upon. He takes the small wooden box out of his backpack, notices that one of the soft edges has been nicked by the avalanche equipment stowed next to it. He slides it open to the small tightly wrapped plastic bag whose granular contents are the size of a walnut and whose color varies between white and gray. Looking out over the contours of the Wasatch Mountains that hem them in, he lifts the bag out, carefully undoes the tie and waits for a breeze. He holds the bag up, rustles the the ashes, and is letting them fly when Mike says, "Why are you doing it that way?"

He's right. Some bits fly back and sting Sam's face and he actually laughs. But most of the ashes catch the wind and are carried aloft like heavy motes of dust. He closes his eyes for a moment, thinking how Luc had always wanted to ski this slope with him, thinking how ironic it was that they'd never actually skied together. And then the odd, breathless feeling comes over Sam, a firm pressure just below his rib cage, almost like a body thrust upon him.

This time he's first. But fear isn't there the way it was before, just anticipation, an edgy, adrenalized hyperawareness. It occurs to him that he has less to lose now, not that he wants to lose it, but that he's had a good run so far, and if he's taken—earlier than expected—he's fifty-one years old now; it'd be hardly the tragedy of a young man like Luc Flanders perishing in his prime. But with this recognition of mortal inevitability comes a certain kind of detachment that allows him to assess risk without worry, to begin his descent as he would some twisty, narrow steep trail back in Vermont, getting freshies with a bunch of his buddies before the crowds wade in, cutting into a perfect, untouched icing of snow and whooping it up as skiing becomes sailing and zigzagging between trees trussed up with powder. Here at Black Diamond Fall, there is one headwall that scares him, but Sam is down it almost before it even registers, and, his mind synced to his body, he turns quickly with great precision and then he's in the wide-open face, taking a traverse before executing a few more turns. At one point he catches an edge and, trying to recover, feels the weakness in his once shattered left leg and a shooting pain, and all he can do is pray that he can hold it together. Soon, the ride is over and he's safe below.

At the bottom, he glides into a wide swale and swivels around to watch Mike whipping down as gracefully as a swan doing figure eights on a pond. At one point, Sam is shocked to see Mike tumble, but miraculously nail an acrobatic recovery, then continue to ski down. He almost wonders if what he has just witnessed is some sort of hallucination. When Mike is at the bottom of the final slope and traversing toward him, Sam exclaims, "Wow, that was close! That could've been the finale of your midlife crisis."

"Talk about a reversal," Mike says breathlessly. "Me instead of you." He grins wildly. "But then Gina wouldn't be able to kick me out! She'd have to nurse me!"

"Or bury you," Sam says.

And then he finds himself remembering Luc's pale, disconcerting gaze, the tottering way he walked into a room with his head bowed, the slight waddle to his gait, the one soccer game against Bowdoin that Sam had watched and Luc scoring a goal, and everybody jumping all over him, hugging him as children hug a father while Sam remained quietly in the stands, not wanting to attract attention but brimming with pride and just yearning to embrace him. Yes, he supposes this love, in all complexity and depth, does resemble love for a child—if he'd had one—but, of course, it's so much more. They are two people reaching to one nother over a gap, or maybe climbing the face of Black Diamond Fall and losing hold and trying to save a fatal fall, and at some point just having to let go as, at some time in the future, someone will have to let go of him. But then there is the placid, surprisingly intimate look in Luc's eyes when he is finally freed from the river, when he lies at final rest in Sam's arms.

ACKNOWLEDGMENTS

I'd like to thank the following people who either gave their time reading the manuscript, or, through sharing their personal history, helped me better understand the situations, people and settings in this novel.

Mitchell Waters
Diane Mott
Todd Melendy
Emma McKay Thorpe
Connie Gaylord
Beth Kanell
Evelyn Toynton

Special thanks to Lori Milken

And thanks to Jason Pinter and Polis Books

And thanks to Todd Wolk — for everything